TALES OF KINGSHOLD

Book 1.5 of the Wildfire Cycle

D.P. WOOLLISCROFT

For Mum and Keith.
I think you would have liked these stories.

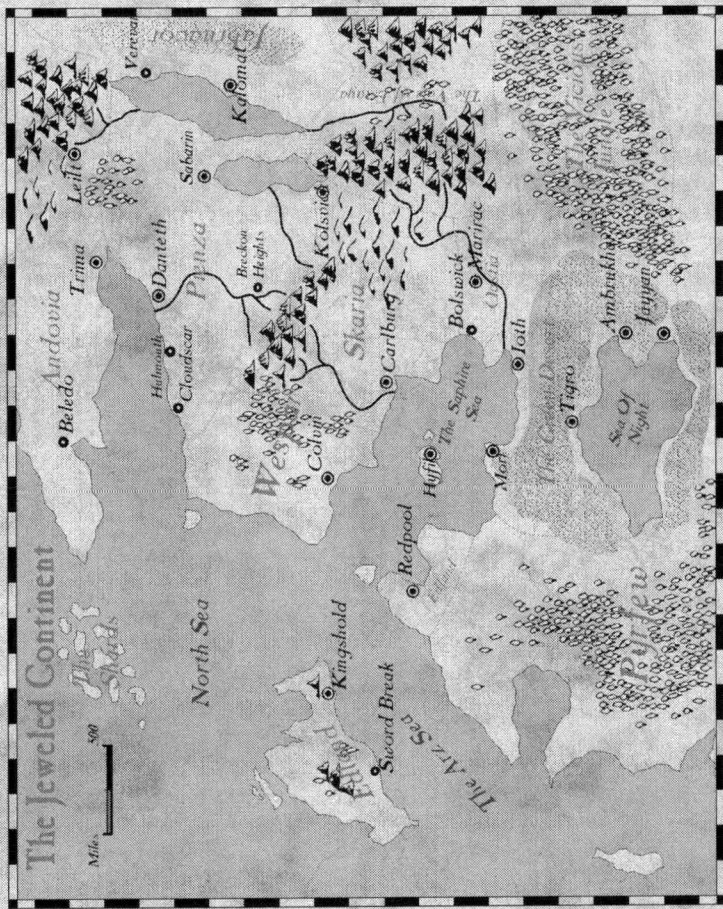
The Jeweled Continent

FOREWORD

Welcome to the *Tales of Kingshold,* a collection of shorter stories that accompany the novel *Kingshold.* And yes, this book is titled book 1.5 of the Wildfire Cycle. So what does that mean?

Well, first of all, these novelettes and short stories all stand alone as intriguing explorations of the Jeweled Continent.

But these tales are also extremely relevant to the overall story I am telling. They provide more color or backstory to some of the major and supporting characters, they answer some open questions from *Kingshold*, and they introduce new characters who will appear in book two and beyond. And though these stories are relevant, I did not want them to bog down either *Kingshold*, or book two (titled *Ioth, City of Lights*) with either additional 'points of view' or asides.

I intend for this to be a pattern for publication going forward. A major book that will be primarily focused in one location and a condensed timeframe, followed by a collection of *Tales* linked to the events of that book.

I hope you enjoy the stories and another visit to the Jeweled Continent (and the sneak peek of *Ioth, City of Lights*). As ever, I would love to hear from you, in particular about what you think about this format, so please find me on Goodreads, Facebook or Twitter.

Thanks for reading,

D.P. Woolliscroft

AUTHOR'S INTRODUCTION

It has been many years since the events of that fateful summer in Kingshold when Jyuth called the very first election in Edland's history.

So long.

The world is different now than it was then. And so am I. Neither drunkard nor victor. But still, I find myself alone. Missing friends and loved ones.

I am alone, with only these stories for companionship. Stories that I collected from my former friends, lovers and even my enemies.

As I scoured my notes in creating this tome, I was reminded of how many years I lost at the bottom of a bottle, my awareness of the passage of time muddied, both before and after these events.

Some of these tales were gathered when we all lived in the Royal Oak, eager to change the world; others I heard in my first months as Lord Protector when we turned the world on its head; but others required hunting down many years later, when the world had taken its revenge, scavenged from archives or told over glasses of whiskey watered with tears.

Now, the night draws close for me and these tales and their memories are my only joy.

There are morals or truths in these tales you would do well to heed. I was told history is a repeating visitor, and though it may have new clothes, it brings old problems. Do not be surprised when it appears at your threshold.

MARETH BOLLINGSMEAD

FROM FATHER TO DAUGHTER

The morning sun streaked in through the window of Neenahwi's bed chamber. She had not slept well. And not just because the merriment of celebrating the election results had continued until well past midnight. She knew her father, Jyuth, had left.

Neenahwi rolled across the bed until her outstretched arm reached a sealed scroll. Jyuth had asked her not to read it until he had gone, and for once she had respected his wishes.

In fact, she was not sure she wanted to read it all.

She had her final memories of her father; the joy they'd had flying together for potentially the last time, over the city and around Mount Tiston, dodging drakes that tried to catch them in the air. They had laughed at the sport, the sounds emanating as the shrieks of owl and eagle. But as soon as she opened this letter and read what was inside, those memories could be forever altered. And if she knew one thing about her father, if he didn't want to discuss the contents in person, then it would not be pleasant reading.

"Coward," she said, though she wasn't sure whether she was referring to Jyuth, or simply herself.

Shuffling upright to a seated position, she broke the seal on the scroll and unrolled it to reveal writing that was shaky and, in places, blotched with tears.

Neenahwi,

You are reading this after I have left Kingshold. I do not know if we will meet again, though you will be in my heart always. I have lived a long life, and I am proud of many accomplishments. But it is you that has brought me the most happiness, and peace of mind.

I took a risk in rescuing you from Llewdon. I didn't know you. I didn't know why he wanted you and your brother. In fact, my motivations at the time were only that I wanted to take something he wanted, and to show him that I could infiltrate his home. Not the most noble of motivations, but I am so glad that I let my baser instincts win out. For not only do I think you are important to Llewdon, for reasons I do not know; but, more than this, it brought you into my life.

Oh, you were hell to live with initially. And I can't blame you for that. You were young and had been through so much. Captured by the very person responsible for destroying your family. It was only reasonable for you to think that the old man who came along and spirited you away was not to be trusted. Thank you for eventually giving me the benefit of the doubt.

Neenahwi smiled at the memories of their fights when she had first arrived in Kingshold. Underneath those arguments had been her fear that one gilded cage had been replaced with another. It was only when her threat to leave was met with reluctant approval had she finally accepted that this cantankerous old man bore her no ill will. Now she couldn't imagine what her life would have been like without him.

I TOLD YOU I AM TIRED, BUT I DIDN'T HAVE THE COURAGE TO tell you all of it. My life has been long: more than a thousand years. I learned my skills, and that which I have taught you, at the feet of Myank himself, and I traveled the length and breadth of the Jeweled Continent before forming Edland into the country it is today. I am only human, remember, with a short life. Unlike the elves of course, of whom Llewdon is the last; or even the Alfjarun, your own people. The demon stones have preserved my life for the past four centuries, but my actions before that are some of my most shameful.

As I have taught you, action requires energy. And life requires life. Initially I thought myself superior to others. Later, I thought I was essential in the protection of Edland as a bulwark against Pyrfew. But no matter the excuse, I had to take the life of others; stealing their mana to roll back the years.

I tell you this with great shame but I feel you must know.

It began with people—young people, who wouldn't be missed— and I took away their futures, took away whatever it was that could have been special about them. There was more than one servant from the palace who I used in this way. I believe there is still some trepidation for those assigned to serve me, even today; though it has been many, many years since any of the staff have gone missing by my hand. That was because I realized that greater levels of mana resided in magical creatures, such as dragons, and even drakes; and so I traveled to find these creatures and again, take what I needed. Eventually, I found the demon stones and they removed my need to steal these special lives, but they too came with a cost; dreams of blood and fire, bouts of anger, and ever more difficult-to-resist urges to destroy.

"WHAT?" SHE EXCLAIMED INCREDULOUSLY. SHE KNEW Jyuth had killed in the past. He'd killed the King and Queen just a month past, but this was different. This was a murder of innocents. *How had he done this for so long?* A wave of revulsion swept up from her stomach and caused her to retch. She recalled her confrontation with Gawl Tegyr; the way he had pulled the life out of the men who accompanied him. Was her father no better than that demon?

She almost threw away the letter but her eyes were drawn back to the page and she continued to read in morbid fascination.

I WILL DO THIS NO MORE. I AIM TO LIVE OUT THE REST OF MY days naturally, no matter how short they may be. I am burdened by my regrets but, please, do not let this completely taint your memory of me. It was your influence, your example, and my desire for your pride in me, that led me to this decision.

But I do worry about the state of affairs I leave you with. And I'm sure you must wonder why I have not done anything about Llewdon. The truth is that he is too powerful for me, his servants too numerous. I thought him dead for a while when the elves disappeared, but he returned; and so I have used the resources of Edland to spoil his influences in the rest of the Jeweled Continent. Assassins. Politics. The navy. At other times, open war. These things kept Pyrfew's ambitions contained, but Llewdon's tendrils of influence have spread to your homeland, the Wild Continent, and I worry that we have reached a tipping point where he can't be contained any longer. His threat will only accelerate.

I know you want revenge against Llewdon but you cannot face him. Maybe one day in the future you will have the strength, but you must be patient. Patient, but proactive in attempting to understand his plans.

Therefore, it is important that you know more about Llewdon.

A BALL OF RATTY FUR JUMPED ONTO HER LAP AND STARTLED her. Tuft, her cat. Neenahwi scratched behind his ear, the purring sounds soothing as the anger that boiled inside her switched its focus from Jyuth to Llewdon, self-styled god-emperor of Pyrfew and scourge of her life. She read on, eager for insight; for instruction.

I FIRST MET THE ELF WHEN I WAS UNDER THE TUTELAGE OF Myank. Llewdon was a strong and intelligent wizard; the best of the elven sorcerers, and he was a friend to my master. But theirs was a strange friendship. Llewdon was envious of Myank and the influence he had over the peoples of the Sapphire Sea. Not to mention that he was the elf's equal and only a human. Nevertheless, Llewdon would often visit, and he and Myank would spend days in conversation. I would take my turn to wait on them with fellow students, eager for an opportunity to eavesdrop.

And then, one day, Myank announced that our lessons had ended. From then on, we would need to learn by ourselves. He was leaving for an expedition that we could not join. I would not see my teacher again. I departed, along with my peers, all going our separate ways; and I saw nothing of Llewdon for many years, for rarely did the elves leave their forests, and his friend was now gone. But I heard tales that he had become consumed by the question of where Myank had disappeared to; I assume a terrible fear of missing out had settled in his soul.

Then word came of the great catastrophe; the death of all of the tribes of the elves in a magical calamity. I thought Llewdon had perished too, but a half century later came the first military excursions of demons and magical creatures; taking lands, subjugating people and forming the nation of Pyrfew. I don't know for certain, but I can only assume that Llewdon must have either been responsible for the catastrophe or he had previously abandoned his people, if he was the only elf to have survived.

I don't know what his motivations are. Is it a simple desire for conquest, or something else? How do you and Motega fit into his plans?

These are the questions that you should find answers to, though I have tried and failed.

The only clue I have for you is that Llewdon has always shown a great interest in Redpool. Most people think Pyrfew covets that city because of its position of strategic importance at the mouth of the Sapphire Sea. And that may be part of it, but they are unaware that there may be other reasons.

Myank was born in the fishing village that was there before the city, back when there was still a tidal pool, surrounded by banks of red sandstone, where we would dredge for clams and mussels. And at that time, he had a tower—a place of study and knowledge—that is there no longer. I can't escape the feeling that Llewdon's obsession with Myank's disappearance is why he has sought to add Redpool to his empire for so long.

Many of Llewdon's spy networks in Kingshold are known to me, and I have ensured that they know of my intention to leave, as evidenced by your meeting with Gawl Tegyr. Llewdon will come looking for me. He will not believe my intention to drift away disgracefully, and so I hope that I can prove to be something of a distraction, at least in the near term.

One thing I have learned from being alive so long, is that time can move in cycles. A thousand years ago many things happened that have stood almost undisturbed since then: the rise of the church of Arloth, the founding of Edland, and the catastrophe of the elves. Now I fear that the circle of time is coming back around again, that tumultuous events are nigh and the world will look very different afterward.

So do not dally.

Step on the front foot—as is your want.

Trust your instincts and identify assets that you can call upon, because you cannot succeed alone.

Remember, pair action with patience. Remember that I love you.

And I am so very, very proud of you.

JYUTH

NEENAHWI SCREAMED A CRY OF FRUSTRATION, TUFT leaping away to hide beneath a chair. *Was that it?* Jyuth didn't know anything. There were no answers. Just more questions.

She smashed the letter into a ball and tried to throw it into the fire that smoldered in the hearth. It bounced off the mantel and rolled across the floor, Tuft pouncing on it as if it was a toy.

Neenahwi got out of bed and paced the floor, thoughts racing through her mind like a herd of stampeding bhiferg. It made no sense. What was she supposed to do? What did Llewdon want? What was compelling him to be such a scourge for so many centuries?

She grabbed a clay cup and threw it against the wall. Shards reigned down, causing Tuft to dive for cover once more. The fire poker skittered across the floor from a well-aimed kick that left her toe throbbing. She flung open a window and screamed at the top of her voice, "You bastard!"

Of course she was filled with rage toward Llewdon, but as she sucked in a big lungful of air, she realized that her anger was targeted elsewhere.

Her father.

And really, what she meant, what went un-screamed, was *why did you leave me?*

TWIN LIES

"So I guess we won."

"I guess we did," said Florian. "Don't feel right though."

"What do you mean it doesn't feel right?"

"Those kids had nothing to do with this. It's not right, that's all."

"The way I see it, Florian, is if we hadn't done it, there would be a lot more dead right now. Those people in Redpool for a start, suffering, because of the siege. And they didn't ask for it. I didn't like killing a bunch of women and kids either, but who's to say whether this wasn't right," said Joe. He was one of the new additions to Sergeant Morris's squad, a few years younger than Florian and he'd done well with the silent, lethal, work of that morning.

And who knows? In the past, Florian might have seen it the same way. Though he doubted it.

"I don't know," said Florian, "still doesn't make me feel good."

Redpool was Edland's only territory outside of the island

landmass. It was the kind of strategically-important city used to being fought over. For centuries it had changed hands numerous times; tribes and petty kingdoms warring over it, most long since disappeared, becoming consumed into the empire of Pyrfew.

This latest tussle over the city that controlled the trade routes to and from the rich merchants on the Sapphire Sea, was all down to one ambitious governor, betrayer of the King of Edland who had installed him. Claim Redpool for Pyrfew and claim the favor of the emperor. It hadn't worked out too well for him.

Florian and Joe looked down on the battlefield from their perch at the top of a hill, the dead looking like piles of fire-wood from this distance. Captive soldiers on their knees, both natives of Redpool sold a pack of lies and Pyrfew troops, too honor-bound to turn tail and run like some of their comrades. That didn't seem right either. It was the cowards who got away to freedom, while the ones doing their duty bore the brunt of the ill will that had welled up inside the Edland army from weeks of skirmishes and failed assaults on the walls.

The battle had been well matched until Eden's cavalry arrived. They had been the deciding factor. Trapping the opposing army between the pike wall and the stampeding hooves of the horses had assured only one likely outcome. Of course, the army occupying Redpool would never have taken the field if it hadn't been for the Ravens.

Florian's squad had infiltrated the city to kill the gover-nor's family while he was out there talking to Eden under the white flag. Enough to drive a normal man to make bad deci-sions in the name of revenge. Another thing to add to the list of injustices. But that hadn't stopped Florian from following the orders.

A squad of pikemen came walking up the hill. Some were laughing while others were quiet with that look in their eyes, that recognition that only luck kept them from being another body on the battlefield. Some were walking wounded, but all bore scars inside. They were the fortunate ones who had made it out, and so was Florian. With Redpool free, Florian had done what they were supposed to do. Maybe it was time to get out, before the next war came along.

"Hey, Ham, how are you doing? Haven't seen you in ages," called a man from the pikemen squad.

Florian looked up to see who had called. "Ervin. Glad to see you made it out of there," he said.

"Me too," replied Ervin. "Let's get a drink tonight and catch up. I'm with the Eagle Company. You'll find me later?"

"Sure," said Florian, though he knew he would not seek company tonight. The pikemen walked on past he and Joe, continuing their way to their camp of the past few weeks.

"Why did he call you Ham?" asked Joe.

"It's a long story," said Florian.

"Well, there's not a lot else going on is there? Go on, tell me the story. It might take your mind off all this shit."

"Well, I guess it might. Alright, sure. But only until the sarge arrives."

~

I HAVE TO GO BACK A LONG WAY TO TELL THIS STORY. I have a twin sister. Her name is Aiola. We're not identical, which is good news for her.

I'm a few seconds older, and I got the strength of dad and she got the smarts of mum. Where I picked up the sword quick from dad, she was never any good. But she was half decent with a bow, taught by our dad too. A good thing too.

This all started when we'd become teenagers. We were always close, like most twins, but we didn't spend all of our time together. I had my friends, other village lads. We would play knights, fighting giants or dragons or vicious spiders that protected ancient treasure.

My sister had her friends. A lot of them girls, and they would be falling out over something all the time. They'd get into a fight and one of them would stomp off. I could never understand it.

One day I was playing in the forest, just on the outskirts of the village with a few my friends. We were fighting a demon if I recall, running around with our wooden swords, and I heard her call.

"Florian!"

"What?" I called back. I expected she wanted me to come and help her with something. Something I wasn't interested in. But I didn't want to lose my place in the game, so I didn't come.

"Florian!" came the call again. She sounded a little upset, but sometimes she got upset about things that didn't matter to a boy, like what one of them said to the other. So, still, I didn't move.

I kept on playing but then I heard her call again.

"Florian!" There was a shrill edge to her voice now that was not normal. It was enough to raise the hairs on the back of my neck. I ran to where I thought the sound of her voice had come from.

"Aiola? Aiola!" I cried in return, but there was no answer.

I found her behind a fence on the south paddock. A wolf, hackles raised, and fur bristling, had backed her into a corner. She told me later that she'd been the one to stomp off, when she had noticed something bothering the sheep. Normally, any predator would run off at the sight of a human, but this wolf was determined to eat, and a skinny girl would do just as good as a fat sheep. Aiola screamed again as the wolf leapt toward her neck, teeth bared. She shielded her face with her arm and the wolf's jaws clamped down on her upper arm.

Wooden sword raised above my head, I charged the little shit. And I hit it with all of my strength, just below the wolf's ear. I tell you, it was only a wooden sword but it damn near took its head off. I'm not sure the wolf knew what had been coming, but it let go of Aiola and literally ran for the hills.

I took Aiola in my arms before checking her wounds. The flesh of her upper arm had a series of deep puncture wounds that welled a deep red blood. I tried my best to clean it up but I didn't know what I was doing. She cried deep gasping sobs and moaned my name. And all I could think about was how I wasn't there when she first called. How I ignored her twice.

"I'm sorry Aiola," I said. "I'll always be there to protect you. I'll never let you down." And that turned out to be my first lie to my twin sister.

∾

FROM THAT DAY FORWARD, I PROTECTED HER.

Everyone around the village, and even around the whole

county, knew if they so much as laid a hand on Aiola they would have me to deal with. As I got older, I got bigger and better with a sword than most grown men, so nobody wanted to try anything.

It was about three years ago now, after we turned sixteen, when it happened. I'd been away for a few days, Mum and Dad sending me to find a couple of sheep that were missing. Now, when sheep go missing it can be a few things. It could be wolves, rustlers, poachers; but more likely, they could've just wandered off and got stuck on some hill. I'd grown stronger than Dad and could carry two of the buggers at the same time.

It took a little searching, but I found them sheep, huddled together at the top of a rocky hill, using each other to shelter from the wind and the rain while they kept munching on that sweet untouched grass. I brought them down and back to our house thinking I'd get at least a small pat on the back. But everything was quiet as I approached the little farmstead. I called out, "Mum! Dad! Aiola! I got them."

A few moments of silence passed before I heard my mum call out.

"Florian!" She ran outside to meet me. I could tell something was wrong straight away.

Her hands were shaking and her eyes were red as if she'd been crying some time ago. She ran right over without saying another word and grabbed me in an embrace.

"What's wrong, Mum?" I asked, though I was afraid of the answer.

"Oh, Florian," she said, "It was the army. They came looking for recruits."

Well that sounded okay, I thought. Not bandits, or

thieves, or werewolves, or some other nasty. Just the army, right? The Edland army, there to protect us.

"Don't tell me, Dad signed up again?" I asked. Dad was ten years older than my Mum, and the other side of fifty, but he loved his days in the army. Not sure he ever loved being a farmer.

"It's not your Dad," sniffled my Mum. "They were looking for two recruits from each family. They had records of everyone. They wanted you and Aiola to sign up, no question about talking them out of it. But your Dad, he tried. And he only knows one way to convince someone."

"Dad? What happened to him?"

"They kicked three bells out of him, that's what happened. He's not dead, but he's pissing blood. I'm making him rest," she said looking back to the house.

"And Aiola. Where is she?"

"They took her. Weren't you listening?" she said, panic and frustration clear in her voice. "They took her for the army."

"They took her? She can't join up, she won't be safe," I said, worried about Aiola but also a little disappointed she had gone with them and I had been left behind. I had dreamed about being in the army. Heard the stories from my dad, who only told the good kind of stories, those of brotherhood and heroes and fighting for what's right. Unless he drank too much gin. Then he'd tell the truth of it.

"When did this happen," I asked.

"Two days ago, not long after you left. They carried on down the road to hit the next poor family."

"I got to get her, Mum," I said.

"I knew you would say that, Florian." She stroked my cheek, giving me a half smile. "I knew you would want to.

You're a good boy, and you love your sister. But I won't think any less of you if you stay here. At least I'll have you," she said, tears welling in her eyes.

"I can't, Mum. I got to go."

"Well keep an eye out for her then. You won't get her away. Deserters hang. If you go, you must sign up too. And then I lose both of you."

"Don't worry, Mum," I said, trying to reassure her in a scene I'm sure is repeated the world over when the young go off to fight some stupid war and leave their family behind. "I'll be hard to kill. Nothing will stop me coming back!" I said with as much certainty as I could fake. "Let's go see Dad, then I need to go if I'm to catch them up."

Dad lay in his bed, looking old. Dark blue bruises already turning to a sickly brown. He woke, and we talked; but he didn't make much sense. He spoke about some people he used to serve with, as if they would still be around. Told me to seek them out. I nodded and smiled and then said my goodbyes. Last thing he said was to take his sword, the one above his bed. I haven't let it go since.

~

I SET OUT THAT EVENING WITH MY FATHER'S SWORD, THE bag I had not yet unpacked from my few days away, and the small amount of food my mother could spare; some bread, cheese and a single jug of beer brewed by my father earlier in the summer.

From our farmstead it was a mile to what we called the main road to Ilkestop. A path worn by cartwheels; it was nothing like the roads around the rest of the kingdom. I don't know as I had ever seen a cobblestoned road before. It would be a few days until I set foot on one for the first time.

The grasses were flattened around the cartwheel track, showing evidence of the recruiting team's passage, and following their trail was easy enough. I spent the nights sleeping by the pathway, not bothering to make a fire, just lying down with my blanket and bedroll in the warm early autumn air.

I passed through Ilkestop, Nettering, Little Hampton and Snodden. In each village, the locals told a story similar to the one I'd heard from my mother: two recruits from every family, man or woman, ages fourteen to thirty. Some families took the shock easier than others if they had more than a handful of kids. The mothers missed their babies, but at least they had enough hands to work their farms.

I arrived in Snodden early on the third morning to find I had closed the gap; my quarry having left the village only the previous afternoon. Beyond Snodden was the main north-south road from Aria down to Wombourne. Which way had they gone was the question I didn't know the answer to.

Reasoning they would head north to the town of Aria, Lord Eden's district seat, to assemble with the rest of the army, I turned that way. I thought luck was with me when I saw heading toward me men and women traipsing behind two lead horses and a mule-led wagon.

It dawned on me too late that they were travelling in the wrong direction to be the right squad. But I didn't think about that. Hadn't had too much experience hunting men back then. When you are looking for sheep, you don't give too much thought to which direction they are moving in.

This was how I signed up with Sergeant Morris, all the while craning my neck, looking around to see if any of the sorry-looking souls in the train were Aiola. He wasn't happy that he'd been dragged out for the muster. Normally he picked the cream of the crop for the Ravens after training, but the higher ups had ordered a rapid call to arms and needs must. Flathead and Moley were there to keep him company; and believe it or not, Morris was even more of a miserable bastard thanks to that grunt duty than he is nowadays.

The sergeant noticed I was looking for someone so I told him about my sister. He laughed so hard, and I turned so red, I thought I would pop him one, but I held back my anger. Between his laughs he told me he hadn't been by Shortdrop. Must have been a different crew. Me running to meet the wrong squad was the highlight of his year.

At least until I said I had better be going then to catch up with the other squad, which almost made him piss himself.

"You ain't going nowhere boy," he coughed out between laughs, while Flathead and Moley looked their intimidating selves. "You don't get to decide now. Get back there and get to know your new family."

~

MORRIS'S SQUAD WAS SLOWER MOVING THAN THE ONE I had been pursuing. We only stopped at one village each day on our way down to Crossroads. While the sergeant plus either Flathead or Moley handled the conscription of willing and unwilling alike, the other would lead us in drills.

We ran back and forth across freshly tilled fields, the shifting soil causing many to fall on their faces.

In fields of corn taller than me we would play a version of tag. A handkerchief hanging from the back of our belts the target and the winner would either be the one with the most flags or the last one standing, depending on the order of the day.

And we trained in arms.

Most of the recruits had brought no weapons of their own. I had my sword and there was another boy who also had inherited one. At first the two of us paired up to practice while the three score other recruits received instructions in how to handle a pike and shield, long staves cut from trees along the journey making as substitutes for the real thing.

Matching me with the boy, I think his name was Garth, wasn't the best of ideas. I tried to go easy on him, but the lad had never held a sword. Parrying his crazy flings, I gave him the chance to swing it around but when I counterattacked he threw up his hands to protect his face. And dropped his sword.

It dropped point down, straight through his boot, slicing off three toes. Sergeant Morris was pissed when he got back that night. At Moley who was supposed to be in charge. At me, even though I said I did nothing. Even at Garth. The sarge put his toes in a sack and told him to piss off home.

In retrospect, Garth was one of the lucky ones.

Afterwards, I did double training duty. With the rest I practiced with pike and shield, and my second shift was with Flathead each night by the camp fire. We'd spar, and I'd watch his moves while the other recruits huddled in their blankets, thinking about what they'd left behind. Me, I thought about what I'd found. I was getting better every day, and Flathead, already a veteran of a couple of wars, was not much better than me.

A week passed as we made the slow march down to the second infantry mustering point at Crossroads, and truth be told, I didn't give much thought to Aiola. I was still concerned about her. I didn't want her to go off to this war, but I also knew I couldn't do much about it at the moment. So, I would lose myself in the day's training.

I remember walking with the sarge and Flathead at the front of the train, more than a hundred raw recruits by now. We turned the bend and saw our destination; the camp for the Second.

My heart dropped into my boots, my mouth flapped open, and I stood stock still. Ten thousand people in the field beyond; drilling in squads, cooking around camp fires, great tents pitched all over the place. I knew I was fucked.

The sarge looked down at me then. "Don't worry lad. You might bump into her," he said. "Now shift your arse."

～

"THAT DON'T SOUND LIKE ME," SAID A VOICE FROM BEHIND Florian. "Well the bit about moving your arse does. But not the first bit. Much too caring."

Florian turned to look at Sergeant Morris, flanked by Moley and Midnight. Morris was sharp; in the angles of his face, the bite of his eyes, the sting of his two swords.

Granted, a few long scars interrupted the stubble on his chin, but Florian couldn't recall any other sergeants near forty who still saw action. Florian also hadn't come across any other sergeants who were anywhere near as good leaders of men. Morris was better than most of the captains. It was a mystery why Morris was still only a sergeant; although there was a rumor that the army was his escape route from the gallows, so that could have had something to do with it. Florian had served under Morris for three years but had yet to pluck up the courage to ask him about it.

Morris wore a long shirt of chain-mail under plates of boiled black leather secured by leather straps, which had become the standard armor for their squad. Moley, the man so named because of the star map of moles over his face and body, wore the same. Midnight however eschewed the chain-mail. She preferred padded black leather, her silver hair kept tied under a cap of similar material. Her attire combined with her dark skin had led to her highly original name—grunts were not the most poetic of folk.

"Sorry Sarge," said Florian, instinctively getting to his feet. "We were waiting for you and got to chatting."

"It's all right, Twins. You can sit down. I might join you," he said, as he lowered himself to the ground and stretched his legs out in front of him. "Now it sounded like a story. What's the tale?"

"Some bloke called him Ham, Sarge. He's supposed to be telling me why. But it's not making much sense at the moment," said Joe. "And you and Moley call him Twins, which makes a little more sense I s'pose. Why don't I have a name and Florian has two?"

"Hah, when you earn one, kid, you'll get one," said the sergeant. "And we call him Twins for another reason. I'm sure he'll get to that eventually."

"Aye," said Florian. "I will do, Joe, if you shut up and pay attention."

~

"WE'D JUST ARRIVED AT THE CAMP AND THERE WERE MORE people in one place than I'd seen in my life. More than the harvest festival in the village, more than the county fair even. I'd always been the big lad in the village, everyone knew me. But there, I felt small, a nobody. And how was I going to find just one person? I didn't know what to do. So, I shut my mouth, put one foot in front of the other, and followed the sarge.

The veterans had us set up camp on the outskirts, and then they handed us off to the instructors whose job it was to give a bunch of farmers, smiths, poachers, and tanners enough training so they wouldn't run at the first sight of battle. I settled into the training and the natural winnowing that happens where folks with some ability are selected for more important squads. Over the first week I progressed from pike man, to skirmisher, to armored infantry. All the while I kept looking for Aiola, but I didn't see her.

Didn't see the sarge again either until the next week when he saw me in line for the dinner slops. He told me he'd seen a young girl called Aiola a few days before; looked nothing like me, but he wanted to pass on the information. The sarge told me she was on the far side of the camp with the archers, and it all clicked into place for me. It had to be her.

Once night had fallen and my squad settled around the campfire, I got up determined to find her. Everyone was too sore from the day's bruises to notice I was wearing my sword and had a shield on my back.

Picking my way through a never-ending series of camp-fires, asking directions a few times along the way, I eventually found the archers and my sister.

She was dozing by a fire, back to back with another woman. I touched Aiola on her shoulder to wake her, hoping to be quiet. But I startled her, and her friend leaped to her feet, pulling a long knife and waving it in my face.

"Aiola," I said, "it's me, Florian."

I can still see, clear as day, her eyes going wide as she looked at me, the flames of the fire casting a flickering light on her face. She grabbed me and pulled me into a hug.

"You're here," she said.

Aiola told her friend to put away the knife and I pulled her behind a tent and into the shadows so we could talk.

"Are you ok?" I asked.

"I am now, Florian. I thought I would never see you again. You, or Mum, or Dad."

"I'm sorry, Aiola. I should have been there. I promised."

"You wouldn't have been able to do anything. At least you're here now. That's all I care about. There are some bad people in this army, Florian. If it weren't for Glenda looking out for me, I don't know what would have happened. I can't sleep. I can't even hit a target with this bloody bow because I keep shaking so much."

Both men and women had been serving in the Edland army for generations, and if Aiola had been older or a little more world wise, I thought she'd have known how to look after herself more. Or maybe I was at fault for always protecting her.

Throughout my search for Aiola, I had been thinking about what to do when I found her. I had thought maybe she would be doing alright and I could keep an eye on her. Even if we were in different squads, like my mum had said. But I knew then that would not be an option. I couldn't have lived with anything happening to her.

"Aiola," I said. "We're leaving. Now, while it's dark."

"Florian, we can't desert. I'll be ok." But I could see the bags under her eyes from missing out on sleep.

"No arguments, Aiola. I promised Mum I'd bring you back," I lied. "Get your bow, and let's go."

~

"YOU DESERTED?" ASKED JOE.

"Yep. We both did. Before the sun was up, we disappeared west over the hills and found a little bolt hole to rest in for a few hours."

"So, what happened?"

"Might be good for me to take over for a bit, Twins," said Sergeant Morris. Florian nodded for him to continue. "You see," said Morris, "it was me who figured out this idiot had run..."

~

THE NEXT MORNING, I WENT OVER TO FLORIAN'S CAMP myself. We'd been keeping an eye on him during his training to see if we should bring him into the Ravens. He was much more capable than all but a few recruits and we needed a few more heads.

When I got to his camp, his mates there told me they didn't know where he was. He hadn't been back that night. All of his stuff was still there, the pack he carried everywhere, so they assumed Florian had got lucky with someone and would head back before long.

That rang alarm bells straight away. Seemed unlikely Florian would hook up with someone on the night I tell him to go find his sister. Much more likely he would do something stupid.

I remember it being one of those crisp fall mornings that remind you winter is on the way rather than summer has just said goodbye. I crossed my way through the camp to where I had directed Florian the night before. As I asked around for Aiola, it became plain I was not the first to inquire. A few folks remarked that a big fella had asked the same thing the previous night. Not one for covering his tracks then, was Florian.

Anyway, I found her camp. Although one woman, must have been Glenda, tried to throw me off the scent, it was pretty obvious Aiola too was missing. Took the threat of a flogging to get Glenda to spill the beans, but she told me how Aiola's brother had come for her last night and they'd run off.

Shit, I thought to myself.

This was my fault in a way. I mean it was all Florian's fault, but in some small way I felt I had a hand to play in this mess. So, if someone would have to find the deserters, it should probably be me. I grabbed Moley, Flathead, a woman called Dug you never met, and a few horses, and we set out. Florian wasn't that clever so there was only one place he would go. Home. And he'd already told me he was from Shortdrop.

～

"Thanks for that, Sarge," said Florian. "Appreciate you telling Joe how stupid I am."

"Ah shut up, Twins. You've gotten smarter."

"Still stupid enough to be part of the Ravens though..."

"What did you say?"

"Nothing, Sarge. I was just going to carry on with the story."

~

ME AND AIOLA DID INDEED SET OUT FOR SHORTDROP, BUT we knew enough to stay off the roads. We walked all the first night and found shelter during the day, hiding in the brush of the foothills.

My plan was to head west to the Green Forest, disappear for a few days and then move north once it was safe. We made it to the forest in a couple of days. Aiola and her bow snagged a few hares for our meals along the way, though I let us have a fire only long enough to cook the meat.

In the Green Forest we made a shelter and hunkered down, thinking we were in the clear as we had seen no sign of pursuit.

Unfortunately, sarge had Dug with him and she was a formidable tracker; former poacher if I remember right. They'd gone up the road for a day, assuming I was that dim, before doubling back. Dug could still follow the trail we left behind, even though it was cold for a couple of days. They'd nearly caught up with us before we made it to the forest. We spent only one night in our forest shelter. A night me and Aiola huddled together remembering how we would build forts together in the woods near our home, and we felt close again.

Before the four trackers messed everything up.

It was morning, and I was building a fire while Aiola was hunting for breakfast when I heard the crunch of boots on undergrowth. I saw the sarge and the other three enter our small clearing.

"Hello boy," said the sarge, "where's the girl?"

I stood up slowly without answering and looked back to see my shield and sword propped up against a tree a couple of strides away. I tried to inch my way toward it while I considered my options.

"Stay there," said the sarge. "Don't do anything stupid. If I take you both back now, then I might get you off with a flogging. Do something daft and you'll hang if these three don't carve you up first."

"I'm sorry Sergeant Morris," I said. "We're not going back. I have to take my sister home. I promise I will return afterwards."

"Hah, you hear that?" said the sergeant. Dug, Moley and Flathead let out little chuckles, but I could see they already expected a fight. "I don't think I've ever known a deserter to walk back on his own."

"Look, I wanted to be in the army. But I promised I'd keep my sister safe. And what's a man worth if he can't keep his word?"

"I don't care. And I'm not inclined to stand around here gabbing"

Before he could finish, my boot kicked the fire, scattering the burning tinder and sticks into their faces while I grabbed up my sword and shield and charged.

Dug was closest, and I didn't like the way she was playing with the many knives around her waist and across her chest. Getting skewered by throwing knives didn't sound appealing. Unsure what to do, I charged. I felt a thud on my raised shield, my head ducked behind. She'd got one knife away before I hit her. And I hit her good, launching myself off both feet, raising my shield just before impact to collide with her upper chest and head, bashing her to the floor.

I rolled away as best as I could with the shield looped across my forearm and got to my feet, happy to see Dug was now taking a nap.

Unfortunately, I didn't have much other good news, as Moley and Flathead came at me. Flathead from the left with his sword, and Moley from the right with his axe. Flathead and I had sparred a lot on the way down to the muster point but Moley had never been bothered with the extra training. I didn't know what he could do. The sarge stood behind them both, watching, likely sizing me up, sword in his hand at the ready.

I took a few slow steps backward, careful of my footing as tripping would have been the death of me. And as I backed up, Moley and Flathead were forced together as the forest thickened.

Once they were close enough to each other so I could keep my eye on them both, I charged again, changing direction without warning. And maybe you've noticed, maybe you haven't, but I never yell or cry out when running into a fight. My dad beat that one out of me. "Why let the person who wants to kill you, know what you will do, before you've done it?" he'd say.

So I was quiet, and I was fast.

I faked toward Flathead on the left, but shifted my attention to Moley, hoping my shield would cover the left flank. Like I said, I didn't know what Moley could do with his axe; but I'd seen what plenty of woodcutters and slaughter men could do back home with little more than a strong arm.

Moley swung the axe at my torso as I closed on him, and my momentum and the arc of the blow meant I couldn't dodge. I brought my sword up under his swing. Carrying the movement upwards to his sword arm with the flat of my blade. I just managed to deflect his axe up and over my head.

Moley let go of his axe and it sailed into the air, landing in the undergrowth. While he was clutching his wrist and swearing, I punched him in the face with the hilt of my sword, split his lip and knocked him out.

Flathead wasn't standing around doing nothing. I'd been able to block his first overhand blow with my shield before knocking out Moley, and I turned just in time to see his follow up angle toward my legs and parry it with my sword.

A quick look at the sarge and I saw he was walking over now, having decided to get involved. I had to deal with Flathead quick. Dropping the shield, I held my bastard sword with both hands, knowing I was stronger than him, and quicker too.

I pressed the attack. A couple of strikes he parried, but they forced him back. When he lost his footing a little, it gave me the opening to hit him in the chest with the flat of the sword. Broke a few ribs and knocked him to the floor. I kicked him in the chin and he went out too.

"Well done, boy," said the sarge from behind me. I turned and saw he held a sword in each hand now, and was closing the distance between us. "Like I said, there didn't need to be no fighting. They were going easy on you. We don't make a habit of carving up our kids. But well done all the same. Though you should have kept hold of your shield."

An arrow appeared, sticking out of the dirt just where the sarge was about to step, and we both looked at each other confused.

"Stay where you are," said a figure, appearing from behind a tree. It was Aiola, saving my arse.

"Or what?"

"Or I'll shoot you. I shot this pig," she said, indicating a small wild hog at her feet, "and I bet he can move faster than you."

"You'll kill me? And what are you going to do about my men here when they wake up?"

"I think they might have a problem waking up if we slit their throats." Aiola maintained eye contact with sarge the whole time. I looked back and forth between them like someone watches a game of catch.

Sarge turned and looked at me. "Are you sure this one ain't cut out for the army? Seems like she'd do ok." I shook my head, though at that time I was revising my opinion too. "Well we're in a little pickle then, aren't we? I don't think either of you wants to kill us. Life of an outlaw ain't any better or longer than the life of a soldier. I have a proposition. Want to hear it?"

"Go ahead," said Aiola, clearly still the one with the negotiating power.

"Well, a few folks know Florian is a twin, but no one ever met you. So if I take Florian back with me, he'll do the work of two men on my squad. I mean, he took out three of my crew without killing them. He's a big boy so he can manage. You can walk home and I'll forget ever meeting you."

"That's ridiculous," she said, "how can he be two people at once?"

"I pick the Ravens and I'll say I found two new recruits. As long as I don't notice I'm short a squad member, I'll make sure no one else notices either. Especially if he can act the part a little."

"It might work, Aiola," I said, regaining my tongue.

"What choice do we have? Do we have your word on this sergeant?"

"Aye. Just put the bloody bow down."

~

THE SARGE GAVE US SOME TIME TO SAY OUR GOODBYES. MY confidence in making this plan work disappeared after the standoff was over. It was Aiola who switched view and talked me round; she always could. Like I said, she got the brains.

"What's going to be my name?" I remember asking.

"It's Florian, stupid," she said.

"No, I mean what is the twin version of me called?"

"Ahh." Aiola looked down at the wild hog she'd killed for our breakfast. "How about Hameth?"

I laughed, but it seemed fitting, and so that's the name I used every other day after I got back to camp. Aiola and I hugged. She rested her head on my shoulder and I could feel her crying.

"Don't worry, you'll make it back home ok," I said.

"It's not that, you lummox; I'll miss you."

"I know. Me too." My voice cracked and I felt a tear trickle down my cheek. Saying goodbye to my sister, realizing that I'd miss her teasing, our talks by the fire at night about what our lives might bring, it was worse than coming home to find her gone. "I'll be back. Once this war is over I'll come back to you and Mum and Dad."

She kissed me on the cheek, gathered her stuff, and left. She knew I had lied again.

~

"And so there you go, Joe. That's why Ervin called me Ham and the rest of the Ravens call me Twins. And it's why, even three years later, I have to carry more gear than everyone else."

"Is it all true?" asked Joe, looking to Sergeant Morris and Moley. Both nodded. "You're telling me no one noticed Florian and Hameth were never in the same place at the same time?"

"We keep to ourselves, Joe," said Sargent Morris. "The Ravens get all the shit jobs. Gives us a certain independence. So it's never been an issue."

"Wow..."

"Sarge, seeing as this was a pretty big scrap," said Florian, gesturing down the hill at the battlefield, "what do you think about giving Hameth a decent burial now?"

Sergeant Morris got to his feet, stretched some kinks out of his back, and fixed Florian with one of his stares. "No bloody way. I've been pocketing Hameth's wages for three years now. I've got a wife and kids to support."

And Florian watched his sergeant descend the hill toward their camp as the smoke from the fires burning in Redpool slid toward them on the shifting evening breeze.

JYUTH ON MAGIC - SOURCES OF MAGICAL POWER

These writings are excerpts from Jyuth's hand written journals, gifted to Neenahwi before the election of Lord Protector.

I, JYUTH, WRITE THESE PAGES TO CAPTURE MY LEARNINGS, gleaned from years of study with my teacher and from further independent research. It would be a great shame for all peoples if my knowledge be lost should something happen to me.

~

MAGIC. SORCERY. WITCHCRAFT. CALL IT WHAT YOU WILL, for names do not change the truth of a thing. Magic is simply the manipulation of energy; the application of the wizard's imagination to mold this energy or mana in various applications.

Your first question, much as it was mine, is likely: where does magic come from?

Sources of Magic

GENERALLY SPEAKING, MANA IS ENERGY ALL AROUND US that only the trained wizard can see. And only living things are that source. True, there are a few exceptions when it comes to inanimate objects but I will address those another time. So, it is mana that is the lifeblood of wizardry, and it is the ability to see that energy that surrounds us in so many things, that separates the true wizard from the charlatan. There are five primary sources of magic to consider:

PLANTS AND VEGETATION.

Even the lowliest and meager of plants has mana available. The challenge is in the harvesting, and the time to build the web of connections. Trees are a more fruitful source, in particular old growth which will have surprising depths of power. Care must be taken not to scorch the land. Do not take all that can be taken - plants can regenerate given time, and ours is not the role to be a plague on nature.

ANIMALS.

The nagual or souls of animals can be a potent source of mana but there is no way to harvest it and avoid the creature's death. In fact, the ritual sacrifice of the creature is often required for lesser practitioners who do not fully appreciate that with which they dabble. These same lesser practitioners will attest to the efficacy of certain species—pigs, snakes, calves, doves and so on.

SENTIENT RACES.

All of the sentient races, be they human, giant, elf, dwarf, goblin or other, are difficult sources of mana. Their spark of consciousness brings with it an innate knack for self-defense against the wizard's ability to create a conduit to draw their life force. This takes focused concentration to overcome. There are records of individuals willingly granting part of their own life, but it requires immense trust; as once defenses are dropped then the donor is open to extreme peril.

MAGICAL BEASTS.

Some creatures carry a spark of a different flavor and complexity, and no two are alike. Dragons and drakes, basilisk and salamander, faerie and demon; these creatures are rare and their defenses are strong. In my experience it requires the creature to be subdued to draw on their mana.

YOURSELF.

The most readily available source of mana is the most precious. It is the wizard himself. But the supply of energy is limited and the wizard is literally using his own life. That is why methods to use this energy as efficiently as possible are essential, but that too is a lesson for another day. Beware drawing on your own power too much, as you will perish.

REGENERATION.

Use of your own supplies of energy are unavoidable. Thankfully, as long as your appetite is not lethally great, then your mana can recover with time. Sleep is good. Food is helpful (in particular I have found greasy bacon to be effective). But recovery is slow. With sleep and food, it can take many months to recover from a moderate drain. Faster recovery requires deep meditation and a continuous slow draw from the natural world around you. This is what you must practice.

ALL THAT SHIMMERS

K yle opened his eyes and, as per most days, veritably leapt out of bed. Life was good. He was glad for each new morning that brought him a day ripe with opportunity to hone his talents. Kyle had often told his mother that he didn't want to go to bed, because he'd prefer to keep on working. This wasn't necessarily uncommon behavior for the Deep People of Unedar Halt; a love of what they do. There wasn't any of this strange sickness that Kyle had heard of above ground, where people didn't like or appreciate their lot in life.

But it had been noted by many that Kyle took this enthusiasm to a level that was not often seen amongst his peers.

Kyle's bed chamber was of simple formation; dug out from the rock and dirt under the mountain, it was connected to a basic sitting room that doubled up as a study. He had lived in these rooms for most of the twenty years that he had served with Raghallack, one of the most talented chiselers that Unedar Halt had ever known. There were no decorations. No personalization of this space he owned. And most strangely there was a lack of embellishment or adornment to any of the stone carvings of Kyle's home.

Which is surprising when you consider that the chiseler's role beneath the mountain is not only to dig new caverns, but make them beautiful too.

There was a (generally) healthy rivalry between squads of chiselers for whom could create the most elaborate carvings, and for developing new methods for doing so. Kyle himself had recently become quite renowned for his work on the new Galag Clan expansion: the walls of which had been adorned with branches and leaves of trees that he had never seen in person, rather discovered in a book in the library. When Kyle looked at the empty walls of his home, he envisioned hundreds of ideas of what he could do with such a blank canvas: interconnected geometric shapes; flames rising to form salamanders; a scale map of Unedar Halt. *But when was there time to do something that would only ever be seen by him?*

Kyle ate his breakfast of boiled great-centipede eggs and reflected on his living status. Yes, he was living alone and some of his friends had already found life partners with which to build new caverns. But how did he have time for that either? There was work to be done. Techniques to learn. And new approaches to develop. If he had a life partner demanding his time and attention then he would never have had time to discover the acid that he had used to clear away the stone, one layer at a time through brushed application, that he had used for the Forest Hall.

No, he thought, *there will be time for that later.*

He flung his satchel over his shoulder—it rattled with his tools of the trade—and opened the bronze door to the tunnels outside. Kyle hummed a little ditty to himself as he wended his way on his usual route to the worm pens. Purple worms; a tool that differentiated the chiselers from the other teams that together were responsible for the slow expansion of Unedar Halt.

The chiselers came at the beginning and end of each work cycle. Chiselers carved out the new tunnels and chambers, and then the other teams did their work. Cleaner teams, combinations of warriors and animal handlers, were always close by to a chiseler ready to step in when needed. For new passages would often break through to undiscovered, naturally occurring spaces, and they could be home to the various beasties that inhabited the deep dark.

Chiselers might discover new seams of precious metals or deposits of raw gem stones, and call on a team of miners. These were Deep People experienced in the extraction of the raw materials used by the craftspeople of his city.

All new digs needed to be illuminated; the Deep People had good vision in the dark but could not see in the total black, so gardeners would come along to seed and nurture the luminescent mosses that were everywhere. And then finally, closing the loop, chiselers would be able to scratch their creative itch and bring art to the stone walls of the new spaces they had carved.

And so, the worm-pens was the place that Kyle went every day to collect the one tool that wouldn't fit in his bag, though this was more than just a tool—this was his friend.

Curled up behind a wrought iron railing was Vidin, his purple worm. He was twenty feet of interconnected segments of pulsing pulpous flesh, ending in a hard carapace around the head, with a mouth that could open three feet wide, full of teeth near as hard as diamonds. Vidin was a baby —well, a little older than a baby. Kyle remembered when he had been paired with him at just a few months old. Then he had been six feet long. Now, three years later, Vidin was an infant and growing fast.

The relationship between the Deep People and the purple worms was an interesting one that went back centuries. The worms would bring their young to the dwarves to be raised until they reached adolescence, where it was not unknown for them to be hundreds of feet long and twenty feet in diameter, digging deep underground for reasons that his people had not discovered. The only good answer scholars had developed was a simple one. *Because.*

Kyle opened the gate to the pen and Vidin slithered out to nuzzle up against his handler. Four pairs of eyes around the hard carapace blinked slowly and the creature purred as Kyle scratched at a favorite spot of soft flesh.

"It's good to see you too, Vidin," said Kyle. "I hope you got a good night's sleep. It's time to go to work."

～

KYLE AND VIDIN WORKED ON A NEW TUNNEL BRANCH OFF the great meeting chamber for the Nandaklar Clan, a large family of many generations that had living quarters across many levels that stretched from close to the center of Unedar Halt right to the edges of their territory. The meeting chamber had been there for many years, long before Kyle was born, and it was one of his favorite spaces in the city. The ceiling was decorated with the relief of a dragon—long reptilian body running the length of the chamber and great wings that stretched out across the roof and down the walls—giving the impression that the dragon was sheltering the inhabitants of the room under its mighty presence. The neck of the dragon stretched down one wall where the head turned, mouth open to form the entrance. It had been chiseled by his master in his youth, taking a whole year to complete.

The clan had decided to build out past the meeting chamber in order to house some of the greatest examples of craftsmanship of their family—museums had become something of a new trend amongst the wealthiest clans.

And so, Kyle and Vidin worked away.

The great benefit of the relationship between purple worms and the Deep People was that worms ate rock. And they ate it fast— making them wonderful partners for excavation. Kyle gazed proudly as Vidin rose up and supported himself, his body one long mass of muscle, to reach the higher levels of the rock face. The maws of the worm opened to bite through the stone. The crunching of rock was accompanied with gurgles and sizzling noises as his friend's digestion did its work, each wriggle moving the meal through his stomachs and combinations of chemicals until a grey slurry passed from his rear.

That was why Kyle held what looked like a wooden broom which someone had forgotten to attach bristles to— perfect for spreading the slurry into an even coating that would quickly dry as hard as the rock it had recently been.

A marvel, thought Kyle. *If it wasn't for the worms we would never have been able to dedicate so much of our lives to craft, instead of digging.*

As he spread the slurry he kept watch for particular types of discoloration that would be of interest. It was common when digging at this depth to discover seams of metals, and Vidin could digest almost anything he came across (though lead would often give him indigestion). A sign of gold or silver and he would stop Vidin so a mining team could be called in to extract the precious metals; evidence of tin and they would continue, Kyle instead looking to artfully arrange the glinting slurry.

Kyle stooped to pick up a rock that had passed through Vidin and landed in a puddle of sludge. A sapphire. Raw and uncut, but the blue was visible through the slurry that coated it. He wiped off the grey slime and tucked it away in a pocket. This one could be polished up and put into Kyle's wedding chest to be gifted to his betrothed on the day he married—that was if he ever had the time to visit the gem workers or find someone to marry. For now, it could sit with the other shiny rocks in his room.

~

"YOU DID GREAT TODAY," SAID KYLE, PATTING VIDIN ON the head. The worm nestled against the dwarf as he rested, leaning against the wall of the tunnel they had carved out that day. The creature was warm to the touch from its digestive exertions, and he knew that it would want to sleep soon. But Kyle wasn't done yet.

"I know you're tired, but I'm going to ask that you just take a little rest? I can tell there is a chamber just the other side of here. Don't you want to see what it looks like?"

Kyle could have sworn that Vidin nodded. He smiled. Kyle found it exciting to discover new caverns in the deep of Unedar Halt. Many times, the rock formations and stone faces that were carved by nature put the Deep People's industry to shame, and he wanted to see what today might bring. But first he had something to do. There was a protocol to follow.

"Wait here, Vidin; I'll be back with a cleaner squad."

~

"ALRIGHT, KYLE, LET'S GET GOING. IT'S NEARLY TIME FOR dinner you know."

"I know, Fola," said Kyle to the dwarf standing behind him. She was dressed in boiled leather armor, inset with metal plates across the chest, abdomen and thighs. She held a crossbow at the ready, and a short wide sword hung from her hip. Her three crew members were dressed identically.

Fola was an old friend of Kyle's and he was glad that her crew had been on duty. They went back a long way, friends only of course, though sometimes his dreams—and his insides whenever he spoke to her—told him that he would like that to be different. In any case, it was good he had found her, as the comment about dinner time was no joke: plenty of other squads might have turned down the job because of an impending meal. But Kyle wasn't hungry; he had a lightness in his stomach from the excitement of what they were going to discover.

Kyle patted Vidin's tail three times and the worm wriggled forward to take a massive bite out of the wall. Bite followed bite, only to discover more rock. Kyle looked back at Fola who gave him a small smile.

More butterflies.

Vidin continued to chomp away at the rock. Chomp after chomp. Kyle spread the slurry so it wouldn't dry in a lump and ruin the floor. He turned when he heard a noise behind him.

Fola tapping her foot.

Kyle smiled sheepishly. He really had expected that it would not take too long to break through. Usually he was so good at estimating these dista—

Crack.

Boom.

A cloud of dust swept forward to envelop Kyle, Fola and the cleaner squad as Vidin broke through and the tunnel wall partially collapsed in a shower of rubble.

Kyle held his breath while the dust settled, he'd had years of practice in avoiding inhaling and then the inevitable coughing up of stone dust, thankful that his eyes were protected by his leather framed glass goggles. Vidin wriggled clear of the rubble and moved into the chamber ahead. Kyle followed him without having to duck.

He emerged into the middle of a great cavern, longer than it was deep, that tapered at one end. Stalactites hung from the ceiling and a large ridge, some ten feet across, ran down the center of the cavern. Kyle could see all this without using his shuttered lantern, for the walls were covered with a combination of the naturally growing luminescent moss and, most interestingly, swirling streaks of shimmering bright blue embedded into the far stone wall that shone with a light rarely seen by the Deep People.

"Granthium," breathed Kyle, mouth hanging open at the discovery of the most precious of all the metals that the dwarves worked with. Granthium, the substance that the master smiths and crafters, working in tandem with the high priests of Varcon, could enchant into magnificent artifacts. He turned to look at Fola, expecting to see her face lit up in joy at his discovery.

She emerged from the break-through, and Kyle saw her face become as hard as steel. She raised her crossbow to sight down its length toward him.

Kyle raised his hands in alarm, and stepped backward. *What? Why? They could share in this find...*

A noise from behind Kyle drew his attention to the center of the chamber. The ridge was rising into the air, accumulations of dust and dripped salt cracking away as it moved. At first Kyle thought it was another purple worm trapped in here, like Vidin but three times larger. But though the general shape was similar, it was clearly different. Mutated. Corrupted.

Its skin was not the vibrant shade of purple that was typical to purple worms; it was doughy and white, hanging off in places to reveal green flesh beneath. Tendrils reached out from all over the creature's body—long stretching appendages groping in the dark for prey. And the creature's many eyes blazed with a bright blue light that mirrored the granthium.

The monstrosity's head rose thirty feet into the air, still not reaching the roof of the cavern. A screech filled the air and to Kyle, it was like someone had driven iron spikes through both ears and into his brain. He clamped his hands over his ears to stop the bombardment. Fola and the cleaner squad ran forward, shooting their crossbow bolts with practiced accuracy as they formed a protecting wall in front of Kyle.

The worm-like abomination crashed down, still screaming.

Its mouth opened, more tentacles coming out of the maw to grab a dwarf and pull him inside. The massive teeth came down on a second dwarf and bit him in two from top to bottom. Kyle averted his gaze from the savagery.

Fola and her sole remaining team member grabbed Kyle, each by an arm and made to drag him to the break-through hole.

"No!" screamed Kyle. "Where's Vidin?"

He didn't have time to hear a response, or be able to do anything else as the worm abomination charged.

~

"IS HE WELL ENOUGH FOR ME TO SEE HIM?" ASKED A VOICE that Kyle did not recognize. It was dark.

Were his eyes closed? No, but he still couldn't see anything. Blind?

"He has not yet awoken, Forger," said a gruff voice.

The Forger? Was he asking after him? He had never had the honor of speaking to the leader of the Deep People.

"I'm awake..." came a feeble voice that Kyle was surprised to discover was his own.

"See, Nurse Kenan. The lad is awake," said the first voice again.

"Five minutes. No more," harrumphed the nurse.

"How are you feeling lad?" asked the first voice again. That must be the Forger.

"Am I blind?" asked Kyle, trying to flex his hands but feeling bandages wrapping them into tight parcels.

"No, Kyle. At least we hope not. Your eyes are wrapped up, like most of the rest of you. You had some terrible injuries."

He breathed out slowly, the panic subsiding. "What happened?"

"I was going to ask you the same thing. We lost two squads of cleaners down there. Damn fine ones too."

Two crews? That meant that Fola was dead too? Kyle would have cried if only he had the energy. Silence was the only remembrance he could manage.

"Kyle, I need to know what happened," insisted the Forger.

"I-er- I don't know if I can remember everything. We found a huge cavern, beautiful it was. There was granthium in the walls, Forger," said Kyle, some excitement returning to his voice as he remembered the discovery.

"Granthium, you say, eh? No one has found any granthium in decades." The Forger didn't sound convinced, like he wanted to move on to things of more importance. "It was probably just the light. A different species of moss."

"No, I swear! It was granthium."

"Kyle, that doesn't matter right now. Tell me what happened next."

"There was a creature there. I didn't see it at first. And then I thought it was just a purple worm, but it was horrifying. It looked dead and its eyes glowed blue. And tentacles reached out from all over its body. It pulled one of Fola's men into its mouth before it ate clean through another." The vision of the dwarf being ripped in half like a butchered umbral cow played out on the dark of his eyes at the memory.

"And then I don't remember anything more. What happened?"

"I don't know the details. That's what I'm trying to ascertain. I do know the cleaners did their job and got you free. They tried to keep that beast from being able to get into Unedar Halt. But it was too powerful. We had a juggernaut come and bring down the tunnel, blocked that creature back in where you found it."

"I'm so sorry, Master Forger. It's all my fault."

"Now, now, lad. You did the right thing. Mining is a dangerous business, everyone knows that. We have our protocols to reduce the risk, but sometimes, these things happen. Now get some sleep, I'd best be leaving you alone before I get into trouble."

Something suddenly occurred to Kyle. "Wait, Master Forger. Did you find Vidin? My worm?"

"I'm afraid nothing came out of that cavern alive except you before the tunnel came down."

Kyle lay still. Images of Vidin, Fola and the shorn cleaner floating in the black of his bandaged eyes. He lay still, scarcely breathing.

He did not speak.

And it was a long time until sleep finally paid him a visit.

~

KYLE LAY AWAKE IN HIS BED IN HIS OWN HOME. MANY OF his bandages had been removed before he was discharged from the infirmary. Being able to see was a blessing, but his broken arm remained encased in a cast made from bandages soaked in a thin mixture of worm slurry.

He had been happy to be free of the darkness of his own closed eyes and the visions that it brought, but there was no escaping the memories of what he saw. His imagination conjured ever more gruesome ways to view the deaths of those he did not see. His nights had become a cavalcade of fitful sleep and those terrible visions.

Part of the problem was that Kyle had not been allowed to go back to work. He had been told to rest. *But why did he need to rest when he hadn't spent any time working?* He was not physically tired the way he would be after a hard day's work, and that too made it more difficult for him to sleep.

Poor Vidin, he thought. *I hope he managed to escape that monster. Maybe it wouldn't have attacked something that it used to be? Or Vidin might have tunneled to safety. Though surely, he would have returned by now.*

Staring at the ceiling of his room, his mind thankfully wandered away from the gruesome fate of his companions, and settled on the other thing that had been weighing on him.

Stone walls, streaked with glittering blue. Granthium.

Kyle was certain that the cavern where that monster lay did have a deposit of that most rare of metals, even though the Forger was skeptical. Granthium was naturally strong—stronger than steel—and once forged by a dwarven smith any weapon would be unbreakable. The edge of an axe would never dull.

Most importantly, granthium could absorb the blessings of Varcon, the god of the Deep People, and become imbued with fantastic abilities. It had been granthium that was used to forge fabled weapons that would be encased with fire, or as cold to the touch as the freezing ice on top of Mount Tiston.

And if there really was granthium in that cavern then his people needed it. Many of the best craftspeople of Unedar Halt had never had the opportunity to work with granthium. Surely that was not fair; that they would not be able to test their abilities in the most exceptional of circumstances?

It wasn't fair.

For the good of the Deep People, he had to work out how they could mine the fabulous blue ore.

And so Kyle—chiseler, not warrior—had to know how to beat the monster.

~

THE ARCHIVES WERE KEPT IN THE HOUSE OF VARCON, ONE of the twin-peaked buildings in the center of the vast main cavern of Unedar Halt. The House of Varcon was part temple, part place of learning, and though the priesthood lived inside the needle shaped building, it was open to all of the Deep People.

Not that Kyle visited very often anymore. Feast day celebrations were typically held in large public spaces, either there in the central chamber or in clan meeting areas such as the one he had been recently expanding. But Kyle had spent time in the archives in the past, back when he was the student of Raghallack; who it seemed, at the time, took enormous pleasure in tasking Kyle to research the answers to his own questions, and would not let him return until he had discovered a satisfactory answer.

Which sometimes would take weeks.

And every time, when Kyle returned with an answer, Raghallack would nod his head in agreement at the results of his study, obviously knowing the answer himself.

Initially that had been very frustrating to Kyle. If Raghallack was supposed to be his teacher then why wouldn't he simply tell him the answers? Wasn't that the point of being a teacher? But now, as Kyle passed through a series of staggered entrance chambers, each door booming closed behind him as he would wait for the next to open—safeguards against any contaminants that could damage the books— he knew that Raghallack had prepared him for this moment.

"Good morning," said a young dwarf in dark blue robes, beard and hair shorn to a stubble—the mark of an initiate. "Can I help you find what you are looking for?"

Kyle paused to survey the vast archive in front of him, wondering where to start. Low shelves of books and study tables were arrayed in neat lines that disappeared almost into darkness at the far end of the room; and that was only the first level of this chamber. Pillars interrupted the stacks of books to support the next layer, similarly arranged with shelves, books, tables and columns, further floors repeating in open construction up to the cavernous ceiling. Twenty-seven layers of the archive, all connected with iron ladders, housing the collected learnings and histories of the Deep People.

Remembering the initiate who had spoken to him, Kyle turned to address him. A smile on his face for the first time in weeks. "No that's fine, thank you. I don't know what I'm looking for yet."

∼

RESEARCH DID NOT BRING QUITE THE SAME SENSE OF fulfillment to Kyle as when he was chiseling, but it did give him purpose. That brought a spring back into his step, and untroubled sleep came once more from long days poring over books. The gruesome visions that had been invading his dreams began to fade.

Kyle had lost count of the number of days he had been coming to the archives. In fact, there hadn't really been a need to keep count in the first place. There were no other demands on his time. And he had lost himself in the stacks of books; most bound with metal plates, the pages thin, almost translucent and made of the skin of various subterranean creatures.

He discovered histories of the Deep People that were rarely read. Much of it would be considered mundane—the Deep People were avid historians and kept records of everything—writings on the key events of Unedar Halt; births, deaths and marriages, mining records, ever expanding multi-paged maps of the city.

He learned of Sefu, mother to twins some five hundred years past. Twins! The only known occurrence of a dwarven mother giving birth to more than one child at once.

He read of the skirmishes with Kingshold, petty arguments with Kings who looked to bring the Deep People under their sway.

And slowly, he found teasing little parts of the puzzle that he pieced together.

The archive began to feel like a new home. And like a new home, he began to recognize his neighbors. There was one old lady, Eanrind, he would see every day. Retired from her prior life as a smith, but with her mind still sharp, she had taken on the task of creating a family tree, tracing back centuries to illuminate the deeds of her ancestors. There was a steady stream of initiates, pulling specific tomes and then hurrying back to whomever of the priesthood had tasked them with the job. He saw younger versions of himself—disgruntled young dwarves, sent there by their masters to answer their own questions. But most peculiarly, he saw a female human wandering the aisles, paging through book after book.

Other than old Eanrind, she was the person he saw most often. She was taller than he, though not as tall as he had heard some humans could be, with long dark hair that hung in a braid down her back. She wore simple purple robes and carried a small leather satchel with her at all times. After the fifth time they had seen each other she had smiled at him, and he had nodded good day. By the tenth time they had crossed in the stacks, they were at the "good morning" and "fancy seeing you here" stage.

Yesterday had been a good day. A book entitled *Occurrences Requiring The Guard* from more than a thousand years ago had proved to be a revelation. Or so Kyle hoped. A record of a creature that bore an uncanny resemblance to the monster that Kyle had loosed. They had called it a *spectre*, a creature not dead nor alive, tainted by magic and a bringer of death.

Finally: progress.

This spectre had come from deep tunnels and rampaged through clan living quarters, killing tens of Deep People before the guards had been able to contain it and then kill it, but not without the loss of life. Frustratingly, *"Occurrences"* did not provide details of how the beast was defeated or where it came from, it instead named each of the fallen on that sad day; but it provided some hints as to the nature of the beast and it was that Kyle had as his goal to pursue that morning.

His day passed one book at a time, searching for another mention of the spectre. The earlier forays into the annals that morning had not recovered much; but that was the way with research in the vault—whole days could be spent without finding what you need when you don't know what you're looking for.

But despite all of this, Kyle was enjoying himself. He walked to a far-off corner of the vault, searching the shelves for his next target, whilst whistling a little ditty (though the initiates might pretend to be upset, he knew they enjoyed it really). Turning a corner, he found the human woman standing in front of him, holding a book in her hands. The cover read *Sourcery and Deamons in the Darke*. The book he was looking for.

The woman looked at Kyle and smiled. "Good afternoon," she said.

"Oh, yes. Good afternoon, miss," said Kyle in return, offering a little bow. He was a little apprehensive talking to the human, but he didn't want her to move on with his book. Who knew if she would put it back in the correct place? In any case, she seemed to be approachable.

"I see you here all the time. I am Neenahwi."

"I see you too, miss. I mean, Neenahwi. A pleasure to meet you. My name is Kyle."

"Do you work here?" she asked.

"Oh, no, miss...Neenahwi. I am a chiseler," said Kyle, his back getting a little straighter and standing a little taller. "I'm just here trying to answer some pretty serious questions. Er... are you finished with that book?"

"What, this one?" she said, holding it up in the air like it was a surprise it was in her hands. "You are a strange chiseler indeed, to be interested in these kinds of magics."

"Well, maybe that's not the right book then," he said, suddenly nervous at the question. "It probably doesn't talk about the *locus seeds* anyway."

"I remember seeing a page on that," said Neenahwi. She flipped through some pages, balancing the heavy book on the shelf and holding it with one hand. "Wait a second... Here. Is that what you're looking for?"

Kyle moved to take a closer look. He nodded. "Yes, that looks very interesting. I can come back and get the book when you are finished."

"Oh, that's ok. Reading these books is a lonely business,

don't you think? Come, let's find a table and you can tell me more about what you're researching. I'm fascinated."

Kyle nodded and allowed himself to be led away by the friendly human, continuing to make small talk until, before he realized it, he was telling her all about his shame of releasing the spectre. She nodded along as he told his story, not interrupting—even though dwarven stories typically came with a lot of background and technical details about the craft—until he reached the part about his recent findings.

"So, you believe that the creature you found was a spectre? A worm tainted by magic?" she asked.

"Aye. And I think it's these locus seeds that do it. I have a theory that it's those seeds that create granthium too."

"What are locus seeds, Kyle?"

"That's what I wanted this book for." He slid the book across the table over to himself and read quietly for a few minutes. "I have found few references to them. They are described as small stones that have been found when mining. Extremely rare, and unbreakable—only two known instances throughout the history of Unedar Halt. And magic is very strong around these stones. That's why they are called locus stones. Ah, yes!" He exclaimed in triumph. "Look here, the author thinks that the magic leaks out."

Kyle looked up from the book to see Neenahwi staring at him with wide eyes, her mouth hanging open. "Are you ok?" he asked.

Neenahwi shook her head, returning her attention to the book which she slid over to herself to read the same passages. Once she had finished, she returned her attention to Kyle, the intensity of her expression surprising him.

"And what do you think this has to do with the spectre?"

"I don't know how much *you* know about purple worms, but *I* know a lot. Worms will eat anything they come across, and they can digest almost everything. Except precious stones. Too dense, you see. Now, I saw a worm once who had a diamond as big as your fist get stuck in his stomach. It wouldn't pass. Poor thing was going to die but the worm-keepers, they operated on it and pulled it out. What if this other worm ate one of these locus seeds, and it got stuck? All of that magic leaking out into its body wouldn't be a good thing."

Neenahwi exhaled in a slow whistle. "I never thought there could be one so close," she mumbled. "And you think it's still inside the spectre?" she asked.

"Don't know. It could have passed eventually, I guess. We won't know until we cut it open."

"Kyle. I knew there was knowledge in the vault that I had to find. But I didn't expect to find you," said Neenahwi. "I want to help."

～

KYLE AND NEENAHWI WAITED ON A LONG, LOW CARVED stone bench in a corridor covered in reliefs of the great and the good from Unedar's long history. A brass door beside them opened, and out walked an old dwarf. Old, but not ancient. This dwarf was still strong in the arm and shoulders; once a great smith, the decades of pounding with a heavy hammer had developed muscle that was only now turning a little soft. His job was no longer to create works of art; for many years it had been his job to bring the clans together.

"Come in, you two," said the Forger, issuing them into his office and closing the door behind them. It was a simple room; smooth stone walls, unadorned with etchings or decorations, separated shelves built into the walls that were overflowing with books and loose leaves of paper. In the center of the room was a wooden desk and chairs—such a rarity to see wood from above ground in Unedar Halt—and it was here he asked Kyle and Neenahwi to sit.

Kyle ran a hand across the polished surface of the desk without thinking, marveling at its construction and solidity, before he noticed the Forger looking at him appraisingly. Kyle snatched his hand back.

"That's ok, lad," said the Forger. "It is a beauty, isn't it? It was a gift, long ago, to one of my predecessors. I believe it was from your father, Neenahwi."

Neenahwi nodded and smiled.

"Now, I don't think you two have come here to discuss furniture. And I don't remember saying it was ok for you to be colluding with young 'uns either, Neenahwi. I thought you wanted to use the vault."

"Master Forger," she began, "it was not my intention. But I believe that Kyle has made a significant discovery that aligns with my own inquiry. And I'd like to help him."

The Forger turned to regard Kyle. Kyle had promised himself not to show his nervousness at this meeting, and he took deep breaths to calm his somersaulting heart that he hoped were not too obvious.

"What is it then, Kyle? I haven't got all day."

"Forger. I have been researching the creature we discovered those weeks ago. It's called a spectre, a creature that has been corrupted by magic. Once it was a purple worm and now it's something not alive or dead—"

"—but still bloody dangerous!" interrupted the Forger.

"Yes. Yes, it is. But me and Neenahwi, we have a plan

about how we can kill it."

"No, no, no. Absolutely not. We lost too many good people last time. We have it locked up, and it doesn't seem like it has any intention of eating its way out of its hole. So, let's just leave it there."

"But who knows when it might decide to break through?" blurted Kyle. The Forger shook his head again, the gold earrings in his great lobes jangling together. "And there is granthium there. I am certain of it."

"How are you *certain?*"

"I have a theory," said Kyle, confident in his work and now eager to share. "The same magic that mutated the worm created the granthium. We think it could have been a locus seed. And Master Forger, there was a lot of granthium."

The old dwarf narrowed his eyes and leaning on the desk he stared at Kyle, looking like Varcon himself. *Breathe. Meet his gaze.*

"A locus seed you say? Very doubtful. Very rare. This spectre could have just eaten the granthium," said the Forger. Kyle and Neenahwi exchanged a glance. They hadn't thought about that possibility.

"Well, if that's the case," said Neenahwi, "then the granthium would still be where the spectre is."

"Yes, yes. You've got me there, Neenahwi." The old dwarf sighed in resignation but didn't shift his attention from Kyle. There was silence for a moment, and then the Forger leaned back in his chair, and Kyle felt a great burden lift as the Forger regarded them both equally. "So, what do you need? The guard?"

"No master Forger," said Kyle. "I just need a new worm, and we need a... we need a juggernaut."

~

KYLE AND NEENAHWI WERE ESCORTED DOWN THE LONG main corridor of the House of Varcon by a priest that had collected them from the vault. They hadn't introduced themselves but he knew who they were. Word had come from the Forger.

The priest opened a door and ushered Kyle and Neenahwi in before him. They entered a small circular room through its only door. Neenahwi shot him a look and he nodded not to be concerned. The priest closed the door behind them, and pulled a lever set in the wall nearby. The floor momentarily lurched upwards, a thrumming noise in the background.

"Is this room moving?" asked Neenahwi.

"Yes," said Kyle. "It's called a lift. There are a few in the city, though I don't know where this one is going."

The floor lurched again and the thrumming noise stopped. The priest opened the door, waiting for them to exit. Kyle and Neenahwi stepped out into another, greater, circular chamber, ringed with archways open to the city allowing a view of the central chamber of Unedar Halt from high. Kyle turned around on the spot, taking in the workmanship of the tall columns and the relief-covered ceiling.

He marveled at the sight of the great stone statues arrayed around the chamber. There were eight in total. Half of them were stone renditions of Deep People, all armored and some wielding great steel weapons.

"What are those creatures?" asked Neenahwi, pointing at the other statues.

"That one there is an umber hulk," he said, happy that Neenahwi demonstrated such curiosity, as he pointed to an insectoid statue standing on two legs. "That's a blind spider, they only hunt by vibration and smell. The one with the big clawed forearms, that's an armavole." Kyle whistled in admiration as he pointed to the final statue. "And that's a deep drake." The deep drake was his favorite; it reminded him of the children stories of dragons. Though, of course, he knew they were quite different.

"I thought drakes had wings. I've seen them on Mount Tiston."

"Oh, they do. The winged ones anyway. Deep drakes have forelimbs instead. They hunt in the passageways that the adult purple worms carve out. There's a whole world of things that live down here, you know." Neenahwi nodded and smiled.

The priest walked over to the statue of the deep drake. Kyle and Neenahwi followed, eventually noticing another priest in black robes standing by the large reptilian head of the statue. As he neared, Kyle could see the detail in the work of the statue. Overlapping scales from the nose to the top of its tail. The sharp teeth visible in the open mouth were not stone but a metal of some kind—sharp as any blade. The statue was large, each stubby leg about the same size as Kyle, and he estimated the drake to be thirty feet long from snout to the barbed end of its tail.

"This is Torkel," said the priest who had escorted them from the library. "I will leave you in her capable hands."

Torkel stepped forward to shake Kyle's hand. She had a round face, her hair was braided in many small plaits that she had tied together on the top of her head—they hung down in cascading ropes, like a geyser erupting from her crown. Torkel was thinner than many of the Deep People, taller too, but Kyle was not sure how much of that was hair and how much was dwarf.

"Nice to meet you, Kyle the Chiseler," she said warmly.

"The pleasure is mine," said Kyle, bowing his head.

"And this must be Neenahwi," said Torkel, taking the human's hand in hers. "I have heard much about you."

"All of it good I hope," laughed Neenahwi.

"All of it interesting," said Torkel smiling. "It is not often we have a human amongst us, and the daughter of the great Jyuth of course!"

Kyle's attention snapped to Neenahwi. In developing their plan, they had discussed her magical abilities but her parentage had not come up. The great Jyuth. A human who had lived longer than any dwarf, and proven himself to be a friend of the Deep People numerous times. Neenahwi shrugged.

"There is a friend of mine who was quite unhappy not to be chosen to help you," said Torkel, still talking to Neenahwi. "He is taken with the surface world. That is his juggernaut over there." She pointed to a great statue of a dwarven warrior across the room, armored, with massive gauntleted hands held together in prayer. "But I was chosen, or should I say, the Forger thought that the drake would be most useful to you."

"This a juggernaut?" asked Neenahwi, inspecting the statue of a drake.

"Yes. Or it is when I take control. I am the pilot. Right now, it's just a rather beautiful statue."

"Thank you for your help, Torkel," said Kyle.

"Not a problem, Kyle the Chiseler. Now, let us go down-stairs so we can eat and you can tell me your plan. And hope-fully, Neenahwi, you'll let me ask you some questions about the world outside Unedar Halt. My friend has given me a list..."

~

Pavak, as he had been named by his usual handler, was bigger than Vidin. Two years older and half as big again. He made quick work of the rubble that had been packed into the tunnel that Vidin had previously carved out.

After he and Neenahwi had met Torkel, Kyle had gone down to the worm pens to arrange the last thing they needed. Pavak occupied the pen next to the empty one that used to be Vidin's. Kyle had stopped and stared at that empty pen, remembering the warm welcome that he would always receive, the memories that were now tinged with sadness at his missing friend. He remembered how some mornings he'd seen the two worms attempting to nuzzle together through the bars separating each of the pens, and so it had been Pavak that he had asked to join them.

Pavak was nearly thirty feet long, so there was not much in the way of telling a worm that size what to do; you asked and explained. Kyle knew the worm would listen. Pavak was worried about his friend and wanted to help.

It was not long before the previously carved tunnel was back to its former size and length, only a thin wall separating them from the cavern where the spectre had been lurking. Kyle asked Pavak to move aside so the juggernaut could step forward. The stone drake moved with nary a sound, except for the thud of stone on stone with each step—Torkel remaining in the House of Varcon but able to see through the eyes of the juggernaut. This was where the plan started in earnest.

Kyle looked at Neenahwi, who nodded in return.

"Do it," said Kyle.

The drake lowered its head and rushed forward, stone-taloned feet gouging rips in the floor as it gained purchase for its dash—Kyle would need to fix that later. The deep drake crashed into the thin wall and it crumbled around it; boulders, fist sized and larger, bounced off its stone skin. For a moment it looked like the juggernaut was buried under the rubble, until it gave itself a shake and the debris scattered all around.

Now would be the time to see if their assumptions from their collective research were correct. Neenahwi had said that magic is attracted to magic, and inside every living thing is a little bit of magic. The spectre was likely to be very old, it's eyes no longer useful to see. Kyle remembered the tentacles waving in the air, as if searching for its prey. Obviously, it was an effective method as evidenced by the fate of the two cleaner crews, but Neenahwi had hypothesized that it did this by sensing the life force, or magic, in each of the Deep People that had come to his aid. And so, keeping this assumption in mind, there were two major elements of the plan at this stage.

First, the juggernaut, a massive living statue of magic, would be the flame to attract the spectre's attention.

Secondly, Neenahwi could disguise the life force of herself and Kyle, creating an illusion that would render them invisible to the spectre against the cavern walls.

It was time to see if their plan was going to play out.

Neenahwi grasped Kyle's hand in hers and he led her, clambering over the piles of rubble, past the deep drake that was standing still in the entranceway to the cavern. The chamber was as he remembered in his dreams—vast, walls streaked with shimmering blue, great stalactites dripping down to the floor. And there, in the middle, was the monstrosity that had killed his friends.

The specter's worm like mouth was closed, the head's wedge shape visible, and a writhing mass of tentacles along its body waved in the air. Neenahwi gripped his hand tighter. Or was it the other way around? It looked like the spectre was looking right at him, and he felt his limbs freeze, unable to move. *This is insane! It will see us!*

"Move," whispered Neenahwi, "it's looking at the juggernaut. Not us."

Kyle's body unfroze, and he inched along the wall away from the deep drake, leading Neenahwi behind him. Afraid to release his hold on her in case the magic would stop protecting him, they moved away from where it seemed the spectre was looking. Kyle was relieved to see that it did not turn.

Fifty feet or so away from the drake they sprinted across the cavern to the far wall, where the blue streaks were at their widest. Kyle ran his hand across the stone, feeling what lay beneath. He licked the blue with his tongue and felt a shiver of a spark in his body. *Granthium.* He had been right! Had Kyle been mistaken about the granthium, their plan had been to beat a hasty retreat and seal up the monster for ever more. But now the prize was real, they had to go about claiming it.

"It's what we came looking for, Neenahwi," said Kyle. "Time to see if Varcon is with us and get rid of this thing."

Neenahwi nodded and reached one hand into the satchel she wore across her body. She pulled out three arrows, made completely of steel, fletching replaced by sharp razors. Neenahwi had shown these to Kyle when they had been planning, and though he was not a metal worker, he recognized the work of the Deep People when he saw it. She'd even demonstrated what she could do with them, much to his amazement.

Neenahwi squeezed his hand three times, the signal that their cloak would end, and released his hand. Kyle dashed twenty feet away, drawing a short-sword from his waist. Though he trained one day a week on the drilling fields as all the Deep People do, he never considered himself a warrior, and he was unsure what eighteen inches of steel was going to do to a beast so big. But it was better than having his hands in his pockets.

She threw the arrows up into the air, which then flew away in different directions. Kyle followed one as it arced upward—a silver blur in the dim blue light—did a loop, and descended toward the spectre. He struggled to follow it now as it moved so fast, a shiny buzzing hornet that lifted into the air once more, a tentacle dropping to the floor with a wet thud in its wake. Two more tentacles fell to the floor, victims of the other arrows, squirming a final squirm before they lay still.

The spectre screamed and twisted its head round to see what was attacking it and Kyle found himself staring into its great open maw. His feet became rooted to the spot, but he was at least thankful that the wax pressed into his ears had dulled the spectre's cries; as he would be on his knees again otherwise. The great body of the spectre rolled and twisted as it turned, and Kyle knew that it's charge would soon come. Neenahwi's silver arrows continued to sever flailing appendages, but the spectre appeared to be staring right at him. *Could it sense Neenahwi's magic?*

The juggernaut, the statue of the deep drake, had been

still since it had broken through the wall. Its magic had drawn the attention of the spectre, neither creature making the first move. But now that the spectre had turned and exposed its soft body, the deep drake launched itself forward with a great kick of its hind legs. The massive jaws of the deep drake opened to reveal the knife-sharp teeth; and before the spectre could charge down Kyle, swallowing him up in to the circular mass of teeth, the juggernaut attacked. The deep drake's mouth closed on the spectre's flesh, just behind the hard carapace of its head, gripping it hard and stalling its charge.

The specter screamed again, louder this time—a cornered beast attacked from multiple sides. He could see the stone of the juggernaut's mouth bulging where the muscle would be in its real-life counterpart as it clamped its jaws down on the soft flesh. The head of the spectre raised into the air and it twisted and rolled, the juggernaut hanging on even when it was lifted into the air and came crashing down on its side. But still the deep drake held.

The spectre twisted. Tentacles reached forward from its mouth and sides to grasp the stone juggernaut, but Neenah-wi's arrows buzzed through the air, slicing them away. More tentacles grew in their place.

The juggernaut's forelegs raked at the spectre's flesh with its long stone claws, rending putrid flesh that fell to the floor. The spectre screamed and rolled sideways, its whole body rotating over the top of the deep drake. The juggernaut disappeared under the great mass of the spectre before it emerged on the other side and was flipped over the spectre's body. The stone statue came crashing down with a great noise, a huge chunk of the spectre's flesh coming away in its bite.

Kyle could see the vast wound in its side, the doughy white flesh oozing and crawling—like a million maggots lurking below the surface of the skin. *Maggots truly or was it the tentacles that continued to sprout anew even as they were cut?*

The juggernaut flung away the rotten flesh in its jaws, scrambled back to its feet, and the two titans met head on. Tentacles, ten of them. No fifteen. Too many to count, shot out of the spectre's mouth and wrapped around the limbs of the juggernaut, pulling it toward the great mouth made perfect for eating stone. The juggernaut tried to brace itself but it was being slowly, inexorably, dragged forward. Kyle nearly called out to Neenahwi but caught himself just in time. Instead he waved frantically in her direction. She could not see what was happening, the great bulk of the spectre blocked her view. She turned and nodded at Kyle's beckoning arm, joining him where he stood, and now she saw the danger the deep drake was in, only feet from the crushing, grinding, circle of death.

The silver arrows flew to the juggernaut's aid, tentacles no longer pulling the drake, instead hanging off it like garlands on a festival day. Free now, the juggernaut jumped forward again to bite at the spectre—upper jaw scraping against the hard carapace of the head, blind eyes bursting from the pressure, the lower jaw grasping the spectre on the inside of its mouth. For a moment it seemed like the drake once again had a firm grip but the spectre had been waiting for this moment. A chance for it to test its own bite.

The great worm mouth closed around the lower jaw of the juggernaut like a baby's lips around a stone teat, the screech of stone being sliced by razor sharp teeth filled the air and then the deep drake toppled to the side. It crashed to the floor, its jaw shorn away. The spectre moved in for the kill as the juggernaut clambered back to its feet. The deep drake swung its head to bash into the side of the spectre like a flail, the force of the blow visible in vibrations down the spectre's worm-like body. But the size difference was too great, and though the spectre was a corrupted purple worm, its body was still made to withstand crushing weights of stone.

Unfortunately, the drake was not similarly constructed.

Kyle watched on in ever increasing horror as the spectre lifted its head high into the air, before crashing down onto the juggernaut. The hard carapace around the spectre's head slamming once, then twice against the deep drake, and with a resounding *crack,* a foreleg of the juggernaut snapped in two.

What had he done? Thought Kyle. He was going to be responsible for the Deep People losing a juggernaut. At least he was surely going to die and not have to deal with the shame.

The juggernaut was down. Its limbs broken, it tried to regain its feet but it was no use. And the spectre knew it. Leaving the lame construct, the spectre's head turned slowly to face Kyle and Neenahwi. Its mouth was gouged from the deep drake's bite, and severed tentacles oozed a clear ichor. It roared a greeting to its new prey. The spectre advanced.

Without thinking, Kyle put his fingers in his mouth and whistled.

The spectre moved forward, tentacles reaching out, searching for them, ignoring the attacks of Neenahwi's arrows. And then, from the tunnel back to Unedar Halt, a long purple shape burst forth. Pavak! The purple worm bit at the rear of the spectre, and though it was smaller than the undead beast, it was able to brace itself against the rock of the tunnel. It held the spectre back, away from Kyle and Neenahwi.

The silver arrows had stopped their buzzing. Neenahwi was picking fist size rocks up from the floor. Kyle shook his head—that wasn't going to do anything. She held the rock in her hand and it began to glow orange, then bright red. Neenahwi threw the rock at the spectre's head. It exploded on contact, chunks of flesh sent flying. Kyle mouthed a silent prayer to Varcon at this unexpected talent of his companion.

Kyle bent over to pick up more rocks for Neenahwi and began to hand them to her.

"What are we going to do?" he shouted.

Neenahwi shrugged. "Get ready to run." She looked unsteady on her feet, her exhaustion apparent, and so Kyle moved close to support her.

Suddenly, from the ground near the spectre's head erupted another purple shape. Smaller than Pavak, its mouth opened wide, it bit into the spectre near its head. The smaller worm's body scrunched back onto itself as it tried to reverse its course into the hole that it had come from, pulling the spectre down with it.

"Vidin!" cried Kyle. *Vidin was alive?* "Don't hurt that one," Kyle pleaded to Neenahwi, pointing, "that's my worm!"

She nodded, and threw another red stone at the spectre's head.

The spectre was pinned down now. Pavak held it in place at the rear and Vidin the front. But how long would these two smaller worms be able to last against something that wouldn't tire? Could Neenahwi kill it with the exploding rocks?

He wasn't sure.

Kyle looked around the cavern, looking to see if there

were other options to get out of there, to see where they could flee. They were closed off from the tunnel to Unedar Halt, and Kyle couldn't lead the spectre into the city anyway. They'd have to escape through another passageway and hopefully draw the worm away. Maybe they'd be able to find their way back to Unedar Halt again one day, though he knew that was unlikely.

Slowly scanning the cavern, Kyle's eyes were drawn upward to the ceiling. To what hung ominously above the spectre.

"Neenahwi!" shouted Kyle. "Stalactite!"

She nodded and switched her target. She threw a red rock toward the base of the stalactite, the flight of the missile incredibly straight and true, surely enabled by magic. The rock exploded where the stalactite began at the cavern ceiling, rubble blasting into the air. And though the stalactite quivered, it did not fall.

Kyle picked up a larger rock, as big as his head and handed it to Neenahwi. "Try this."

Neenahwi blew out her cheeks and took the rock from Kyle. She did not look good, her face was flushed and speckled with sweat, her eyes tracked slowly.

Neenahwi held the rock between two hands and it slowly changed color as she poured in magical energy; first orange, then a bright hot red. The red turned to a brilliant vivid purple. *The rock must contain granthium!*

She threw it into the air with some difficulty, and its path was neither as straight or fast as the previous missile, but Neenahwi closed her eyes and its course became truer the closer it got.

Boom!

Crack!

The stalactite was shorn from its root and plummeted to the ground. Kyle watched wide-eyed, time slowing as he saw the tip of the stone stalactite pierce the specter's flesh. Its body was ripped apart as the ever-broadening spear of stone fell to the floor. The great remains of the root, twice as big as the juggernaut, engulfed the corrupted worm's body and threw up a cloud of dust and rubble. Kyle covered his eyes, holding his breath.

The dust thinned and Kyle saw the severed head of the spectre slowly rolling away from a pile of rubble. Great chunks of rock covered the spectre's body closest to them. Where Vidin had been holding on.

"Vidin!" cried Kyle, stepping away from Neenahwi and making to rush to his friend.

"Kyle..." said Neenahwi as she lost her balance. Her eyes rolled back in her head, and she cascaded to the floor.

~

KYLE HAD A SOLID GRIP OF NEENAHWI'S HAND AS HE looked into her eyes. "Good bye, Neenahwi. Thank you."

She looked nearly back to health now, though it had been more than a week for her in the infirmary. They had been so concerned that the Forger had even called the old wizard to visit. Kyle did not leave Neenahwi's bedside, and sat surprised at the wizard's appearance; and even more surprised by the brief inspection which concluded with an exclamation of "Silly girl, you'll be fine." He had kissed her on the forehead before leaving once more.

Now she was on her feet and ready to depart for Kingshold.

"You're welcome, Kyle. And don't look so sad. I'm sure I

will be back."

"I'm sorry what you were looking for wasn't inside the spectre. The locus stone." Once Neenahwi was well enough, they had gone back to the spectre, it's body now a green mess of rapidly rotting flesh. It smelled revolting, but Neenahwi insisted on carving it open and searching through its entrails herself. But there was no sign of a locus stone; whether it was long lost or his theory was wrong, Kyle did not know.

"That's OK. I suppose I didn't expect it to be that easy. I have some leads to follow from my research, so I'll find one. Eventually."

"If there is anything I can do to help, you only have to call," said Kyle, finally releasing her hand.

"Oh, I'll hold you to that," she said, chuckling. Neenahwi reached out and gave Kyle a tight hug, his face blushing at the unexpected affection. The great brass doors of the mountain gate opened a crack, and light from the outside world shone in, making Kyle squint. Neenahwi waved and disappeared into the sunshine.

Kyle sighed a deep sigh. He had places to be. Torkel wanted to show him how the repairs to the juggernaut were coming along, and she even asked him to do some of the detailed carving work—a great honor for one as young as him. And he needed to check on what the miners had done with his cavern, see how big that seam of granthium was. Kyle would be a rich dwarf now; his share of the claim would set him up for life.

But what he really wanted was to start training a new worm.

He had a good name in mind.

Fola.

JYUTH ON MAGIC - INANIMATE
SOURCES OF MAGICAL POWER

T hough I previously stated that magical energy resides only in living creatures, upon further research, there are some examples of non-living things that I have found to contain magic of a sort. I do not attest to this being a comprehensive list, it is only what my studies have unearthed so far.

MAGICAL OBJECTS.

I have discovered a small number of inanimate objects that have been imbued with magical energy for various reasons, but by whom I do not know. The process of doing so must have been extremely arduous and time consuming, and would likely have required considerable amounts of mana. I have found no commonality in the objects that have been enchanted; in either their purpose, quality, or function. From magical weapons to cloth shirts as hard as steel; jewelry that slowly poisons the wearer to a pot that is always full of a foul porridge; their existence is a rarity. I would postulate that as they have been imbued with magic, they could be contrarily drained. Though why one would destroy objects of this special nature, I do not know (except for the aforementioned porridge bowl).

LOCUS POINTS.

The earth, rocks, stones, sand. All are without mana. Dead to the wizard.

But the world is alive with magic, and there do exist places that amplify magic. I have heard rumors of a number of such places, but I know one well; the city of Ioth, the heart of the church of Arloth. Whether it is cause or effect from this city being home of a God I do not know. Are these loci fonts of magic spilling from the core of the world, or are they zones of amplification for the natural abilities of the wizard? I do not know. My teacher knew of more such places but would not share their precise locations with me. I should note that I have long suspected that the elves have one such location in their realm.

DEMON STONES.

There are unique rocks or gems that completely bend my rule that stones are lifeless. Demon stones instead act as reservoirs or conduits of great power. They are extremely rare and quite impossible to identify for the lay person as they are known to look like common rocks or precious gems. Where they come from I can only hypothesize, but for some reason they are highly prized by demons from other realms —which is why I have named them thus. Accessing the power of these stones is fraught with challenges. Anger and blood are the only ways I have discovered to unlock them. And when they are used I am left with a residual anger which takes some time to dissipate.

Demons are beings of anger; does this attract these stones or do the stones create these demons? Are they even part of a demon? I do not have these answers, though I hope that they are not the leftover parts of demon eunuchs.

OF BUCCANEERS AND BARDS

K olsen looked up from his bunk, eyes opening at the approaching sound. Brook, the one and only guard, opened the cell door and led another poor sod into the small bare room. He was a sorry-looking character: bedraggled beard, unwashed hair, eyes glazed and red-rimmed, with dirty, grease-smeared clothes. The man stumbled to the floor, thought about pushing himself up, but couldn't manage it; so he curled up and put his arm under his head, and closed his eyes.

"Ah, I see you brought me another fine cellmate," said Kolsen.

"Shut up, scum," Brook growled, closing the cell door and leaving the lockup.

In truth, Kolsen realized he did not appear too much better than the new arrival. Three days had passed since he'd shaved or washed, and his pink shirt was still torn from the stupid tavern fight that had gotten him into this mess. But surely he didn't smell like a distillery, like this one. At least, not anymore.

Kolsen got up from his bunk, walked over to the prone man, and nudged him with his foot. "Hey, what's your name?" he asked.

The man stirred, opening his eyes to reveal unfocused pupils, before he coughed out a sticky glob of brown phlegm onto Kolsen's once-shiny black leather boots.

"Urgh. Well, I guess you're not going to help pass the time." Kolsen lay back down on the bare wooden bunk and resumed his contemplation of the roaches on the ceiling.

~

THE SIGNS OF LIGHT COMING FROM THE SMALL WINDOW set high in the exterior wall told Kolsen it was morning. His new guest was awake on the floor, knees pulled to his chest, staring at nothing in particular. Kolsen sat up, swung his feet to the ground, and regarded him. The man didn't look up or say anything. Just kept up the dead man's stare.

"So, how are you?" asked Kolsen.

"I don't want to talk," muttered the formerly drunk man, who Kolsen knew must be hurting right now.

"I'm Kolsen, Vin Kolsen. I know how you feel, I really do. I was there myself a few days ago. You feel like somebody put a tap between your eyes and your brain is trickling out. Your mouth tastes like the pissy sawdust from the tavern you were in, and your stomach is as empty as my purse." Kolsen appraised the man. Last night, he'd pegged him for just a drunk. He was dirty, but his boots and belt looked like quality and his empty scabbard pointed to someone who could at least afford a length of steel.

"There's not much I can do to help you with any of that, though. The guard might bring some food and water later, but it's not good. The guard is also the cook. Meanwhile, you're gonna have to suffer. Though, I can at least help pass the time. We're stuck here until the next traveling magistrate comes through, and it could be weeks. Who knows, we could be best friends by then."

"I don't want to talk," said the man more forcefully this time, looking Kolsen in the eye.

"Suit yourself. Only trying to be neighborly."

~

FOUR DAYS STUCK IN THIS SHIT HOLE, AND NO ONE HAD come to get him out. He'd only come into this backwater port because the rain barrels were dry and the chickens had all died of some mysterious pox, one after another. It seemed like a good idea at the time: resupply, give some of the crew a little shore leave, and then head back out to do their jobs. It was his idea, the captain going along with it because Kolsen knew about this fishing village, even though it was unmarked on his maps. He'd been here once before, a while ago.

The village was called Little Eaton and it was nothing special, but it had served as a place to hide out for a while back then. He hadn't expected to be remembered quite so clearly by the locals, though; and it was definitely something of a shock when he discovered, while enjoying just his second drink, a young woman and a three-year-old girl behind him.

"Vin, that you?" asked the young woman tentatively.

Kolsen stared at her. Probably early twenties, plain ruddy face like many of the locals in those parts. Soft in the arms, chest and belly. "Aye, that's me, lass. But who are you?"

"It's me. Eara. You don't remember me? This is Neria. She's yours, Vin." And she pointed to the little girl standing there with wide mooning eyes, dressed in a nightshirt and wearing sandals.

He had taken a moment to consider this, his shipmates around him watching this exchange intently. It probably was nearly four years ago he had been here last, but this was neither the time nor the place to have this conversation. What did she even expect him to do about it? Did she think he had come back to whisk her away, or to marry her and settle down, here at the end of the world? Not likely.

"I'm afraid you must have the wrong man. It's so easy to get us handsome people mixed up when all of you look like a walrus' backside in these parts." Kolsen turned back to the crew, who joined him in laughing while the woman cried, only to be led out by her daughter.

The rest of the evening had been going swimmingly. The ale and the rum had flowed freely and the crew had hung on his every word, many of them asking why he wasn't captain instead of just second mate. It had been going swimmingly until three oafs, resembling hairless trolls to Kolsen's eye, shambled into the drinking hovel looking for trouble. Unfortunately, he was the trouble they were looking for. Overprotective brothers with stout pieces of wood. Not the way he liked to end an evening.

And so there had been fighting, Kolsen's crew standing shoulder to shoulder with him. Blows traded, tables broken, glasses smashed. All good fun until one of them had landed a vicious left hook to Kolsen's cheek. It stung something fierce, and Kolsen could feel blood running. Once he got up from the floor he ran the oaf through with his cutlass.

Apparently, the locals didn't appreciate that. The dozen men standing by watching, placing bets on the outcome of the fight, did not enjoy the disemboweling of Fred or Tom or

Joe or whatever his name was, and soon their little landing party was outnumbered. Kolsen, who prided himself on being one of the best seamen in the northern waters, knew when the tide was turning. It was time to beat a hasty retreat to the longboat and the ship anchored offshore.

The crew behind him, Kolsen ran for the door only to trip over the outstretched leg of an old lady sipping her summer wine and enjoying the show. Villagers piled on top of him, holding him down and ripping away his sword while his crew escaped.

Four days had passed, and no one had come to break him out. Or bribe the villagers. Or do anything except leave him here to languish, waiting for the magistrate and the noose to follow. *Pirates,* thought Kolsen, *they're just not reliable.*

~

THE NEXT MORNING THE WOODEN CELL DOOR BANGED open once more. It wasn't Brook, the part-time watchman for the village. This one looked like a pirate. The only problem was it wasn't one Kolsen recognized.

"You two. Get out here," he shouted.

"Hello, I'm Kolsen," he said, standing up and walking over to shake his hand as though they were meeting for the first time at church.

"Shut up you. Get outside and line up with the others." Kolsen was more certain of his initial appraisal regarding this man's profession. He had the aura of cockiness of one who has made a pact with the devil and is quite enjoying the way it's working out.

The clothing gave him away, too. The mismatched waist-coat and trousers with a billowing frilly blouse sprouting from underneath were evidence of the magpie-like nature of the common corsair, collecting what they thought of as finery as they went and wearing it proudly. Each new addition to their outfit was as much a badge of honor as the ears worn around the necks of goblin hunters. Tucked into a belt around his waist, the pirate had two short knives. Slung across his shoulder was a miniature crossbow, something he was probably particularly proud of as they were expensive and difficult to obtain. Kolsen had seen better.

Kolsen's cellmate walked out the door first. He followed and joined the short train of four men and a woman proceeding to the main dirt square of the village. It was early morning.

Scores of villagers had assembled, many dressed in nightclothes and some even in just their breeches. Families and friends stood in groups opposite thirty or forty North Sea corsairs. Two teenage girls were pulled from their families by a handful of viciously armed pirates, much to their father's protestations, for which he received a sword hilt to the face. His wife held him back as he spat teeth. Kolsen had seen these scenes many times before. The wife was wise to hold him back, even as the daughters were dragged off into a nearby house.

Behind the pirates were stacked a variety of supplies: crates, sacks, and barrels. It was probably all they would have to show for a raid on a village this poor, though Kolsen knew they would still want more.

"We'll be on our way if you cooperate," said a man dressed all in black, clearly in charge. "Don't try any funny business or hide anything from us and you will make it to the end of the day. And then we'll be gone. And we promise we won't come back, at least for a while. Eh, boys?" The crew members around him laughed on cue, many jeering menacingly at the villagers.

"Bring us what weapons you got and bring us any coin you have. We'll take your food. And in case you weren't listening, you will not do anything about it. Unless you want to dig some graves." The pirate leader pointed to where Kolsen stood with his fellow inmates. "These folks here from the gaol, we're taking them with us as slaves, and you should be thankful we're not doing the same to you."

One woman stepped forward and pointed at the woman in the group with Kolsen. "That's my sister," she said. "She's not even supposed to be in the gaol. She's only there because she was protecting herself from the sorry excuse for a man she married. You can't take her!" Other families called out about Kolsen's fellow prisoners; though he noticed Eara didn't beg for him to remain, nor did anyone for his silent cellmate.

"Shut up!" the pirate hollered until there was silence. "This is not a negotiation. We take them or we pick from you lot. Any arguments?" There were no arguments. Becoming a slave was the worst thing these people could imagine. Kolsen had seen worse, but he wasn't exactly enamored by this change in circumstances.

"Good. Now, any of you boys and girls want to join us? Many of us were like you, growing up in a piss pot by the sea, weren't we boys?" More jeers and cheers as the crew remembered the latrines they had clambered out from (into what, Kolsen wasn't sure). "Join us. Make your fortune. Live a real life. Not just gutting fish and watching the years steal away your youth. Who here would join us?"

"I will," said a boy, maybe fifteen years old, though big for his age. He was broad-shouldered and one of the few dressed like he was ready to go. He had the look of someone who had already spent several years on the fishing boats and would have been heading out this morning. Smart boy. Not much of a life in fishing.

A boy standing next to him, shorter, skinnier, altogether less of a boy, looked at his friend with concern etched on his face. Then he, too, raised his hand and called out, "And me. I want to come, too."

The first boy turned to the skinnier one and said, "What are you doing, Karr, you ain't even been on a boat. How are you going to be a pirate?"

"You never been a pirate either, Creed. And I don't want to be left here without you. If you're going, I'm going, too."

"Well, boys," said the pirate leader, "look at these two lads having a lover's quarrel before they part. Come on. You can leave your ma and da here. We'll take you both. Need someone small to get up the rigging." He waved over two of his crew to escort the lads to their new life. The villagers contained, he turned to address the raiders. "OK, pick it clean boys. Find everything and get the cargo on board. Miss Carliss, there's five new mules for your oars. Get them settled. I want to be gone before dusk."

～

MISS CARLISS HAD TO BE THE OFFSPRING OF AN OGRE. SHE was over six feet tall. The prow of the longboat, where she sat, dragged in the water from her bulk. Mean, beady black eyes and a thin mouth were just about visible between the menagerie of warts and sores on her face. She barked orders in a high-pitched clip like a yapping terrier. Her whip proved her bite was even worse than her bark.

Once on-board ship, Kolsen surveyed his new home, starboard oar number five, first seat. It had a well-worn bench, chains to keep him in place, and the lovely aroma of urine the previous tenant had nurtured so well. And luckily for him, he was well-acquainted with his neighbor.

"Well, how are you liking it so far?" Kolsen asked his former cellmate.

The man didn't look to be enjoying himself. His head was bowed, resting on the oar handle in front of him. Kolsen looked around and saw that the new guy had managed to fit in quickly. Though the older hands were sleeping rather than questioning the life choices that had led them there. The man looked up at Kolsen and sighed.

"Mareth."

"Pardon?" asked Kolsen.

"You asked my name before. It's Mareth."

"Nice to meet you, Mareth," said Kolsen, reaching out a chained hand, "I'm—"

"Kolsen. I was listening before, and I'm good at remembering names. Why are you looking so happy? We will die here."

"My friend, I am happy because this is an improvement in my surroundings. I was wrongly accused of murder back in that stink-hole of a village, but no magistrate would have sided with me. Besides, this ship is a 60-foot galleon, and it will be well-stocked. We'll likely eat better than those fools left behind. And it's not like we have to row all the time."

"We don't?"

"No. The oars are used only when the sea is becalmed or for coming into port. And maneuvering in battle, of course."

"How do you know?"

"I have spent a lot of time on the seas. Once, I was a

merchant seaman and saw many vessels like this." Kolsen carefully considered his words and the truth of them. As a young man, he had spent many years traveling the trade routes with different merchant vessels. He had merely chosen to leave out the fact that he hadn't been in that line of work for a while now.

It was a particular affectation for Kolsen, and especially for a pirate. He was always careful not to lie. He remembered seeing a Priest of Marlth asking for alms on a street corner in his home city of Ioth when he was a young boy. He had a bright shiny copper coin in his pocket from a neighborhood lady he called his grandmother, and he was going to buy a honey stick. When the priest had asked him for a donation, Kolsen had said he was penniless. Somehow, the priest had known he was lying. The young Kolsen was grabbed by the earlobe before he could run away. The priest had screamed in his face that he was a liar and a sinner and that Marlth would put out his eyes and eat his tongue in the next life if he didn't change his ways. That kind of early experience can really impact you.

This did not mean Kolsen was honest. Far from it. He had no qualms about misleading people and creating illusions the unwary could choose to follow. Experience had led him to realize that the truth, edited for the audience, was far more effective than lies.

Mareth nodded, buying the story, but Kolsen could see he was slipping back into his own thoughts again. "So how did you end up in the cell back there?" he asked, trying to bring Mareth back.

"I think I hurt someone. Didn't meant to. Hallucinations. Skyweed."

"I thought you were drunk when they threw you in the gaol. What did you see?"

"I *was* drunk. I tried to stop the visions by drinking fast until I blacked out. But it didn't work. Made it worse, I think. You don't want to know. I was an adventurer, and we saw some bad stuff." Mareth's thousand-mile stare returned as though he were remembering something. "Terrible. It killed all of my friends. I should be dead, too. Well, it won't be long now, I suppose."

"There's looking on the bright side," said Kolsen, meaning it. "You never know what will happen. As long as you're breathing, you're fighting. And there's no better way to get cleaned up than being chained to an oar."

~

BEING AN OARSMAN (KOLSEN REFUSED TO CALL HIMSELF A galley slave) on a ship like this wasn't that bad. It didn't smell too good, what with there not even being a pot to piss in, but the food was not terrible. It was certainly more plentiful than in the gaol and the work was not too backbreaking.

The first day had been the worst. Getting into the rhythm of the other oars when Kolsen and Mareth were a new pairing had not been easy, and they had both received a couple of lashes of the whip from Miss Carliss. Not that Kolsen blamed her. How could she keep order without using a bit of the whip? Once they had matched the beat of the oar, the ogress changed her tune and began saying they could earn their freedom. *Ha!* He'd never heard of any slave doing that on a pirate ship before. Sounded like gull shit to him, and an unnecessary motivational technique. A swig of grog and no whip would have been incentive enough for most in his position.

On top of all that, Kolsen had been forced to give up his boots. They would have gone rotten in the bilge of the rowing hold anyway, but it was still a wrench. They were good boots, been with him a long time. Lived through a few soles. He'd always considered boots to be better than people. More than a few people could do with re-souling, himself included.

Mareth noted Kolsen's webbed toes as he, too, took off his boots to hand over to Miss Carliss. Kolsen explained that when he was born with the webbing between his toes, his mother knew he would be destined for a life at sea. He didn't share how the other villagers steered clear of him, thinking him devil-borne. It drove his mother so mad. Mad enough that they had left the fishing village of her birth to move to Ioth, another home by the sea. Kolsen thought she also felt a guilt for passing on her own deformity to her child, and wanted to protect him from the mocking she suffered.

Kolsen noticed Mareth's boots. They were a good pair, but not as nice as his. Well, he thought, they will be going to some other man now. Maybe the merchant's patter in Trima would prove true and they would last longer than him.

Things improved steadily from the second day through day twelve. Even Mareth got used to his new role in life and embraced the simple peace of knowing your place. Captain makes the order on deck, oar rope is pulled, bell rings, woman yells, and you row.

And when you row, you are just a single cog in the human machine. If your oar is out of pace with the others, then accidents happen. On the second day, one of the other new rowers from the gaol fell out of time and hit the oar in front of his, the handle hitting him in the face. It wasn't pretty, nose like a smear and what remained of his front teeth bashed in. Nearly choked on one of them, too, until Miss Carliss came along and thumped his back with her big plate of a hand until he choked it up. Then she whipped him to make sure he had learned his lesson.

Times like these always made Kolsen philosophical, and he didn't mind sharing his thoughts with others. Given the seating arrangements and lack of mobility, Mareth was the natural receiver of much of Kolsen's wisdom. There was a lot you could learn about life from being an oarsman. It taught you to be watchful of the timing of others, to conserve your energy for when it was needed, to value good, honest, simple exercise and look out for your partner. What went unsaid was bide your time, assess your surroundings, and then be ready.

Mareth became more talkative, too. The second and third days had been rougher for him than Kolsen, what with getting off the skyweed. He'd complained of his head hurting like the seven hells, and he'd vomited down his shirt more than once, causing him to discard it and go shirtless.

A few more days had passed when Kolsen enquired about the scars on his chest. Mareth opened up about his life as an adventurer. A bard no less, looking to make famous tales of himself and his friends. But all they had managed to do was go from one terrifying situation to another until he had been the only one left. Seemed to sum up Kolsen's life pretty well too.

~

THEY HAD BEEN TALKING ABOUT WOMEN. THE OARS WERE

in. Kolsen and Mareth leaned forward to rest on the worn wooden handles, heads conspiratorially close together as they shared tales of lost beauties and brief flirtations, when a shout went up from on deck. A call to starboard.

In the past fortnight, there had been only two moments of action. A pirate's life, much as any other sailor's, could be weeks of boredom and monotony interrupted by moments of terrifying and intoxicating danger.

The first time they had rowed to position the ship offshore from Hulmouth, a town Kolsen recognized after peering through the oar hole. *The Scythe* had joined up with four other corsair vessels to raid this large town, and he and Mareth had watched as longboats had taken scores of pirates ashore. The crew had returned many hours later, laden with a haul bigger than they'd managed at Little Eaton, crowing so loudly about their success it could be heard below deck.

The other time they had been called to action was to man the oars and ram a merchant ship on the open sea. The impact and the ear-splitting squeals and shrieks of timber and man unnerved Mareth, who had not known what to expect. Kolsen had found himself grinning, even though he knew he would not be waiting at the railing to leap over and see what chance had brought them today.

"Can you see what has been sighted?" Kolsen asked Mareth once he heard the call. His oar mate leaned to the hole in the hull and peered out.

"I can't see anything. Just the sea and the sky."

Another cry, muffled at first but clearer as it was repeated.

"Pienza Navy!"

Kolsen sighed. That was not good news. Raiding towns and villages always led to trouble. He had little time to reflect on shifting fortune though, as the whip was cracked and they rowed for all they were worth.

～

"WHY DO WE ROW WHEN THERE IS SO MUCH WIND TODAY Kolsen?" asked Mareth between strokes.

"I don't know for sure, but it's likely the navy ship is faster than we are. More sails and so it will catch up."

"Shut up!" screamed Miss Carliss, and the whip flicked out and hit Kolsen on the back of his neck, blood mingling with sweat as it trickled down between his shoulder blades. He doubled his efforts, silently imagining ways to gain his revenge on this banshee.

Pulling the oars when the sea was so choppy was difficult, and there was little respite. Lunch came and went with only a brief begrudging break for water and to wolf down a biscuit after one of their fellow oarsmen keeled off his perch. The captain of this vessel and his crew were clearly desperate. These oars would not save them unless the weather shifted.

"If the navy catch them, then aren't we going to be free?" asked Mareth, chancing another question when Miss Carliss was prowling the stern.

"Maybe," said Kolsen, "but don't bet on it. They rarely care about distinguishing between who wants to be on board and who doesn't, unless you are clearly of means and have been kidnapped. Likely as not we'd still be explaining it while they put the ropes around our necks."

Mareth screamed as the whip left a long red mark across his shirtless back.

"Shut up and row, you worthless shits!" screamed Miss Carliss. This time Mareth stopped with the questions.

~

BELLOWS FROM ON DECK SIGNALED THE PURSUER WAS close. Shouts rose as the crew riled themselves up for the fight to come.

Then the port side oars slammed backward into their teams with a sickening crack as men and women were crushed against one another. The boat listed to the starboard side from the collision. Oil lamps swayed from the ceiling of the rowing hold, sending shadows spinning in different directions and painting the grisly scene of crushed bone and spilled blood in a sickly yellow light.

"Hold your oars!" screamed the ogress. Too late, though. Too late for the poor souls who were unlucky enough to sit on the far side from Kolsen. "Stow!"

Miss Carliss waited long enough to see that her order had been carried out before disappearing up the stairs. Water began to slosh into the ship through cracks in the ship's hull. He tried to move but Kolsen was still chained to his post; the best he could do was stand and listen to the sounds of battle from above, but they were strangely muffled and remote to the denizens of the hold.

Kolsen had heard others talk about the chaos of large battles on land where one army would throw itself against another, the maelstrom of chaos you would find yourself in; but he didn't know about that. He only knew what it was like to fight on a ship when the deck moved beneath your feet, when the fires started, and when there was nowhere to run. Kolsen had seen big men, men who had told him about fighting for hours in some idiot's war, last no more than five seconds in the middle of a fight at sea.

He didn't know which way the fight was going, but he could hazard a guess. This was not a large pirate vessel.

Mareth was quiet as he tried to free his chains. From up the stairs, Miss Carliss returned with two men in tow. One set to work unlocking the chains; the other left behind a box of boat hooks, mallets, cudgels, and chisels before disappearing back up to the fight. "Get upstairs and fight! If you live, you're free. If you don't, you're dead," she called.

Kolsen and Mareth rubbed life back into their feet before being hauled to stand unsteadily. Tools repurposed as weapons were pressed into their hands and they ascended the stairs, Miss Carliss and the other pirate right behind them.

The final flight of stairs was like being born again, but into a world of hell and thunder.

The Pienza naval ship was an additional deck taller than the pirate ship. Its golden prow decoration of a screaming eagle, wings swept backward, loomed across the deck where the ship had crashed into the mainmast, which now leaned at an angle. Marines had boarded and engaged the pirates. They fought tooth and nail for their lives and all they owned, but the odds were against them.

Along the naval vessel railing stood a row of crossbow men, picking their targets and firing into the melee. Kolsen saw one bolt whistle across the deck and take a man in the neck. He fell gurgling to the floor. It was Creed, the boy who had volunteered from the village.

The man accompanying Miss Carliss rushed past Kolsen to help their comrades, and Carliss pushed Mareth forward to join them.

There's no way I'm wading into that, thought Kolsen. He

turned and took Miss Carliss by surprise, burying his chisel in her eye, through her skull, and into the brain.

Mareth turned and saw what had happened, a question on the tip of his tongue. "We've got to get out of here," shouted Kolsen. He picked up the sword Miss Carliss had been holding and Mareth did the same with a discarded one at his feet.

"This is my sword. The one they took from me at the gaol," said Mareth.

"Well, isn't it your lucky day?" said Kolsen. Mareth looked idiotically happy. Kolsen looked over his shoulder and signaled to the stern. "Come on."

The fight was clearly turning against the pirates. The mainmast was leaning over to the side and its weight was causing the ship to pitch. Only the attacking vessel's proximity kept it close to level.

Crossbow bolts thudded where Kolsen and Mareth had been standing, but they ran to the stern where Kolsen had seen a longboat tethered. Working together, they cut the ropes holding it down and pushed it over the rail.

"Come on!" Kolsen called above the noise of battle and jumped into the sea. He swam to the boat and pulled himself out of the dark waters, looking for Mareth.

Kolsen pulled his oar mate on board and noticed another figure struggling to swim amongst the waves. Back at the oars once more, they rowed away from the scenes of ship-borne carnage.

"Kolsen, it's the boy, Karr, from the village. We have to get him."

"No, we don't. We have to get away."

"How far from land are we? We need another set of arms to row."

Reluctantly, Kolsen let the boat be steered toward the boy thrashing around in the water. Mareth reached over to grasp his flailing arm and pull him in to the boat. The boy lay there in a sodden lump, his coughing and spluttering turned into tears and blubbering.

"Creed," he wailed between gasps of air, "he's dead. I saw him die."

"Shut up, boy," hissed Kolsen, "or I'll throw you back and you can join him. If you must mourn your friend, do it in peace."

Mareth regained his seat, and he and Kolsen rowed away from the lurching pirate ship. Fire arrows, launched skyward from the navy ship, caught its sails. Flames licked high into the night sky. They could not turn their eyes away, knowing the pirates would be dead or captured to pay publicly for their attack on Hulmouth.

So, they said nothing but focused on the long pulls of their oars. They were free now, but chained to their destiny just the same, unsure whether they were heading toward land or out to the North Sea.

~

"How much farther do we have to go?" asked Karr. His blubbering had turned to snores last night, only to be replaced by annoying questions once day broke and he took his turn at the oars.

"We don't know," said Kolsen. "We haven't been above decks in two weeks. You were in the crow's nest. What do you think?"

"I don't know which way is land. I was only to keep lookout. I didn't even want to come." And the boy sniveled and whimpered once more. To Kolsen's mind, it seemed he didn't know how to row either. What kind of kid grows up in a fishing village and doesn't learn how to row? But he thought for once it was better to hold his tongue, especially as he was the one resting.

"Well, that way is east. East is guaranteed to be land, but north or south could be faster depending on where we are..." Kolsen let the sentence hang, its meaning clear. Without food or water, they would need to hope luck was on their side.

∾

NIGHT FOLLOWED DAY AND DAY FOLLOWED NIGHT AS IS the way of the world. No food and no water. The boy had tried to drink the sea and Kolsen had hit him, too tired to explain his stupidity. Karr had cried again.

Then Mareth had sung. He had told Kolsen he was a bard, but he'd kept his songs and stories to himself, even when asked. It had seemed like a strange moment to get into the festive spirit, but Kolsen was happy for a way to help pass the time.

Mareth sang of feast days, winter tide, and summer solstice, harvest festivals, and spring celebrations. The words conjured images of roast lamb and squash soup, of sausages and sticky cake thick with dried fruit, glasses of mead and tall mugs of foaming ale. Kolsen's mouth watered. At first this brought annoyance, but it quickly passed, as strangely, he forgot about his hunger and thirst.

∾

THE SEA CONTINUED, ENDLESS, NO SIGN OF LAND OR SHIPS.
Days passed. Like automatons of some mad wizard, or maybe
more like the dead made to shamble around by a necromancer, they worked the oars.

And Mareth still sang. The bard wet his mouth occasionally, swilling sea water and spitting it out. Kolsen knew
Mareth was still killing himself with the salt, but what did it
matter when they would all die. Unless they killed the boy.
The little shit looked in better condition than Mareth,
though. Probably better than Kolsen, too. Damn his youth.
Wasted on the young. He'd outlast them both.

~

THINGS WERE GETTING BAD. GIVEN ENOUGH TIME AND
lack of sustenance, hallucination was inevitable. Kolsen
could see a triple-masted ship heading in their direction. It
looked so beautiful. The ship he'd always wanted to captain;
big but fast, like the boxers in the pits who dance around
their opponent, weaving away from blows before exploding
with a fist out of nowhere. Atarah, goddess of sailors and sea
wives, teased him.

The ship got closer. The bright blue sails stiff in the
strong wind, the red and black pennant atop the mainmast
billowed. Hah. A pirate ship. She was rubbing his nose in
it now.

"Ho!" came a call from the ship.

"Kolsen," said Mareth, "we need to turn to meet
the ship."

"You see it, too?"

"Of course. It's massive. How could I miss it?"

"I thought it was all in my head." *My dream ship*, thought Kolsen, *come to save me*.

～

THE SHIP WAS CALLED *THE ICICLE*. CAPTAIN GILSTRAP MET the three visitors at the rail once they had been pulled from the longboat, too weak to climb.

She was tall, having a few inches on all of her crew and she carried her sinewy frame with well-practiced grace. Her hair, the color of honey, was pulled into a bun that sat at the nape of her neck, below a wide-brimmed red felt hat. Once they were on board, two crew clambered down to secure their small boat.

Another woman, a crew member who would have been quite a looker if it weren't for her milky white eye and the broad scar from eye socket to jawline, gave them wooden cups of water which the three devoured.

"What are you doing out here in the North Sea with that?" she said, indicating toward their most recent home.

"We were on *The Scythe*. It was destroyed by Pienza Navy," said Mareth.

"And you escaped?"

Kolsen shot Mareth a look he hoped conveyed the message to let him do the talking. "Aye. No profit in death."

"Heh, that's true," she replied.

"It was dark," continued Kolsen, "so we slipped away a week past. Figured there might be others joining us but we saw no one. Do you have need of some experienced hands? We're grateful you came along."

"Might be we do. Mister Talbot, can you make use of these three?" She directed her question to a man of middle years, broad in the shoulder and chest, with a curly mustache, very much giving the impression of a well-to-do walrus.

"I think so, Captain, if we fatten them up. These two have swords, so I assume they can use them, and this one looks like a climber. Could always do with another climber."

"So be it. But you're on probation. Half-share until you prove yourself. You'll listen to Mister Talbot. He'll tell you the rules and set you to work. Welcome aboard, gentlemen."

❧

KOLSEN HAD BEEN THE FIRST OF THE RAIDERS TO LEAP over the rail that afternoon, same as he had been for the three other unlucky recipients of a boat-load of pirates over the past few weeks.

Today it had been a shipment of tea that had traveled all the way overland from eastern Jabruacor to Carlsburg, loaded onto a clipper bound for Kingshold before it had fallen into the hands of Captain Gilstrap.

The hold of *The Icicle* was full to bursting, so Kolsen and the crew stacked crates on the deck. Soon it would be time to return to whatever port Gilstrap used to sell her ill-gotten gains; the tea and the bolts of fabric, the bales of cotton and the assorted exotica bound for customers all around the Jeweled Continent.

Kolsen passed Mareth, heading in the other direction with a crate in his arms. The bard did not look well, his face a deathly white. In truth, Kolsen had not spent much time with him recently, which was hardly surprising now they weren't chained together. Mareth had been by his side for the first raid and not far behind for the others, excited and nervous but wanting to prove himself to the crew, which was smart given he didn't have a lot of other options right now. And for the most part, it had been smooth pirating. Most merchant ships would have a crew of around a score, and when you're one of them, faced with two hundred screaming corsairs, then you know the best thing to do is lay down your weapons and get it over with as quickly as possible.

Today had been a little different, though.

Everything had been proceeding to the usual 'intimidate them until they hand everything over' game plan until Nail, an evil-looking bastard with a squint and teeth filed to a point, had dragged a screaming girl on deck to present to Mister Talbot, the first mate.

But Nail, the idiot, hadn't completed his search of the ship, too enamored with the heaving bosom of the girl. Out burst two Jayyan mercenaries, followed by an officious-looking bald man with tiny half-moon spectacles. Jayyan mercenaries are not only expensive but notorious for choosing to die rather than fail a mission; and the two fell on the boarding party like a whirlwind.

Nail lost the arm holding the girl. Four other pirates ended up on the deck before Kolsen could draw his sword and engage the Jayyans. Kolsen killed one and two other crewmembers, Ley and Dubh, got the other.

Talbot was pissed. He screamed at his men that they'd all gone soft. They needed to be more professional. He grabbed the one with the spectacles and questioned him about what was precious enough on board to merit Jayyan mercenaries.

Turns out it was the girl, the daughter of a merchant in Carlburg. She was travelling to marry a rich old banker in Kingshold. That was enough to consider her part of the cargo, and she was taken kicking and screaming aboard *The Icicle* to be ransomed.

But Talbot wasn't done. He was mad the bald man hadn't controlled his contractors, and he held him responsible for *The Icicle's* five crew left in various states of butchery.

A rope was tossed over the yard arm and a noose put around the man's neck. Kolsen had witnessed a few quick hangings in his time. Some for mutiny, and others like this, when they needed to make an example that would spread far and wide when this crew finally got back to port. There were always plenty of boxes around to make a simple scaffold. Kicking a box out from under someone worked as well as a trapdoor. But Talbot threw the other end of the rope to his lads and just told them to haul him up.

They pulled, and the man lurched up into the air with each tug, tears running down his cheeks as he suffocated. He clawed at the noose but couldn't do anything.

It's a shitty way to die, going purple with your tongue sticking out like a snail coming out of its shell, instead of a nice quick broken neck. Talbot believed in the old ways, though, and if there's one way to improve on a hanging, it's a disemboweling. Mareth, watching along with the rest of the crew, lurched to the side of the ship and puked his guts overboard.

And that, thought Kolsen, was when the pirate life got real for Mareth.

～

NIGHT HAD FALLEN AND THE TEA CLIPPER HAD BEEN LEFT behind. The wind was good, and they were in open and clear waters by the time the sun set in a brilliant array of oranges and purples.

Captain Gilstrap had been happy with the haul, and so the celebrations were suitably boisterous. Kolsen could see Mareth across the deck, playing dice and stopping only to walk over and fill his wooden cup from a cask of brandy, spoils from last week.

Kolsen sat in a small circle with Talbot, Ley and Dubh, sipping the dark brown drink.

"You've been doing well, lad," said Talbot. "You're not stupid, which is actually a pretty high bar for this lot."

"Thanks, Mister Talbot," replied Kolsen. "I like it on *The Icicle*. You think I can be off probation soon?"

"Already spoke to the captain. You're good. All three of you."

"Thank you, Mister Talbot," said Kolsen. "Can I ask you a question?"

"Course. Anyone can ask anything here. It's not the bloody navy."

"That's what I would ask about. You didn't seem worried about the Pienza Navy when we told you what happened to us. Why's that?"

"Hah! Well, for one, we're not stupid enough to go raiding Pienzan towns. And then, we've got a writ from the grand duke himself saying we can do whatever we like. We're not pirates. Well, not officially anyway. We're privateers."

"Pardon?" asked Kolsen as Dubh and Ley grinned, obviously in the know about this particular tale but not leaping in to do the telling.

"It's ten years old but we've got a writ, issued by the grand duke from when Pienza was at war with Edland, which says we can do anything to disrupt them. And seeing as most trade goes through Kingshold at some point, we can do pretty much anything. As long as we give a quarter to the duke and we don't get too greedy. That's the most difficult part. Isn't that right, boys?" he said to the other pirates sitting with them. "If we're too prolific, then Edland will complain and then we'll end up with both navies down our necks. There is no longer a war after all. So, we take a good part of the year off or some head down south."

"Where do you go? You go down to the Sapphire Sea?"

"Nah, we go up to The Shards. There's a place up there called The Pit, the seediest, dirtiest, most contagious little ball of fun you've ever had. No taxes. No guard. No rules except the corsairs' rules. I guess you never heard of it. Your other crew must have hailed from down south. It's only for the North Sea lot."

Kolsen's mind raced. A pirate town? A pirate country? "So, who's in charge? Is there a king?"

"Hah. Ain't no pirate king. Hasn't been for centuries. Who wants that? Nobody fucking tells us what to do." Talbot stood, a little unsteadily. "I need a piss," he said over his shoulder as he wobbled toward the railing, already unhitching his trousers.

〜

THEY WERE HEADED TO CLOUDSCAR, A COASTAL CITY OF Pienza with a busy, deep-water port. A place where ships from all over the North Sea would go to replenish their victuals and trade with merchants who considered themselves superior to their counterparts in the capital city of Danteth. It was the Duke of Cloudscar who Kolsen discovered was the captain's sponsor in maintaining her writ of privateering. The hold of *The Icicle* was full, and the crew were restless to have coin in the pocket and to live their other lives.

Kolsen stayed close to Talbot. The first mate was more knowledgeable and respected than most captains he had served with, and Kolsen could see why the crew were content to be led by him and Captain Gilstrap. After all, on a pirate ship, leadership was a popularity game. A captain could have their rank stripped away by vote or worse, by mutiny. But as long as a crew was successful and well-fed, they were usually glad to pay the greater share to the leadership.

Kolsen was back on his feet now, his sea legs happy to be free of solid ground and his lungs free to breathe the fresh air, though he didn't intend to be just crew on a North Sea Corsair ship for the rest of what would be an inevitably short life.

But he knew, be patient and opportunities would arise.

~

"SHIP SPOTTED! TWO O'CLOCK!" CAME THE CRY FROM THE lookout on the crow's nest.

"What is she flying?" called Gilstrap from where she stood at the stern. She pulled out her own looking glass to mirror what Karr would be doing from above. It was a beautiful day, blue skies and a stiff breeze sending wispy clouds racing.

"It's a big one, Captain! Four masts. Looks like blue and yellow pennants," called Karr. He was calling out what he spied, but what he didn't know was those colors meant an Edland ship, likely sailing out of Kingshold.

Kolsen watched Captain Gilstrap and Mister Talbot

confer, intrigued as to what they were going to do. An Edland vessel, as long as it wasn't navy in disguise, would likely be a handsome catch. But their ship was already fit to burst.

Gilstrap laughed, placing an arm on Talbot's shoulder, saying one more thing in quiet before she turned to face the crew and hollered, "Change heading to intercept! But take it slow, we don't want to spook them. Drag anchor and raise Ioth colors. Let's go and see our friends from the west!"

~

THE RUSE WAS A GOOD ONE. KOLSEN AND MARETH WERE both selected to remain above deck while the majority of the crew hid. Coats of a common gray appeared as if by magic. The mounted ballista remained covered under tarpaulins and within a few minutes, *The Icicle* looked much like any other merchant vessel. Pennants of green and gold for Ioth stood to attention on the breeze, and joining them was the black and white checkered flag for a parlay.

As they neared the Edland vessel, it changed course to meet them, moving faster than *The Icicle* due to the anchors dragging in their wake. As they neared, Kolsen could identify the name of the vessel, *The Dolphin's Prize*. He took in the swivel ballista on the foredeck; fabled to be dwarven made, it was a weapon unique to the Edland Navy. He almost expected a call from Captain Gilstrap to change tack and get away before it was too late, but it didn't come. That's when he noticed there was only one such weapon and only a sparse crew on deck. Kolsen realized if he had been captain, he would likely have made the wrong decision in that instant. Something to learn from.

The captains of the two ships greeted each other from a distance of fifty yards, calling out through metal cones. The captain of the merchant ship was comfortable enough with the illusion they presented that they neared each other and threw ropes to bring their ships together.

The Dolphin's Prize was a beauty, probably no more than five winters since it was built. It was big but with a sleek hull and a full rig that gave it speed across the open waters. A copper dolphin, just beginning to tarnish green, leaped from black waves carved of ebony on the ship's prow. A score of seamen manned the sails and the rails as they neared, with more arriving from below decks to see what the day had brought.

The shouts of welcome and friendship from the crew of *The Icicle* changed once the ships were secured to each other. Kolsen's outstretched handshake grabbed hold of the man opposite him and pulled him into the jab he powered into the unfortunate soul's face. Kolsen's sword was out of its belt as corsairs appeared and vaulted the rail to take the crew of *The Dolphin's Prize* by surprise.

Kolsen was up and over the railing a few seconds later. A seaman still had a boat hook in his hand and jabbed at Kolsen's face. Kolsen backed away, wary of the polearm, and circled his opponent.

Thwum. A three-foot bolt of oak and steel ripped through the body of a corsair near Kolsen, blood spraying into his face. It continued on its journey, severing the outstretched arm of another pirate before taking a fat one in the gut and sticking him against the aft castle.

Thwum. Another bolt shot across the bows, miraculously missing the corsairs still climbing over the rail and smashing through the wood of the forecastle of *The Icicle*. Screams of surprise were audible over the sounds of battle.

Thwum. The ballista had been swinging from pointing out over its own deck to coming around to face *The Icicle*. This missile hit a group of pirates trying to get away. It busted through chests and faces before hitting the foremast with an almighty crash, splinters and debris exploding into the air.

Swivel ballista were deadly at range, and at these close quarters, they were doubly so. The ballista had a three-man crew, one to aim and two to wind the winches that mechanically loaded the missile and drew back the string. And this crew looked to Kolsen like they were experienced.

However, take one of the crew out and the weapon becomes unusable, as the shooter quickly realized when a wincher was struck in the eye by a crossbow bolt from on high. Karr had a good aim.

From when the machine had started firing to when it had stopped had been no more than a minute. Both pirates and *Dolphin* crew had stopped their struggling to either gawp at the power of the ballista (like Kolsen) or get out of its way and find cover (almost everyone else).

Unfortunately, Kolsen's opponent had not been one to scatter. All of a sudden, Kolsen's head exploded in pain. He fell to the floor, looking up at the grinning man wielding his boat hook. A flappy piece of skin and gristle that looked suspiciously like an ear, attached to the end like a tiny pennant. *Bastard!* That was his favorite ear.

The seaman raised the polearm into the air to strike Kolsen in the face with the butt of the handle when a sword went through one side of his body and out the other. The skewered seaman reminded Kolsen, hilariously so at that particular moment, of a kebab on a Tigrone street-vendor's grill. And Mareth was the chef.

~

THE REMAINS OF *THE DOLPHIN'S PRIZE'S* CREW LINED UP ON their own deck. Armed corsairs loomed behind every man and woman.

Kolsen had regained his feet after being saved by Mareth, and he had continued laughing throughout the time it required to seize the ship. Now he sat on a crate, watching the proceedings, his head bandaged and a cup of rum appearing from somewhere to take the edge off the burning on the side of his head. Captain Gilstrap surveyed her captives, able-bodied men and women, honest seamen like she had once been. At their fore, held by two pirates, was the captain of the vessel.

"Take what you want, woman. My crew have suffered enough," said the captain, in his late thirties, blood showing on his shirt from a number of cuts. At least here was a captain who would fight with his crew, unlike many they had recently come across. "We will put up no more fight."

"Thank you, Captain. I do appreciate it," said Gilstrap. "However, I am faced with a quandary. You have a ship full of goods bound for Kingshold. I want said goods. The only problem is my ship is full. You see, we are very good at our work. So how can we, as they say in Trima, have our cake and eat it, too?"

The Edland captain looked visibly troubled but refused to answer.

"Yes. I think you know the answer. Captain Ba, you are hereby relieved of your vessel. And so, you and your crew suddenly find yourselves without jobs, or a home, in the middle of the North Sea. But never let it be said Captain Nini Gilstrap is not one to help fellow sailors in a time of need. You can join us if you like, on probationary terms, of course."

Captain Ba spat at her feet. Kolsen admired his balls, if not his good sense. "Never. Edlanders don't make pirates. You can all rot in hell!"

"I was afraid you might say that." Gilstrap nodded and the pirate minders of each crew member drew knives and set to work. She turned away from the carnage and shook her head. "Mister Talbot!"

"Yes, Captain," called her first mate.

"You are captain of *The Dolphin's Prize*," she said, gripping his hand and shaking it. "See it to Cloudscar. This has proven to be quite the profitable season. Choose your crew, clean up, and then be on your way!"

~

TALBOT TOOK A CREW OF TWENTY-FIVE ABOARD *THE Dolphin's Prize*, and he named Kolsen as his first mate. Mareth and Karr came along, too. He wasn't sure whether Talbot had chosen the two of them because the new captain assumed Kolsen had a connection to them or if he just wanted to keep an eye on the other new guys.

It didn't matter to Kolsen. He certainly wasn't going to feel responsible for them. The only thing that did matter was that he was first mate, even if only for the week it would take to sail to port. Opportunity presented itself again.

Mareth looked increasingly out of sorts. He'd had a haunted look in his eyes in the days since the old *Dolphin's*

Prize crew had been disposed of, and Kolsen had noticed him keeping to himself. Kolsen had approached him the night before with a cup of rum, only to find him two cups in and looking surly. Well, it wasn't his fault if Mareth couldn't handle it.

Karr, meanwhile, had been adopted by all the crew as a lucky token. It had been his shot with the crossbow that had taken out one of the ballista crew and allowed enough time for others to respond. Apparently, the wiry little streak of snot had been something of a crack shot hunter working with his da, more at home in the trees of the forest than out on the sea.

As the sun set that night, Kolsen was enjoying his dinner, sitting on the deck with Talbot and a few others. The new captain preferring the company of the crew instead of the former captain's quarters of the Edland ship. Kolsen saw Mareth approach from the corner of his eye. The bard touched Kolsen's shoulder and bade him to follow to a quiet spot away from listening ears.

"What is it, Mareth?" asked Kolsen.

"I need to get off the ship. I can't do this," said Mareth, his eyes darting from side to side, a twitch appearing at the corner of his mouth. "How can you stay here? You saw what happened to those people."

"Mareth, I didn't want to tell you before," said Kolsen, resting his hands on the bard's shoulders and looking him in the eyes. "I made my decision for this life a long time ago. Before we met."

"You were a pirate before? Is that why you were in jail?"

"No. I told you the real reason I was there. But I was a pirate before, just as I am now. And I'm a good one. It's business. People get hurt in mines, or in wars, even minding cattle. Piracy is a risk of working at sea. It's always been that way. There's nothing personal in it."

"Nothing personal?" Mareth tried not to shout, his voice coming out as an angry whisper. "Did you see those corpses after they'd all been stabbed a dozen times? I need to get off, and I need you to be able to do it. You owe me. I've saved your life twice now. Once back there when you lost your ear, and you and the boy wouldn't have made it in that rowboat if it wasn't for me. You owe me two."

"I got you off *The Scythe*," hissed Kolsen. "You'd be hanging from a Pienzan gibbet."

"Ok. That's one. So, you still owe me one, Kolsen."

Kolsen looked down at his feet. He hated to admit it, but Mareth was right. Now the question was, did he have to do anything about it?

"What are you thinking?" Kolsen asked reluctantly.

"We make off in a longboat again. It's a week to Cloud-scar, but less to land if we head south. We can be prepared with food and water and a sail. But I need you to sail us."

"How would we get away? Are we going to shout 'look over there' and then make a run for it?"

"I have a plan. Tomorrow night, when everyone is drinking, I will put them to sleep." Mareth paused when he saw Kolsen's face. "You remember how I stopped us all from getting hungry on the boat. Well, I can put people to sleep with a song, too. Especially if they've been drinking. Not much call for it normally, wanting your punters to go to sleep. But I can do it. You believe me, right?"

"I believe you," said Kolsen, his mind racing, considering the alternatives. "OK, we can do it. Tomorrow night. You get the supplies ready and I'll get everyone in one place."

"Thanks, Kolsen, I mean it. You will save my soul."

"Don't thank me yet. Still a bloody crazy plan."

Kolsen walked back to the group assembled around Captain Talbot, once more entering the ring of laughter and bawdy humor.

"What's up with your mate, lad?" asked Talbot. "He's had a bit of a sulk on him. Is he missing someone from *The Icicle?*"

"No, nothing like that, Captain," said Kolsen. "He's an artistic type. A fully trained bard, and he misses performing. He'd like to sing for everyone tomorrow night."

"Well, of course he can. It's about time we had a proper celebration for capturing this beauty," he said, gesturing at the ship. "We can afford to take it easy for one night. We're well ahead of Captain Gilstrap, what with her damaged mast. Tell him we'll have a proper party, and he can be the center of attention."

"Aye, aye, Captain," said Kolsen, a smile spreading across his face as he snapped a salute.

~

THE SUN HAD SET, THE SAILS HAD BEEN TAKEN IN, AND A barrel of ale and a cask of rum had been brought up from below decks. Cups were full, and a freshly slaughtered goat provided a rich stew better than anything eaten in weeks. Dice were rolled, arms were wrestled, and so began a pirate party.

Kolsen stood on a crate midships and called for attention. Eventually, Talbot banging on the floor with a stout stick did the trick.

"Good evening, ladies and gentlemen," he called, and laughter followed at the honorific. "Captain Talbot promised

you a piss-up and a piss-up you shall have. And so, to enter-
tain you this fair evening, I bring you, all the way from the
Bard's college in Longford: Mareth!"

Mareth walked out from the aft castle, dressed in the
previous captain's finery and carrying a lute found somewhere, its owner no longer of the ship. He had washed and
shaved, his hair tied loosely at the nape of his neck, and he
looked to Kolsen more alive than at any time since they had
met those many weeks past. Mareth sauntered over to take
Kolsen's place on the makeshift stage. He bowed once and
strummed a chord.

The bard launched into an old sea shanty which got the
feet stomping. Someone sitting next to Talbot tried to join
the chorus with his cracked voice, but the captain clouted
him with his stick and he quickly stopped to let Mareth sing.
Song followed song, drink followed drink, and Kolsen smiled,
not knowing if it was from the drink or Mareth's voice. He
saw the same joy in the faces of his comrades, and people
soon got to their feet to dance.

A full moon rose in the deep blue night sky, filled with
twinkling stars. Mareth paused only to take an occasional sip
from a cup of ale. Kolsen danced, too, though he was tiring
and wanted to stop. Eventually, he was exhausted and
flopped onto a coil of rope to take a breath.

What was he doing? he thought. Mareth had told him to
put wax in his ears and he had forgotten to do so. He pulled
two pieces of candle wax from a pouch, warmed them in his
hands until the material became malleable and pushed them
into his ears, which instantly dulled the noises of the celebration and allowed him to hear the sound of the sea in
his head.

All around Kolsen, the other pirates were collapsing onto

makeshift seats or the bare deck to rest. Mareth stepped from his stage, and though the sound was now muted, Kolsen could sense the tempo change in the bard's singing. A feeling of warmth and contentment nagged at the edge of his weary muscles. Kolsen took to pinching himself on the arm to maintain his focus, as one by one the pirates fell asleep.

~

MARETH STOPPED SINGING AND GENTLY PUT DOWN THE lute, leaning it against the mast. Kolsen could see Mareth's mouth move, but he couldn't hear anything over the rushing of the waves in his head or through the veil of fog that had descended over him. Kolsen breathed deeply until the veil lifted enough for him to realize he needed to pull the wax from his ears.

"They're all out," said Mareth. "Let's go."

"How do you do that?" asked Kolsen as he struggled to his feet, his left leg tingly and half-asleep.

"No time for chit-chat. I'll get the supplies, you get the boat ready." Mareth disappeared down the steps to below deck while Kolsen stood waiting. He was in two minds about his plan. He owed Mareth, but there was an opportunity here. His indecision took root and held him in place.

"What are you still doing here?" asked Mareth once he returned a few minutes later to find Kolsen rooted to the spot.

"Mareth, I—"

A cough came from behind them. They both turned to see Talbot getting to his feet. "Gotta piss," he slurred. The captain looked around at the sleeping pirates before seeing Mareth and Kolsen. "Bloody lightweights!" And without waiting for an answer, he stumbled up the stairs to the aft castle, already trying to untie his trousers.

"Shit," exclaimed Mareth, "look we've got to g—"

Kolsen sucker punched him in the jaw. The bard's eyes rolled back in his head as he melted to the floor. Kolsen dragged him over to lean against another slumbering corsair and made a passing attempt at making him comfortable.

"I'm sorry, Mareth," said Kolsen, though the bard was unconscious. "I will not pass this up. Let's say I owe you two now."

~

CAPTAIN TALBOT LEANED AGAINST THE RAILING, SIGHING as a hot stream of piss sailed out through the night sky and into the sea at the rear of *The Dolphin's Prize*. Ever since he'd been stuck by a pointy little rapier in a particularly nasty scrap, he'd had a problem of needing to piss every couple of hours, even during the night. He had cursed it to any who would listen, and Kolsen should have remembered.

That was the thought occupying Kolsen's still foggy mind as he willed his tired limbs to creep as silently as possible behind his captain, holding a wrung staff claimed from the carpenter's supplies. That was the thought that occupied his mind and made Kolsen's reactions a second too late.

Talbot had finished relieving himself, unaware of the threat creeping up behind him. He leaned over to pick up his trousers from around his ankles at the precise moment the length of stout wood whizzed over where his head had been seconds previously.

Kolsen, expecting Talbot's head to do the job for him, was not braced to stop his swing. He spun with the momentum, allowing Talbot's danger-experienced subconscious to take over. The captain let go of his trousers and made a grab for Kolsen. He dropped the staff, and turning, punched the older man in the stomach. The wind left Talbot in a rush, but flinging up an elbow, he caught Kolsen in the side of his head, where his ear once was, the wound still raw.

It hurt like hell. Kolsen's stitches had busted. One hand foolishly went up to defend his non-ear from further attack, opening himself up to Talbot's rising knee, which drove into his balls. Kolsen revised his opinion. *That* hurt like hell.

And then the world lurched. Kolsen felt one hand on his groin and another on the shirt about his neck as he was lifted bodily into the air, above the captain's head. With a grunt, Kolsen was jettisoned from the ship.

The pain in his head and his bollocks felt unconstrained by the physical world, existing only in a bubble of himself sailing through the air. He hit the surface of the water hard, the shock of the impact twisting his neck. Kolsen sank below the waves as Captain Talbot collapsed onto his bare behind, breathing hard and wondering what the hell was going on.

~

KOLSEN PLUNGED INTO THE DARK WATER, HIS EYES OPEN but his arms and legs not responding to his brain's desperate pleas to claw his way to the surface. The pain in his groin had disappeared, along with any other sensation below his neck.

This is how it ends, he thought, though he continued to hold his breath as if there was still a way he could propel himself to the surface to gulp more sweet fresh air.

He noticed shapes darting around him; sleek grey blurs, moving fast. Sharks. What would be a better way to go?

Drown or be ripped apart? But as he saw the creatures more closely, he saw their smooth, vaguely canine faces. Seals.

Seals were always considered to be lucky by the common seafarer, so much so he'd seen many a seafarer wearing a seal-skin cloak, although how that was lucky for the seal he'd never understood.

The mammals swam around him, and then one came straight toward him, and though he knew he was slowly sinking, it stayed with him.

As Kolsen gazed into the eyes of the seal, the face flickered to reveal a beautiful woman with dark hair waving around her head like a halo. She was clothed in a robe that sparkled like starlight, the ends of the fabric floating like tendrils sensing the deep. Her hands and feet gently moved, swimming, as Kolsen so desperately wanted to be able to do, webbing visible between her fingers and toes.

"Greetings, Vin Kolsen," said the selkie. "You have returned to us too soon. Why are you here?"

Kolsen didn't know what to do. He found himself compelled to respond, and though his chest burned, he didn't want to release his breath, and he couldn't gesture when his arms wouldn't move.

"You can speak," she whispered. "Nothing more can happen to you now."

"How?" Was all he dared try at first, but no water rushed into his lungs. Confused, he continued. "How is this possible?"

"Because I willed it. Here at your end, you remember your heritage."

"I will die then?" he asked, shocked at the confirmation, though he already knew it was true.

"You are already dead," said the selkie. "You failed. You had so much opportunity, but it has been wasted."

"What did you say about my heritage?"

"You are of the selkie. Your mother was my half-sister, did you not ever wonder about your feet?"

"I wondered. Children said I was cursed. My ma always said it was because I would be a famous seaman. Can I change shape like you?"

"Ha, you are funny, Kolsen." She tilted her head as she looked him, her brow furrowed and the barest upturn of her lips made him think of his mother, when he was a child and she would try to reassure him that everything would be ok. "No, you cannot. I had hoped to meet you one day, to point you in the direction that would please me and your family. But it looks like I was too late."

"What would you have had me do?"

"Sow chaos on the seas. At a greater scale than you have done before. These humans grow too quickly, they poison our seas and steal our fish. They club our kin and wear their hides as trophies. I know you cannot wipe them out, though I would like it if you did, but you could have made a mark."

"Yes," said Kolsen, suddenly understanding what had been driving him all of his life. "Yes. Let me do this for you."

The selkie tilted her head to look at him. "You are dead; though I could fix that." She considered him. "You need to command this ship. You must move faster. I am tired of waiting."

"That's what I was doing. The bloody bard made me too sleepy. I can take care of Talbot, but the ship's not mine then. It will be sold when we reach port. The crew will never let me steal it."

"If you need the yellow metal, then I can give it to you.

To the south, there is a bay with trees all around and four rocks which step out to sea. The bay is deep, and a ship of southerners is there, full of shiny metal. They are repairing their ship after getting caught in a storm. They have come from the west. Take them and get what you need."

"It must be a Pyrfew ship," Kolsen said to himself. Plans bubbled up again, like his never-ending last breath rising to the surface. "I shall do it. Thank you. Tell me, what is your name?"

"I am Xataniel. Go." Kolsen's aunt grabbed him by the face and pulled his lips toward hers. Powerless to resist, he thought a kiss on the lips a strange goodbye, but it was no kiss. She sucked the air from his lungs with one deep breath until everything went black.

~

KOLSEN STOOD ON THE DECK OF *THE DOLPHIN'S PRIZE*. The staff in his hands, and Captain Talbot sat in front of him on his bare buttocks, breathing the deep-contented breaths of someone dreaming.

Kolsen held the staff high above his head and brought it down with a *crack*.

~

MARETH STOOD ON THE DOCKS OF CLOUDSCAR AND WAVED goodbye to the departing, newly renamed, *Juniper*. He couldn't see if Captain Kolsen waved back, but he doubted it. Bastard.

Mareth had awoken on board *The Dolphin's Prize,* the crew desperately looking for Captain Talbot. No one found him.

Kolsen took command, of course. He was first mate, and with such a skeleton crew, there wasn't anyone else who wanted to challenge for it. He ordered the crew head southeast instead of northeast, arguing it would be better to stay close to land.

And wouldn't you know, they happened to come across a treasure boat from the Wild Continent, full of slaves and gold. It had been undergoing repairs in a secluded cove, away from any escort it must have lost in the same storm which caused it to need two new masts.

What a lucky bastard, thought Mareth. *Why does that never happen to me?*

As he thought about it, he'd been pretty much at rock bottom when he'd met Kolsen. Now, with the benefit of time, having partially forgotten what had happened to some of their poor victims and with a jangly purse full of gold, Mareth recognized that some of Kolsen's luck must have rubbed off on him, too.

But that was some luck. The treasure boat had been basically unprotected. Most of the crew were on land, organizing the slaves hard at work crafting new masts. *The Dolphin's Prize* sailed right up to the ship in broad daylight. The crew climbed aboard and took what they wanted, keeping the slavers at bay with the ballista.

When they eventually got to Cloudscar, they saw *The Icicle* had arrived before them. The inventory was sold, debts settled, and the prize shared amongst the crew. A larger share went to Captain Gilstrap and the biggest share to her backers.

Kolsen had seem depressed when he handed over *The Dolphin's Prize*, but only Mareth noticed. The others were too busy melting away to their families in Cloudscar after another privateering season done, or getting ready to move on to The Shards and pick up with another crew.

Gilstrap asked Kolsen to stay on and travel with her to The Shards, but he turned her down. He said he would stay in Cloudscar for a while with Mareth, his old mate.

Of course, before Mareth had even turned around, Kolsen was gone. Mareth had thought the pirate gone for good, a week having passed since then, until a note turned up at the inn where he lodged.

It's not The Dolphin's Prize, *it's mine. Come to the docks at two.*

There was Mareth, on time. But there was no handshake or embrace. Just the sight of *The Juniper*, formerly *The Dolphin's Prize*, rowing out of the harbor. Kolsen was putting on one last show, and there was no bloody wave back. Just the last words of the note.

I still owe you one.
Kolsen.

JYUTH ON MAGIC - WEAVING

I spent my childhood years on Edland. My family were sheep farmers, and I have discovered that being a wizard is much like the life of a sheep farmer. We had to attend to our flock, ensuring they were safe and never taking too much to feed our family so there would be sheep for tomorrow. We would shear the sheep, cutting their wiry woolen fleece, which we would then tease into long strands that could be used for weaving. My mother and sisters would use simple wooden looms to weave the thread into yards of fabric that we would use to clothe us and keep us warm at night, or to barter and trade with other families.

For the wizard, it is the same. It should be obvious to you by now, that the sources of mana around you are your herd. They must be tended, and not exhausted, otherwise the wizard will starve and die. And the mana is the woolen fleece, which must be pulled and stretched into long threads, ready to be woven into whatever wonders you can imagine.

All of the magic that I have learned requires the ability to take these threads and mold them into the form needed.

And, like weaving a blanket, this process can take time for the unpracticed wizard and it always requires concentration. But in moments of stress or strife, it is often time that you do not have.

And so, I have learned how to do many different things at once.

There is a children's game where they try to rub their stomach and pat their heads at the same time. For a long time, their hands want to do the same thing; both hands pat, or both hands rub. But eventually they learn the trick of starting one process and then layering on the second. Well, I spent two years studying how to do that in a different way.

The mind is a strange tool that must be mastered by the wizard. If you were a knight it would be your sword; your loom if you were a weaver. And so you must constantly train, practice, hone your skills.

The first thing that is realized is that the mind can be split, consciously and safely, creating independent thinking and operating units within your mind. The different selves can focus on different tasks; such as carrying on a conversation, and at the same time drawing thread and weaving it to create a shield, or drawing the wind under the wizard for flight. The ability to concentrate on these separate magical tasks while going about your normal life, be it reading a book or running from a bear, is what makes a true wizard.

I cannot begin to convey on parchment how you would do this—you need to have a teacher to show you the steps of mastering the mind through meditation, and you will have to practice them your whole life to keep them both supple and sharp. And if you are my student then hopefully you now understand why the first task you had to master was something that most children think of as a game.

NARROWING IT DOWN

P etra was out of breath. The brisk walk from the Narrows back to the Cherry Tree district—on top of a whole day pounding the pavement drumming up support for the district meetings that needed to be held—had left her exhausted. But if she had been able, she would have run the final length of the Lance.

After all of the hard work of the past days, those two knuckleheads could mess up everything. This was the type of problem that needed to be fixed.

Quick.

As she arrived at the Royal Oak, Petra saw Alana approach from the opposite direction. Petra waved and got her attention before she entered the inn.

"Petra, are you ok?" asked Alana. Petra's sister's face was still puffy; a blue and yellow bruise visible through the powder that Jules had applied to her face. Petra realized that the sight of her hustling through the streets had made her sister think about the attack that she had suffered just a few nights past.

"I'm fine," huffed Petra. "Seriously, I'm well. But we're in trouble. Dyer and Lud have decided that they don't want to work together. And Dyer says that if Lud is going to support Mareth, then he's not going to."

"What? Why?" Dyer and Lud were the district supervisors for the Inner and Outer Narrows, and they had both shown their support the other night when many of the supervisors had agreed to come together and see if they could influence the election. The fact that they hated each other, typically not agreeing on any topic, did in retrospect mean that their concurrence was peculiar.

"No bloody good reason. Other than pig-headedness. Stupid men."

"We've all got to work together," said Alana. "If one district isn't on board then the others might decide to do something different. We should tell Mareth."

"I know that, Alana. But he's not here. They went to Unedar Halt this morning when you went to the palace for your shift. And we can't tell him yet anyway. You heard how he was questioning if we could win last night. If the district support is not there, that will knock him on his arse."

"So, what are we going to do?"

"I don't know," Petra shook her head. "That's why I was rushing. To find you. Thought you would know what to do."

Alana tilted her head and looked up into the sky for inspiration. Petra knew her sister so well. Her mannerisms. This was her thinking, and Petra gave her some time to consider.

"Why don't they like each other?" Alana asked. Petra wasn't sure if she was asking a question or talking to herself.

"I don't know," she sighed, taking it for the former and tired of being asked questions she didn't know the answers to. "Everyone says they used to be friends. But that was a long time ago."

"Maybe if we find out, we can fix it." Alana reached out and laid a comforting hand on her shoulder. "Get them to be friends again. Then they'll work together."

"I guess that could work," said Petra. "But how do we find that out? Neither of them even wants to talk about the other."

"We could talk to others who know them. Everyone in the Narrows loves to gossip."

"Alright, let's give it a try. I'll take Dyer. You take Lud. See you back here this evening and we can compare notes."

~

PETRA WAS ALWAYS ABLE TO TELL WHERE SHE WAS IN THE Narrows by the contrasting surroundings. Having started off as shanty settlements beyond the Outer Wall of Kingshold, it would be reasonable to assume that the area closest to the Outer Wall was the oldest, and it was true that the Inner Narrows, as it was known, had been in existence for the longest time. But the district that she was in now had gone through more changes than the Outer Narrows since Crandall's Curtain had been drawn around all of the Outer Hub settlements. Now, interspersed between the wooden buildings that were still aggregations of various pieces of salvaged materials—which did give their appearance a certain organic quality—were some new buildings. These stood upright, all straight lines and sharp corners. Wealth from the Middle had been slowly trickling through the twenty feet of Outer Wall. So now, surrounded by the new, that meant the oldest part of the Narrows, and surprisingly the inhabitants took pride in both of those things.

Dyer lived in one such house of newer construction, though the whitewashed facade was faded and peeling in places. Petra had been there that morning to talk to Dyer, the district supervisor of the Inner Narrows, but he wasn't her target now. She wanted to talk to his wife.

Standing behind a cart selling unidentified grilled meat snacks, Petra waited until she saw Wenda leave the house, and move off down the narrow pedestrian pathways. Wenda wore a dress that was simple of cut, but adorned with tiny cross stitch flowers, her signature that everyone in the Narrows knew. Wenda was short, getting a little rounder around the waist from making an acquaintance with middle-age that had also gifted her with more than a few gray hairs.

Petra hurried after her.

"Excuse me, Wenda," she said, tapping her on the shoulder. "Could I speak to you for a moment?"

"Oh, hello, Petra love. You're back again?" she said. "Dyer's back at the house if you want to see him."

"I'd like to talk to you if I may?"

"Whatever for?" she asked, one eyebrow arched. From reputation she knew that Wenda was not a favorite of the women in the neighborhood, and so she hardly contained her surprise at Petra's request.

"You've been with your husband for a long time. I wondered if you knew why he and Lud don't like each other? I remember hearing they used to be friends."

"Well I don't know about them being friends. Weren't ever the case since I met him. Dyer didn't like him then," said Wenda, before adding with a shake of her head, "and after that night at the Giant's Toe he made it clear what he thought of that Lud!"

"Tell me be about that."

"Well, it was a long time ago. Twenty years nearly. Dyer was playing in a skittles tournament during the mid-winter festival at the Giant's Toe. And he was good; still is," she said proudly. "But this was his first time getting to the final. There was a bloke from the Outer Narrows who won every year, but it looked like Dyer had a good chance of beating him." Wenda paused for dramatic effect and conscripted her hands to aid in the telling of the tale that she launched into. "The tavern was packed. Supporters from both sides filling the common room and spilling out on to the street. Back then I was a bit of looker if I do say so myself. Always had plenty of the lads sniffing around like horny dogs. But I was already in love with Dyer.

"So, I was there supporting him. Standing right at the front, when Lud inched his way through the crowd and started talking to me. It was obvious he was trying to chat me up, but I wasn't interested." Petra nodded along, having a fair understanding of what 'not interested' would have been like. "I kept trying to ignore him but he'd start up some more conversation, commenting on the game or someone in the crowd he knew. He was definitely a bit of a charmer. He tried very hard. Well, you know what I mean love. You must have them buzzing around you all the time like flies.

"Anyway, Dyer noticed that Lud was trying to talk to me. Knocked him off his game it did. And then he couldn't bear to keep seeing Lud trying it on with me—not that he had a chance—and so he came over and told Lud to bugger off."

"And that was it?" asked Petra.

"Oh, no! There was a right bloody argument, there in the

middle of the tavern. Lud was saying rubbish about being there to support him, when Dyer knew he was there to throw him off his game. Argument started inside, but it finished outside with their fists. Dyer might have lost the skittle match, but he wiped that smarmy smirk off Lud's face. Anyone can tell you that." Wenda finished with her hands on her hips as if in triumph, pedestrians of the Narrows walking by craned their necks to see if there was some juicy gossip they should be gathering.

Petra gave this some thought. A fight between Dyer and Lud was hardly news. Hardly a year went by without some gang fights between the Inner and Outer Narrows, and when the two of them were younger men, they would be there at the front. Now they were more likely to be at the back handing out clubs to the youngsters. But, maybe this was the first time they really fought?

No. Wenda said they weren't friends, so it sounded like they had problems before that she didn't know about.

"Thank you, Wenda," said Petra. "That's very helpful."

"Well, I'm happy to help, love." Wenda leaned in conspiratorially. "And you know what? I enjoyed talking about the old days. Nice to remember that men used to fight over me."

Wenda walked away appearing taller, with a sway of her hips and a smile on her lips.

~

ALANA STOOD IN THE DOORWAY OF A LONG ROOM; A fireplace at the far end with a pot of bubbling water, and metal tubs lining the length of the room. Neighborhood women and children crowded around the tubs, rubbing wet cloth against wooden boards, scrubbing the grime of the city out of their meager clothes. Alana was familiar with wash houses like this one, even though this was not her local one. For a few coppers you got a big tub of hot water, and most importantly a bit of soap. And, a good bit of gossip too.

She threaded her way through the working women— young children hanging off their skirts or trying to climb into the grey water—until she reached a middle-aged lady standing by the cauldron.

This was Madge, wife of Lud and owner of the washing house. She was taller than Alana, and though she'd had four children, she was lean; ropey muscles visible in her arms as she poked at the fire and placed another large log on top. Madge barked orders to a boy and a girl, who ran around tending to the customers. In the light of the hearth she looked like a fire giant of legend. Alana swallowed down her fear.

"Mistress Madge," shouted Alana over the hubbub of the wash house. "Can I have a word?"

Madge turned and appraised Alana. "Alana, I don't have time for any of this election rubbish."

"Please, I need your help. Five minutes. That's all I need."

"Alright," she conceded with a harrumph. "Come back here where we can hear each other without shouting." Madge led Alana into the back room, passing out orders to the girl to mind the shop. Closing the door behind Alana, thankfully muting the shouted passing of local news, Madge offered Alana a seat at a simple table. Though she didn't go so far as to put the kettle on.

"What is it then?"

"You've been with Lud for a long time..."

"Aye. Married twenty years. Courting since we were kids."

"Did you know Lud when he was friends with Dyer? Folks have said they used to be friends."

"That was a long time ago, before I knew either of them. But I know that Lud was bothered by it. He didn't talk about it much but I could tell he missed his friend. He was always interested in news about Dyer, though who knows what he saw in him. One mid-winter he went to go and do something about it too. Got it into his head after a few drinks that they could be friends again." Madge shook her head, at the foolishness of boys in their cups or in anticipation of what was to come, Alana wasn't sure.

"He knew that Dyer was playing in a skittles tournament at some tavern somewhere, so he went to give him some support. I didn't go. Can't stand skittles. But he told me all about it after he came home and I had to help his mum clean him up."

"What happened?" asked Alana.

"That cow, Wenda, is what happened." Madge's head continued to nod like she was watching one of her customers scrape the dirt out on a wash board, but this time Alana could tell that her displeasure was aimed at Dyer's wife. "She said Lud tried to hit on her, but he was just being friendly to his old friend's girl. And then she came on to him. He had to push her off! Everyone knew that Wenda was a slut. Walking around, swinging her arse in everyone's face. Dyer couldn't help notice, but he didn't lay the blame with her. She was his girlfriend. He pointed the finger at my Lud and came out arms swinging. Well, Lud had to teach him a lesson then."

"Wow," breathed Alana. "Did Lud try again to make friends with Dyer?"

"'Course not girl!" said Madge, exasperated by the question. "Waste of time it was then, and waste of time it would have been after. At least that little episode got it out of his system to want to be friends with that arsehole again. Now then, is that all you wanted? I have punters that need seeing to."

"Yes, Mistress Madge. Thanks very much for your time."

≈

"I HATED THAT INNER LOT WHEN I WAS A KID. ME DA always told me to watch out for them."

Alana sat across the rickety table from Orman, Lud's best friend, in the Kingshold's Glory. How the original founder had decided on that name, given it was now a smoky, dirty, dive of a bar was lost to history. The fact that the locals called it the Glory Hole, or sometimes just The Hole, was much more appropriate.

"Not that I hold that against you, Alana," continued Orman. "You're on the border, you could be one of us. I knew your dad and he were a decent sort."

Orman was a short man, shaved head attempting to disguise that his hair had gone the way of his youth, and with a pot belly from too much time spent in taverns. It was early afternoon and here he was, already a few drinks into his day, illuminating the fact that he didn't have what you would call a *profession*.

If you were to ask he'd say he did 'odd jobs'—code for he'd help you get money back from anyone who owed it to you for thirty percent of the take. Everyone knew what it meant if Orman came to call, and his extended girth and sallow complexion didn't seem to be impacting his business. A man could live off the reputation of his younger self for a long time.

"That's fine, no offense taken," said Alana. "So, you knew Lud since he was lad?"

"Yep. We grew up on the same street. Knew him when we were just old enough to get into trouble."

"Did you know if Lud and Dyer used to be friends?" asked Alana tentatively, she didn't want to get him defensive, or even worse, offensive.

"Yeah, I guess so. But he doesn't go 'round talking about that much anymore." Orman stopped talking, and Alana let the silence hang in the air, waiting for him to continue. "Never understood it me self."

"I'm not going to tell anyone, Orman. I promise. But this is important. How did they become friends?"

Orman grumbled, took a big gulp of the dark brown ale and let out a burp. "I guess it can't do no harm in telling. Like I said, me and Lud got to know each other as soon as we were old enough to make trouble. To start it was just us two and then as we got older, more kids glommed on. We had a right little gang, all Outer kids."

"We got a bit older, and the knocking on doors or nicking stuff got to be less fun. Needing something else to do, we got into playing kick."

Alana nodded. Kick was a game played in the streets of Kingshold. Teams of varying, and not always equal, size would kick an approximately round object to the target of the other team, usually several streets away. There were no rules as she could tell, in fact most of the kicking seemed to be aimed at the opposing players.

"It wasn't long before we started playing against a gang from the Inner. Dyer was on that team. Him and Lud were the best players by far. They could knock a ball off a wall to go 'round another player," Orman pushed his chair back and stood to mime the moves, suddenly becoming alive, "or lift it up over their heads, and they'd both be able to get 'round without having their feet knocked from under them.

"I guess that's why they started hanging out. Spent less time with me then, did Lud." Orman sat back down with a thud, his excitement disappearing and replaced by the look of a toddler who had his favorite wooden toy taken away. "Only cared about games of kick. And it wasn't long before they started to mix up the teams, Inner and Outer Narrows kids playing on the same side if you can believe it.

"I didn't like Dyer. Like I said, my da told me to watch that Inner lot. 'They think they're special', he said. And that was Dyer alright. Thought his dad shit gold he did. But his dad weren't anything special. He didn't have any hustle, no side game. He just worked for a merchant down the docks."

"I'm sure you work very hard, Orman," said Alana, stroking his ego. She could see bringing up the past and the fickleness of his childhood friend was agitating him. And she needed him to get to the good stuff.

"Course I do," he exclaimed. "Not many who can do what I do. Got to have stomach. And balls." Orman took another swig of beer. "Anyway, one day it stopped. Lud lost interest in kick, and he stopped talking to Dyer. That's when the fighting started. Same gangs would meet up and knock three bells of shit out of each other. Now, that was more my style."

"So why did that happen?"

"Dunno. Maybe he just grew out of it. I wasn't complaining. Got my best mate back, and I bloody hated kick." Alana contained her surprise at Orman's declaration of not enjoying the game given his previous demonstration, but he quickly explained why. "Wasn't any good at it. I do remember it was right around the time Lud's dad died though. Guess he thought he had to be a man after that."

Alana thought about what she'd heard. She was so close to getting to the answer, but Orman didn't really know what happened. He'd never thought about why his friend had come back, just that he did. Maybe it did have something to do with Lud's father's death. Alana was all too familiar with how a death in the family meant that *some* people had to grow up quicker than others.

∼

HANDCARTS WERE HOW EVERYTHING TOO HEAVY TO CARRY got moved around the Narrows. The narrow confines, abrupt turns, and throngs of humanity on the streets at any time of day or night made it impossible to get a beast-led cart through the streets. A mule with some bags on its back would work, but who in the Narrows had money to feed another mouth?

Petra walked alongside the handcart being pushed by Aymer—a friend of Dyer's—being careful not to get caught under its wheels as he would zig and zag around people and the large muddy puddles that could often be deeper than the harbor. Aymer had tanned skin from being out in the sun all day, but somewhere in his family's history he probably had roots from somewhere south of the Emerald Sea—no one really gave any mind to that in this part of the city, no one had two coppers to rub together and that made them all the same.

The cart was full of cabbages, already turning brown. Cabbages that were not good enough to sell in the main market anymore, but good enough for the people in the

Narrows. In fact, it hadn't been too long ago, after Petra and Alana's parents had died, that they'd had to scrounge to buy a cabbage like this to make soup. And it would last them a week.

"What do you be wanting with me then, Petra," said Aymer in his raspy voice. "I don't want word to get back to the missus that I'm walking out with a beauty like you. She might get the wrong idea."

Aymer laughed at his own joke. Petra flashed him one of her best smiles.

"Very true, Aymer. I don't want to get on the bad side of Mildred, now do I?" Petra laughed along too, nudging his arm with her elbow. Aymer nodded, with more seriousness than Petra expected. "I thought seeing as you have known Dyer for so long, you might be able to tell me how him and Lud became friends. And then why they stopped?"

"And why do you want to know that?"

"Oh, I'm writing a book on the history of the Narrows," replied Petra brightly.

"Heh, good answer," said Aymer, catching on. "Well, it's not every day I get to help a scholar now is it? I think we originally got to know the Outer Narrows lot when we would play kick against them. Bit of fun you know, keep us out of trouble for a bit. Excepting that it would often turn into other trouble.

"Especially when Dyer and Lud started being friends. Kick would turn into nicking stuff. Always Lud's idea. Like they say, apple doesn't fall far from the tree."

"What do you mean?"

"Lud's dad. He was a thief. Everyone knew it. He lost an ear once at the Judiciary after getting caught for something."

"How long were they friends?" asked Petra.

"Oh, must have been a couple of years. Thick as thieves they were." Aymer laughed again at his own inadvertent joke. "Then one day, Dyer didn't want to see him anymore. So, we went back to playing kick with just us Inner lads. Until the Outer gang jumped us one day. Cowards had sticks and gave us a right hiding." Aymer stopped pushing his cart, and pointed to a scar above his eyebrow. "But we got 'em back. Then that was it—always about the fighting it was. Working out plans when to ambush them. Pick off their lot when they were on their own. Even when we got old enough to get interested in girls and ale, there'd still be fights."

Petra considered this. Was she getting anywhere? She could talk to twenty people and hear as many stories again about them fighting. "But why did they stop being friends?"

"Dunno. I know Dyer's dad didn't like it much, him hanging around those Outers. Might have had something to do with it. Heh, you could ask him but you'd have to go out onto Corpse Hill with a witch to help you. What with him being dead."

Petra clucked her tongue, a habit from when she was a child—for some reason it helped her think. "Is there anyone around who knew his dad?"

"Hmm," said Aymer, stopping to stroke his chin. "There might be. Haven't seen her in a while though..."

~

"YOU'RE GOING TO HAVE TO SPEAK UP DEAR!" SHOUTED THE old lady from the deep folds of the pillows enveloping her in the beaten oak arm chair. This was Nanny Earma, Dyer's great aunt and his only surviving family member. And though she held a tarnished old brass trumpet to her ear, she was having problems hearing Petra.

"I said, Nanny, that I wanted to talk to you about Dyer and Lud." Petra practically shouted down the open end of the trumpet, slightly afraid she would deafen the old lady, but then realizing that was impossible. Petra called her Nanny because all the kids had grown up knowing her as nothing else. Nanny had never been able to have children of her own, and so she became well known to the children of the Narrows as a kindly old lady who would always welcome someone hiding out, whether from their parents, older siblings or more official trouble. And if you were lucky, sometimes you would get treats.

"Dyer and Lud, you say? Such sweet boys they are. Always coming 'round to help out."

"Nanny, they are both over forty now. I don't think they come 'round to help anymore. That was probably thirty years ago."

"Oh," said Nanny Earma, her face falling at the instantaneous passing of time. "I guess you're right. I don't remember seeing them in a long time. Especially that Lud." Nanny Earma squinted her eyes, the wrinkled eyelids almost meeting, creating the look of something like a pair of walnuts. "Now that I think about it, I'm not supposed to like that Outer Narrows lad. Bad boy."

"Why do you say that?" asked Petra, leaning forward on the edge of the wooden stool, which until recently had been the resting place for Nanny's feet. Nanny had already explained in great detail how her varicose veins had been giving her some trouble today.

"Pooh, he did a bad thing." The old lady shook her head

vigorously, her thin grey hair coming undone from its perch on top of her head.

"And? What was it?"

"Pie!" barked Nanny. Petra jumped involuntarily.

"What do you mean pie?"

"You know Dyer's dad never liked Lud." Petra nodded, wondering at the change of topic. "Never liked him. But Dyer always vouched for him. Said he was different from his thieving dad. But he was wrong."

"What do you mean?"

"Dyer's dad worked so hard for his family. So, so hard. Doing whatever that miserly old Iothan merchant said. Then one day, he had an opportunity! A chance to move up in the world." Petra leaned in as Nanny Earma warmed to her subject; she could almost imagine the flood of memories coming back to her. "A nobleman from Pienza had come visiting Kingshold. Big fat man. Wanted to eat all the Edland food. He'd heard about flying pig pie and he wanted to try it. Dyer's dad had been there when the fat man offered five gold crowns to whoever brought him the best pie."

Flying pig pie. Petra mused on this. A strange dish of pigs' feet and pigeon, both fairly plentiful in and around Kingshold, and it was definitely famous; but that didn't mean she would ever actually eat it. The pigeon was usually stringy —and a bad pie maker was sure to leave some small bones and gristle in there to pad out the contents—and the trotters brought a certain slimy and gelatinous element that some generous folk said helped with swallowing.

"Dyer's dad sent him to the shop he knew that had the best pie. This was his chance, see. His chance to go up in the world. Before Dyer went, his dad sat him down and made sure he knew how important it was. And then, when he got to Dibbler's, there was Lud..."

~

"FLYING PIG PIE."

"Pardon, Miss Nini. What was that?" asked Alana.

Alana had found Lud's grandmother in a small house near the curtain wall, after asking what had seemed like half of the neighborhood for directions. The door had opened itself when she'd knocked, and she'd been invited in with a call to find Nini sitting in a chair by the fire, shawl wrapped around her shoulders and a walking stick leaning against the wall nearby. Nini had thought it was one of the neighborhood ladies coming in to check on her. Alana had to explain who she was, which became a long game of who-knows-who until Nini was happy enough with Alana's ancestry to tell her to put the kettle on and make some tea.

Over tea, Alana had asked about Lud and his friendship with Dyer, and Nini had been happy to talk. Unfortunately, the story started with Lud's birth and Alana's attention had started to wander as Nini told of how Lud once got stuck in a chimney when he was three.

"Flying pig pie. That was Lud's dad's favorite," explained the old lady in a strong but quiet voice that meant Alana had to lean in to fully hear. "Not that I ever used to make it. We couldn't afford that most of the time. But he'd have a slice some times and he loved that crispy pastry wrapped around the meat." She paused in recollection, a beatific smile on her face. "Mmmm. I love a bit of flying pig pie too."

"Did Lud like it too?"

"Oh no, he hated it. Fussy eater." Nini shook her head

and pulled a face at the shock of her grandson not liking something that was so clearly a delicacy.

"So what's that got to do with Lud and Dyer?"

"Well it was Lud's dad's dying wish to have a pie. A whole pie. For the first time in his life. He'd had an accident at work you see. Got a long cut on his arm and didn't go to a good barber to get it cleaned up. Green rot took hold. I can still see it now," she said, her hands clutched to her chest, "the tendrils that crept up the inside of his arm like a vine, closing in on his heart. He knew he didn't have long left, so he sent Lud to the best shop in the city.

"And when he got to Dibbler's, there was Dyer..."

∾

PETRA WAS WAITING IN ALANA'S ROOM AT THE ROYAL OAK when her sister returned. She had taken the opportunity to lie down on her sister's bed and rest her feet that throbbed from walking all over the city. Her eyelids had started to droop, and the siren call of a nap pulled at her when the door to the simple bed chamber opened. Petra smiled to see her sister, but she noticed that Alana's face turned to a scowl as she saw Petra sprawled on the bed.

Too late, she realized she hadn't taken off her shoes. Always a peeve of Alana's.

Petra scrambled to sit upright on the bed, feet on the worn wooden floorboards.

"Alana, I figured it out!" said Petra.

"Me too," said Alana, dropping onto the only chair in the room. "It's all Dyer's fault. What a horrible piece of work."

Petra was momentarily puzzled. She considered her sister, who looked tired too. Those bruises must still hurt, and she'd worked at the Palace that morning before joining Petra on their afternoon investigation. *She must be mixed up.* "No, Alana. I think you mean it's Lud's fault. You must be exhausted and got it turned around."

"I'm not confused, Petra." Alana spoke slowly. Condescendingly. Petra hated it when her sister would assume she needed to *explain* things to her. Petra could feel her blood starting to rise. "I got the whole story. It was a fight over a pie. Can you believe it?"

"I know. But it was a bit more than that wasn't it?"

"You're right," said Alana. Petra momentarily smiled, expecting to hear her sister agree with her after all. She quickly realized she was mistaken. "Lud wanted the pie for his dying father. His last wish. Can you imagine? I always thought flying pig pie was a cause of death, but I guess there is no accounting for folk. Anyway, what could be more important than that?"

"Dyer needed it for his dad too. He had a chance to get new work, make a little windfall and get his family out of the Narrows," said Petra, before she explained the story of the fat foreign gastronome.

"That sounds far-fetched to me." Alana shook her head. Petra knew her sister, once she thought she'd figured something out she'd cling on to it like a randy terrier on your leg. "Why wouldn't this rich nobleman just go and buy it himself?"

"He was a foreigner. Obviously. He didn't know where to go." It was Petra's turn to shake her head. "I'm not saying that a father's dying wish is not important. It is. But we're talking about the living here."

"That's what Dyer said! To someone who was supposed to be his best friend!" Alana exploded, waving her hand dismissively as she spoke. "Of course, you would take his side. Always trusting whoever tells you anything, Petra. Come on. Think for once! His dad was dying! Wouldn't you want to have done the same for our parents?"

"Think? Think! Why don't you think about what you're saying?" Petra had leapt to her feet and was waving a finger in the direction of her sister. "You wouldn't talk to me like that if Mum and Dad were still around. And this was a once in a lifetime opportunity for Dyer's dad. Our Dad would have understood that. He did everything he could for us."

Alana stood too; Petra could see her nostrils flare, her eyes staring wide—signs of danger but she wasn't going to back down.

"Right! Trust you to bring up Mum and Dad. I know you were their favorite. Don't you think I don't remember that every day? Don't you think it didn't stab me in the heart and twist every time the neighbors came and consoled you, and only you, after they died. Come on. Who gets out of the Narrows with a pie?"

"Why not?" asked Petra, pushing her blonde hair from her face, her hands shaking with anger. "The little things matter, Alana. Look at us—"

"—Yes, look at you bloody two," came a voice from the still open doorway. Jules, the owner of the Royal Oak, eyes flitting from one sister to the other, waved a dishrag in air. "What. The bloody hell. Are you two doing? We can all hear you down there," Jules waved in the direction of the common room, "arguing over pies!"

Petra and Alana were speechless. They looked at each other, Petra able to see the anger still bubbling in Alana.

"Sit down." Jules waved them to the bed. They both sat on the edge, as Jules closed the door and stood in front of them, looking down with her hands on her hips. "What's going on?"

Petra, shamefaced, explained the events of the day. Alana followed suit and Petra realized that they hadn't stopped to listen to each other. As she heard her sister recount the conversations she had, Petra didn't really know what was true anymore.

"You bloody idiots," said Jules after they finished. "Look at you. Fighting someone else's battles. Acting like men, when you should know better. That's how wars start. People wanting the whole bloody pie, all or bloody nothing, and usually it's both sides ending up with nothing."

Petra bowed her head, shame showing on her flushed cheeks. She snuck a sideways glance at Alana, who gave her a little smile, just like she used to do when they would get into trouble with their mum.

"You can't fix stupid," Jules said shaking her head, "but you two aren't stupid."

"I'm sorry," said Petra to her sister. As the oldest she felt it was her responsibility to apologize first.

"I'm sorry too."

Petra hugged her sister, delighted to see a smile on her face once more.

"Good," said Jules. "And after the dinner time rush I'll go and see those two Narrows fools and I'll tell them what to do. And they better bloody listen. Now, I have an inn to run." Jules turned and marched out of the bedroom without a farewell.

"By Marlth, we were being so stupid," said Alana, once Jules had gone.

"Yes. I know you think I'm stupid, but I know it wasn't all over a pie," said Petra. "I'm sorry about Mum and Dad."

"It's ok. And I don't think you're stupid!" Alana put her hand over her heart, "I promise. All of this stuff we're doing with the election was your idea. I'm sorry I said that you're gullible. Too trusting. I guess it's difficult how quickly you make friends. Trusting people is part of that."

Twin tears, released at the same time raced down the sisters' cheeks. They smiled at each other. The kind of smile that comes from a deep love, and they held each other for a while.

"I hate flying pig pie," said Petra.

"Me too," said Alana.

JYUTH ON MAGIC - APPLICATIONS OF MAGIC

M ana.
Magical energy.
Whatever you call it, it is a highly flexible resource that is limited by its availability, the time available to the practitioner, but most importantly, the imagination of the wielder. A dullard will never be a magic user of any proficiency. Drawing mana in threads enables the wizard to weave different applications.

I have been told there are many ways to skin a cat, and though I have little firsthand knowledge of that, I do agree that there are multiple ways to achieve your objectives in any situation. In this regard, I have found it essential to focus on the efficient use of magic. Therefore, consider the following applications in order of their magical expenditure.

TELEKINESIS OR THE APPLICATION OF FORCES

THE CREATION OF INVISIBLE FORCES IS BOTH FLEXIBLE AND

scalable. Small amounts of power can be used for the creation of forces to lift small objects or to apply pushing forces. Larger expenditures can create forces powerful enough to cause the wizard to fly or crush steel. In fact, cities or mountains could theoretically be levelled with such an application but the mana required would be immense.

Psychic projection

The wizard can travel at great speed using only their mind, leaving their physical body behind. The wizard allows their consciousness to form outside of their own self, in whatever form they choose and can, for all intents and purposes, 'fly' in order to travel great distances. It is possible to make yourself visible and audible, but corporeality is not possible. Psychic projection does come with risks: the wizard's body is vulnerable while the consciousness is separate; and though the wizard is not able to weave threads while projected, he can be vulnerable to some magical attacks.

Transformation

1. Of self. The act of transformation largely depends on the size of the object being transformed. And in the case of the wizard it can be considerable (especially in my case). A large use of energy may make transformation sound unappealing, but efficiency needs to be measured over a longer period of time. Let me illustrate. Transforming into a bird takes considerably less mana than flying for a

prolonged period of time. Transforming into a lion can potentially be both more efficient and an effective method of dealing with attackers.

ii. Of others. Stories abound of witches transforming people into frogs, toads, pigs and even fish. It is not common for me to discover my own limitations, but I must admit that I don't truly know if these are just stories or if it is just that I have not discovered how to do this particular type of magic effectively. In my experience, I have found that when the wizard transforms themselves, it is as if they weave a new image that they choose to don like clothes. But when attempting to transform others it is apparent that the subject can, much like a child on feast days, refuse to wear the new outfit.

iii. Of things. The world is made of 'stuff" (for want of a better word—it could even be said to be stuffed full of stuff). And stuff can be transformed into stuff of another type, but there are some very clear rules:

- Size matters. The bigger the object, the more energy. And you can't significantly shrink or grow something
- Like for like. You can't change iron into wood or stone into water. But you can turn stone into glass
- The wielder is the craftsman. If you don't know how to make a sword, that iron ingot you make look like a sword will likely not function as well as a sword made by a talented smith
- Gold and gems are difficult. I'm not saying it's impossible to transmute copper into gold, but it is a long and tiresome process. That is why these things have value and I am not rich.

Conjuration.

I shall limit this topic to the conjuration of inanimate objects because the summoning of creatures brings with it certain ethical issues. This is because conjuration literally takes something that is wanted from somewhere else; and whilst I may have not balked at tasks that would have led others to question their own humanity, I am not a thief or a taker of slaves. However, should you need to the means are theoretically straight forward. The wizard weaves the thread into what is desired, and the conscious locates it and pulls it through a magical gate to the wizard. Conjuration uses a great deal of energy (less if you know where the object resides and the distance is not far, incredible amounts for unique objects of unknown location), though it is great for the showman. Some people say there is nothing like pulling a rabbit out of a hat to get a crowd's attention, though I have typically found more efficient means to get all eyes on me.

Pure energy, including fire

For offensive purposes, especially in combat with another proficient magic user or a magical creature (when you can't run) it is important to hit hard. Fire. Lightning. Pure energy.

These weapons are combinations of transformation and conjuration, combining elements that do not exist on-hand with what does. And thankfully it does not require the wizard to understand the physics behind it. Weave tightly to strengthen purpose.

And don't forget some imagination if you want to catch your opponent off guard.

TELEPORTATION

IF CONJURATION WORKS THEN SURELY THE WIZARD CAN send himself to another location through a magical gate.

The answer is no.

A resounding no. This does not work.

THE WORKING DEAD

"And five more makes fifty gold crowns," said the well-dressed woman counting out the reward into Trypp's hand.

Bekah, for that was her name, was a business associate of their usual middleman, Artur Danweazle. Artur was renowned for being able to obtain specific items for the right kind of discerning clientele and while Redpool was his usual home base, his network was a spider's web of similar individuals across the Jeweled Continent. Bekah was the better looking Carlburg version of Artur.

As usual for business dealings: Trypp took point; Florian loomed, acting as a deterrent to any signs of mischief; while Motega remained aware of their surroundings. Motega was happy to let his friend lead in business transactions, each of them well aware of the strengths of the others. Discussions of money was not where he was best suited.

"Thank you, Mistress Bekah. That all seems to be as agreed, though I don't think this price was right," said Trypp, as he dropped the small stamped gold coins into a leather purse, that disappeared into his shirt. "There was no mention that the crypt was haunted."

"Master Trypp," she said, her voice calm and slow, "I didn't think it would be necessary to call that out. Artur made it sound as if you three were professionals. When has a magic object tucked away in a crypt not resulted in a haunting? Magic leaks after all. Why, if someone could just walk right in and get it then why would I need you?"

"A zombie or two, even a few skeletons, we expected. A handful of wights and a shambler are a different matter. We've, maybe, come out even on this job, what with travel and materials. Goblin fire does not come cheap; as you well know."

"Yes, well I understand your concerns," she said. Motega could tell she may well understand but she also didn't plan on doing a fig about addressing them. "Hmm, perhaps I can help you out?" she continued. "I happen to know of another job that should be much more straightforward."

"What is it?" asked Trypp, eyebrows arched.

"There is a town called Stableford near the mountains between here and Kolsvick. They have a little problem I'm sure is nothing. Reports of grave robbing."

"What else?" asked Trypp. "Sounds like a job for the Sheriff. Or a fence maker. What's going unsaid?"

"Well, they had a problem with a necromancer ten years ago," said Bekah. Trypp sighed and Motega and Florian exchanged similar shakes of their heads. "But he is supposed to be dead," she quickly added, "no one has heard of him since then. The town will pay twenty-five crowns to get to the bottom of the matter. And I have an interest in this as well, so I'll add another ten crowns for you."

"What type of interest would you have in a little town like that?"

"There is a new supplier of furniture and decorative objects there. Good quality and great prices. They are selling like hot pies—I just can't get enough for my clientele here in Carlburg. I want nothing interrupting that supply line."

"Well we were hoping to stay away from dead folk for a while. But I guess where there's corpses, there's gold." Trypp looked to Motega who shrugged, the meaning clear to his friend. *It's your call.* "We'll do it for thirty-five gold and you'll sell to us at cost going forward," he said, thrusting out his hand.

Bekah licked her palm, the Skarian way to vouch that your hands were clean, and they shook on it.

~

THREE DAYS' PLEASANT HORSE RIDE HAD LED THEM TO THE outskirts of Stableford. The journey had been a welcome respite after their recent underground exertions; the road well maintained and free of bandits.

Cresting a hill, Motega gazed down at the valley below. Their destination was a small town that nestled between flowing waters from the mountain range behind it. In the distance to the north west, they could see the river Tarm falling down the sheer white cliffs to the valley floor, where it winded its way to meet a large stream that flowed from the east; a stone bridge arched over the stream on the far side of town.

Following the road, the three riders arrived at the river, the shale of the bed visible through the cold clear water; the ford that had led to the founding and naming of this settlement.

Water splashed into the air as Motega led the way through the crossing, his horse snorting at the cool water after the long dusty ride—though he didn't let him stop to play. Through the town they passed an evolution of human habitation; one-story wooden buildings giving way to two-story; wood being replaced by the same white stone from the mountain side. Barge stations by the river became taverns and inns for the traveling soul, and eventually they found a small but thriving market, populated with handcarts, upon reaching the central square.

There was no wall about the town. No gate to stop them, or guards to question them. In fact, their passage went unremarked by a local populace apparently used to travelers passing through.

The Kingdom of Skaria, much like many monarchies, had its own assortment of nobility. If Motega could recall, he thought they were referred to as Greves and Grevindes, though he had yet to find any who referred to themselves as noble born who were worth a fart in the cold. But one thing he approved of in Skaria, was that any town situated on the King's road had to have an appointee of the crown to run the show—nobles had farm land, hunting grounds and serfs, of course—but the thinking seemed sound that at least they couldn't fuck up any place important.

And so Motega asked an old lady, sat on her wooden porch, for directions to the Town Hall. The home of the Sheriff.

~

THE TOWN HALL WAS A SIMPLE ONE-STORY STONE
construct not far from the main market square. Attached to
it on one side was the small-town lock-up and guard house,
and on the other side was the local money lender. It was
Sheriff Garrelont who had put word out for adventurers to
help, and it was to her that Motega, Trypp and Florian were
escorted by a local constable of considerable years.

"If this wrinkled old scrote is all that stands between
them and a necromancer, I'd be putting word out for help
too," muttered Motega to Florian. His friend grinned, but
Trypp glowered at the pair of them.

Sheriff Garrelont's office was sparsely decorated; simple
functional furniture, bare stone walls visible behind plain
green rugs that hung for warmth. She stood and shook hands
with each of them. Motega first, then Trypp, and finally,
being most vociferous in her hand pumping with Florian.
Garrelont was a small woman, and Motega guessed she was
not yet forty by the few wrinkles that were only visible
around her eyes; but she had an air of confidence about her
from which Motega guessed she'd been Sheriff for more than
a few years.

She sat down behind her desk and looked at the big
swordsman. "Master Florian, I am so glad for you and your
employees to be here."

Florian exchanged looks with Trypp and didn't answer
their host.

Motega had seen this before in Skaria, especially once
you got out of the big cities. The country was not welcoming
of foreigners or different faces; all were assumed to be inden-
tured servants or, best case, skilled employees.

The first time they had encountered this, they'd tried to
go with the flow and have Florian take the lead. But after the

soft lad had agreed to help another particular town for free, falling for the sob story and the pretty smile of the mayor's daughter, Florian had agreed not to talk in public. Not until the talking got to talking about fighting at least.

"Sheriff Garrelont, it's a pleasure to meet you," said Trypp. "*I* made the arrangements with Mistress Bekah. The three of us are not from Skaria, but let us reassure you that we are extremely capable. Now tell us, what are your troubles?"

~

"I GUESS IT STARTED A DECADE AGO," SAID THE SHERIFF. "We had a problem with a necromancer up in the mountains. He went by the name of Hrodebert. I remember the day quite clearly. It was a spring morning, the daffodils were blooming and everyone was moving about the town with a spring in their step, happy for winter to be finally over; when he turned up out of nowhere.

"Walked into town with hundreds of zombies and skeletons shambling behind him. He must have come across a goblin graveyard as most of them were only four feet tall, but it was also plain that he was the cause of our grave robbing problem we had back then. I saw my great aunt Gertrude holding a pick-axe, by the love of Marlth!" The sheriff shook her head at the thought, before plowing on, Motega and friends paying close attention. "She'd been dead for years and everyone said afterwards how her walking into town was more active than she'd been in life. Right lump she was. Anyway, that's besides the point. So, there were hundreds of dead things walking around, some of them we knew personally, and so, to be honest, no one put up a fight. We all just ran indoors and hid. The few mercenaries around town scarpered, or hid in a bottle in the tavern. There definitely weren't no heroes.

"Hrodebert took the Sheriff's house for himself and renamed the town to the New Republic of Zomtopia."

Florian let out a chuckle, Motega shot him a smirk. *Why was it that those who liked to spend their time with dead always turned a little peculiar?*

"Oh, yes. It was clear he was three crates short of a full barge, but he was in charge. My predecessor, Sheriff Marley, tried to reason with the necromancer as he marched into town, pleading with him to negotiate. His face went redder and redder as Hrodebert ignored him, jogging alongside the marching army, his paunch wobbling along. Eventually he earned the pleasure of being held by the skeletons after screaming in the necromancer's face. And that's when the poor bugger realized where they were heading; he keeled over and died right there as his family were evicted from their house to make way for Hrodebert. Seeing his wife marched out by a decomposing corpse proved too much for his heart, we reckon. And Hrodebert brought him right back to life again, or whatever you call it. But it was obvious he weren't the same no more."

"How did you get rid of him?" asked Trypp.

"Well, I weren't sure that Hrodebert really enjoyed what he was doing. He didn't seem happy, looked like keeping things going caused him more grief than maybe he expected. Zombies and skeletons aren't that smart, so he had to constantly give them orders. We still had ferry traffic coming through, and though he increased the tariff, the corpses weren't much use as workers so he needed the real people to keep doing their jobs. To be fair to him, he still paid folks; there weren't much in the way of force to get people to do it.

"By the way he walked around town like a man who'd found a copper and lost a crown, you could tell that he was finding it all a drag. And then the summer came. A hot one. In case you didn't know, zombies stink in the heat. Folks got sick too. That's when most of the people died during the reign of Zomtopia. Some nasty diseases went around, even though we tried to have people clean up behind the zombies; bits of green flesh dropping off all the time. Summer was ending when word reached us that King Arlfsson had finally dispatched a squadron to deal with the necromancer. And I'm sure he heard about it too."

"Did they lay siege? Clear the town house to house? How bad was the fight?" asked Florian, leaning in as he listened to the story. Conversation had moved onto military matters—so now he was allowed to talk—and he was always eager to see if there was a tactical lesson to learn from a tale.

"There weren't one!" said the Sheriff, throwing her hands up in the air. "A squadron of a dozen-dozen soldiers readied themselves across the river late one evening, and then attacked the town at dawn. They expected a fight right enough. But the zombies and skeletons just collapsed at their feet. Dropped dead again if you like. And Hrodebert was nowhere to be found. Cleaning up all those dead bodies was the worst, I can tell you. The squad captain told me that he must have ran and once he was too far away from the undead, they had no magic to hold them up."

Motega exchanged a look with Trypp. This was a strange invader, even for a necromancer. Avoiding a fight when by the Sheriff's description he outnumbered the army three to one. *Why did he run?*

"Since then there's been neither sight nor sound of Hrodebert," continued the Sheriff. "The necromancer's tower, where he came from, is still there in the foothills of the mountain nearby, and it's been quiet. But then, a year ago, we noticed graves being disturbed again. Thought they might be just scavengers to start off with, or bandits taken to robbing graves for what they're buried with; but it's been happening too often, and we know there aren't any bandits around the King's roads. So, I asked Johan, he's a tracker here in town, to investigate the tower. Just to make sure there was nothing going on."

"Let me guess," said Trypp. "Hrodebert is back."

"We don't know if it's him. Johan said he got close to the tower and heard an infernal racket of scraping and banging. Got scared for his own hide, and ran back with his tail between his legs. We don't know what's happening and I can't get any more volunteers to go and have a look, so I have to assume he's back and rebuilding his army of the walking dead. I sent messages to Carlburg for help, but they're not interested. Until something happens, or I've got more evidence, they won't march the infantry all the way up here.

"That's why I put the word out for people like you," she said, looking to Motega and his friends. "I need to know what's happening and have some evidence if I need to call for the King's help."

"All we have to do is find out what's going on?" asked Trypp.

"That's basically the job. But if you three are as capable as you say and you can stop Hrodebert yourselves—make him run away again even—then I can pull together an extra twenty-five gold crowns. A clean-up bonus. All of this uncertainty is bad for business in this town."

"We'll see what we can do," said Trypp, reaching over the table to shake her hand. "Now, can you point us toward this tracker?"

~

MOTEGA, FLORIAN AND TRYPP STOOD OUTSIDE A SHOP ON the main square. The swinging shingle hanging outside read "Breckon Trading".

Apparently, Johan the tracker had decided on a career change and was now Johan the salesman.

The dirt square was the center of commerce for the town; handcarts of produce, two taverns, a blacksmith, and the local branch of the Kollskar bank. Locals and transients moved about with intent as Motega surveyed the shop front. By the looks of it, Breckon Trading sold everything you could want that wasn't made in a town of this size. Hanging on racks, or stacked on shelves on the porch outside, were pots and pans, iron bathtubs, rakes, hammers, and a surprisingly large selection of well-crafted furniture and other home decorations.

"I'm no expert, but that stuff looks like what Mistress Bekah was selling in Carlburg," said Motega.

"Aye," said Trypp. "This is the place where she is getting her new produce. It's the supplier she wants to make sure isn't interrupted."

They walked inside the store and faced a grim old man standing behind the counter. Big bushy beard and black hair shot through with gray, his broad expanse breaking out from the sides of his leather apron. "What can I be doing for you gentlemen," he asked, politely enough but his piercing stare clearly said something else—*I can see your weapons and I don't care; don't nick any of my stuff or there will be hell to pay.*

"We're looking for a man by the name of Johan," said Florian.

"And what would you be wanting with him then?"

"The sheriff sent us. We're investigating the disturbed graves. Are you Johan?"

"Nope, that's not me. I don't think them graves anything other than hungry mountain trolls if you were to ask. But I'll get him for ya." The shopkeeper stepped through a curtain into a back room. He called for Johan and a new silhouette, visible through the dirty grey hanging, joined the old man.

"I can't make out what they're saying," whispered Trypp.

"Me neither," said Motega. Maybe it was all above board but, in his experience, whispers led to lies or knives.

"Here he is, boys. Don't take up too much of his time though eh? He's got work to do." The shop keeper pushed a small, wiry man—rather resembling a ferret to Motega's mind—out of the back room with a large paw of a hand. "Why don't you sit down over there to talk," he said, nodding to a table and chairs on display nearby.

In his line of sight, thought Motega.

Johan squirmed on his chair as Motega and his friends sat down, avoiding eye contact, but he squeaked a welcome. "W-w-what can I be doing for you gentlemen?"

"The sheriff said you saw something up at the necromancer's tower," said Trypp. "I was wondering if you could describe it for us."

"I don't like to talk about it, sirs," Johan mumbled, looking from side to side as he spoke. "Given me awful nightmares. I can't go up in the hills anymore. Jump at every sound."

"I understand, Johan," said Trypp, remaining patient. "But we need your help."

"Didn't see much to be honest. There were bright lights burning in the windows of the tower and this new building built next door to it. Lit up the night it did. I would have looked more, but that's when I heard the noises."

"What noises?"

"Terrible screeching sounds. Banging and moaning. That's what wakes me up at night. I couldn't get no closer, my legs froze." Johan looked up from the floor to Trypp for the first time. "Prolly pissed me self too. I'm sorry, sirs, I don't think I'm much use to you."

"That's all right, Johan," said Trypp, resting a hand on the shaking man's shoulder as his gaze returned to the floor. Trypp looked at Motega and rolled his eyes. "Help us out with a few directions and we'll be on our way."

~

THE TOWN CEMETERY WAS ON THE OUTSKIRTS OF THE settlement, a grassy flat expanse bordered by a low white-washed fence. Small mounds of turf, or for the more recently deceased, freshly turned earth, headed with stones or carved wood signifying the final resting places of the townsfolk. And dotted throughout the burial ground, home to centuries of inhabitants, were signs of graves being disturbed and not set right. *Awaiting the return of their owners?* thought Motega.

"Let's split up," said Motega. "See what we can find out here, and then go and get some dinner. I'm starving."

Trypp and Florian agreed and they divided up the field between them. Motega walked through uneven rows of graves, his falcon, Per, clutching his shoulder and tearing at jerky that Motega fed the bird with his fingers. His eyes scanned the markings as he walked, noticing families sharing the same name grouped together. Where the stone had not worn away, there were a few words remembering the soul buried beneath; the size of their family, their profession, in some cases a nickname or other way to remember the long dead body beneath the grass. In war they say that the victors write the history; some gravestones showed that in the war of life, it was the young who were the winners.

Edith Flyss, Barely a mother to Audrey. Royal cow to all. You won't be missed.

Motega wondered who would raise a stone above his head when his time came? He hadn't seen his sister in five years. Likely he was heading to a stone that read 'Brother in name only'. He shook his head. No point getting distracted when he had a job to do. They didn't know if there would be any clues around here, but they needed to be certain and the day was getting long.

Walking up and down the rows it was obvious which graves had been despoiled, the gaping holes topped with an aged marking leaving little doubt, often a wooden box of varying stages of decomposition at the bottom. The open graves were dotted throughout his section of the cemetery, not just close to the edges of the yard which would make it easier for any raider. He counted only fourteen open graves, most with their neighbors untouched, except for one whole family, the Tomrers. How was it known who would have the richer spoils?

"Motty," called Florian, walking over with Trypp at his side. "Are you finished?"

"Yeah, I think so," said Motega. "Any great insights?"

"Not much," said Trypp. "We counted twenty-two robbed graves between us."

"Fourteen for me. Hardly an army with those numbers." He paused, thinking about the strange pattern of exhumation. "The thing that's bugging me... why are the robbed graves all spread out though the yard? Doesn't one dead body make as good a zombie as another?"

"Don't know," said Florian, shrugging. "We were discussing the same thing. Seems like they were picking graves at random."

"Maybe," said Motega, fingers twirling through his braided hair while he thought. "But if so, why did they take this whole family?"

"I don't know," said Trypp. "And I don't think we will figure it out here. Let's go back to the outfitters and stock up ready for tomorrow. We'll go find the tower. But tonight, I want a beer and a comfortable bed."

"Good plan," said Motega, slapping his friend on the back before they strode back the way they had come, to the center of Stableford.

∿

TWO INNS FACED EACH OTHER ACROSS THE CENTRAL square, The Cold Peak and The Boars Head. They plumped for the latter. The common room was empty, except for three people clustered around a table in the far corner from the fire; their friend Johan the former tracker, the shop keeper and a well-dressed fellow who had the look of a traveling merchant. Florian made an imposing figure as he walked across to the man standing behind the bar, cleaning a pewter tankard with a rag that looked more oily than clean.

"What's on the menu tonight, good sir?" asked Florian.

"Same as every night. Boar. 'S good though," replied the barman. "Thas what ah'm known for, and plenty of boars in them forests. You want a drink too?"

"Yes, and we need a room for the night. Three beds."

"Ah think ah can manage that lad. Aht'll be ten silver. Each."

Florian put the money down on the counter and the three friends took a table close to the fire. The barman returned with three wooden bowls full of carved meat and roast potatoes, swimming in a deep brown gravy. Three shiny pewter tankards filled with ale followed.

"It's quiet this evening," said Florian.

"Still early," said the barman. "Those travelling through will be here before long. Lot of the locals staying at home though these days. Weird things going on. Ah heard about you three, that's why you're 'ere. Need things to get back to normal we do, so Ah wish you good luck."

The barman left them alone, not waiting for a reply. Motega and his friends ate in silence. The boar was as good as the inn-keep had said, and they felt replenished to plan for their next day.

～

THE INN HAD A FEW MORE CUSTOMERS BY THE TIME THE three of them clambered up the stairs to bed, but it was hardly busy. Motega could understand the barman's forthright concerns.

Their room was adequate—thankfully cleaner than the rag used to wipe the mugs—with a pair of bunk beds. Taking a bottom berth, Motega climbed into bed and sleep came easily.

Some unknown hours later a scream cut through the night. Motega sprang up in his bed, banging his head on the bunk above and cursing. Trypp and Florian, eyes open, were tensed, similarly upright on the opposite bunks, hands on weapons and waiting for further noise. Another cry came from outside, away from the square.

"Mot. Can you look to see what's going on?" asked Trypp as he slipped from the top bunk and moved to pull his trousers on. "Maybe I'm just a little jumpy but I don't fancy staying here if the town is about to be overrun by zombies again."

Motega nodded, he wasn't particularly excited for that eventuality either, and closed his eyes. Per had been sleeping too, perched near the chimney of the inn for warmth in the cool mountain night air, but he had been woken by the screams. And when Motega's mind merged with that of his spirit animal it was already in the air looking for the disturbance. The peregrine falcon swooped low over the square, before banking to follow the street that headed out of town toward the cemetery. The street was deserted until two figures became visible, one a woman, screaming as she tried to open a door to a house. Behind her was a man, slow moving and stumbling, one foot dragging behind him.

Severing the connection with Per, Motega opened his eyes to see his friends dressed and ready to go.

"The mountain road. Looks like a zombie. But just one," said Motega. His friends made for the door. "Hey, wait for me to put my trousers on too."

~

STABLEFORD WAS NOT A BIG TOWN AND IT ONLY TOOK A few moments for them to reach the spot where Per was perched on the side of a small wooden house, the two figures still in the street below. No one else had rushed to help, though Motega had seen several pairs of wary eyes peering out from the safety of their shutters. Maybe the town folk were on edge too? Or perhaps they'd just pegged the scream for being none of their business. The woman was no longer screaming or trying to enter the house though. The door was flung open but abandoned and she was crouched down on the floor by the other figure, that lay face first in the dirt.

Motega approached her, the tears on her face visible in the moonlight. "Are you alright?"

She looked up, her eyes unfocused and red from the tears. "It's my Petr. It's my Petr."

"Do you know him?"

"He's my husband. He w-w-was," she forced out between gasps of breath.

Motega helped the grieving woman to her feet, gently guided her away from the cadaver and to a seat on the front step of a neighbor's house. The tears continued to fall and Motega could get nothing more sensible out of her until the owner of the step brought steaming mugs of tea for the woman, Motega and his friends.

"He died last winter," she said between sips of brown tea. "It wor his birthday today. I missed him. Went to pay him a visit at the graveyard as the sun was going down. I must have fallen asleep and when I woke, there he was, crawling out of the grave, toward me. I ran. I ran away from him. He kept groaning and reaching for me."

"How did you stop him?" asked Motega, looking back

and forth between the uninjured, though clearly dead, corpse and the unarmed woman.

"I didn't do nothing. I was scared! Tried to get behind the door. But then he just collapsed." Her shoulders shuddered as the tears returned. "And now he's left me again."

~

FOLLOWING THE INSTRUCTIONS OF JOHAN THE tracker/salesman—east road out of town and into the foothills—Motega, Florian and Trypp set out for the necromancer's tower. It was a grey spring morning, a constant drizzle in the air that soon dripped from their faces. Hoods up, they continued without discussing the events of the previous night. During dinner last night they had considered whether there were any less-dark answers for the town's problems than a necromancer; maybe bandits or trolls like others had suggested. The zombie had changed that opinion. But a lone zombie wandering into Stableford was a strange tactical decision for their quarry, though from what they had heard about Hrodebert it would not be possible to rely on him being predictable.

And unpredictable was dangerous.

Though the weather was miserable, the walk was easy enough. A rutted caravan trail that headed to the mountain pass was their path for most of the morning, though they saw nary a traveler. Turning off the main path where instructed, by a lightning struck lonesome pine, the incline increased and for a while the path became overgrown and hard to follow, until out of nowhere a gravel track appeared. It was wide enough for a horse and cart, and seemed either recently made or well maintained. Motega looked at his friends, their shared surprise at seeing the road. He shrugged and set off in front.

Somewhere behind the clouds, the sun was starting its long arc back down to its celestial bed when they neared the mountain range, sheer faces of rock launching from the grassy foothills. The road had been helpful and seemed to head directly to the front door of the necromancer, but Motega and friends all agreed it was time to find a more suitable passage for a reconnaissance mission. Silently clambering up hill and over rocks they reached a perch— discovered by Per no less—overlooking their destination, nestled as it was at the foot of the cliff in a small hollow.

A black circular tower, three stories high, twice as wide at the base than at the flat roof. Lit candles visible through unshuttered windows provided interior light in the shade of the mountain. It looked old. Old enough for the black stone, stark against the grey cliffs, to be covered in moss; ancient twisting vines climbed up one side.

Adjoining the tower was a building of much newer construction. Large, rectangular, and made of the same stone as the mountain nearby; to Motega it had the look of a barracks. Functional and made for housing many people. Squeaks, shrieks, bangs and clangs reverberated around the hollow. *I can see why Johan took a fright*, thought Motega.

"What are those noises?" asked Trypp. The three friends lay side by side on a rock, only their heads visible to anyone looking from the tower.

"Doesn't sound like people," said Motega. "It's a racket, to be sure. But sounds more like construction."

"Well, let's figure out what we're dealing with." Trypp pulled out his brass spyglass, Florian doing the same.

Motega didn't need a spyglass, though he had admired

the matching pair they'd bought in Ioth years ago. He didn't need one because he had Per, and a falcon's eyes are sharper than a couple of pieces of glass. Motega's eyes rolled into the back of his head as his mind melded into that of the bird's. And he flew.

~

THE SUN HAD SET BEHIND THE MOUNTAIN AS FLORIAN, Motega and Trypp descended down the escarpment away from the tower to compare notes. Motega had stayed put for most of the afternoon, flying with his spirit animal; but Florian and Trypp had moved around the hollow, looking for different vantage points from which to observe. Dinner was a loaf of bread, cheese and boiled eggs picked up from the inn that morning, and they ate while they talked.

"There are definitely zombies in that barracks," said Florian. "I counted more than ten through the side windows. It looks like they're building something."

"I saw that too," said Trypp. "Looked like there was a forge inside, which would explain the smoke from the chimney and the glow from that end of the building."

"From the high windows I could see zombies at work benches too, looked like they were working with wood," said Motega between mouthfuls.

"What would they be making?" asked Trypp. "I've never seen a zombie do anything but swing a sword. Slooowwlly." Florian and Motega laughed.

"I don't know," said Florian. "Could be they're making siege equipment? Looked big enough. Maybe he captured a smith from somewhere to make weapons too? Makes sense if you want to plan an invasion."

"Well, old Hrodebert is pretty confident in what he's doing," said Motega. "I didn't notice a single guard in the grounds or on the roof of the tower."

"I saw him through one window. Sitting in an armchair, smoking a pipe and a book in his lap," said Trypp. Motega and Florian nodded in agreement.

"Old guy. Looked like a grandad," said Florian.

"That doesn't make him a nice guy," said Trypp. "When I was a kid on the streets of Kingshold, they were the ones we would watch out for." Motega nodded. He knew his friend had a tough early life, escaping one scrape to land in another —that's why Trypp was always ready with an escape plan. But then again, Motega's childhood could be argued to have been even worse.

"Did you notice the vine up the side of the tower? It's an old one. Tough. And there is a nice-looking trapdoor waiting for us at the top of the tower," said Motega.

"We don't need that. We can note our observations and then head back down to the Sheriff," said Trypp.

"What about the bonus that the Sheriff offered us for just taking care of this mess?" asked Florian. "If we don't make the bonus then we won't make much return on the trip."

"You've said it yourself, there are at least a dozen zombies in there, and who knows how many more?"

"Ah ha," said Motega, "but we don't need to fight them. We already know Hrodebert has to control them. So, we just got to take him out. And, friends, just like an Ambrukhan whorehouse, they've practically rolled out the carpet for us."

"Agreed," said Florian nodding. "Trypp, you're outvoted. Unless today is the day you quit."

"Not today," sighed Trypp, his exasperation evident as he

looked at his two friends. "But we need to do something about these voting rights."

～

THE CLOUDS HAD PERSISTED INTO THE NIGHT, CREATING the perfect gloomy conditions for infiltration and assassination. Lights shone from all the windows of the barracks, its inhabitants still laboring by the sounds audible as they crept close to the tower.

Motega had used Per's eyes again to check that no guards had come out for the night, although the falcon's eyes weren't as sharp in the dark. A few flybys still found the coast to be clear. Scaling the vine was child's play for them, even though it was slick from the rain earlier that day. In fact, from the look of the weathered stone of the tower, Motega thought he could have managed without the vine, knowing for certain that Trypp could have been up the wall like a spider running to dinner.

Trypp crouched by the trapdoor on the roof of the tower, the leather roll of his picks and tools already in hand, expectant of the task ahead.

But there was no lock. Was Hrodebert just incompetent or so self-assured in what he was doing? Possessing an invincibility complex seemed to be a common theme for necromancers. Control over death would probably do that for you, even if it was just a mockery of life.

Shaking his head, Trypp lifted the trapdoor and waved Motega and Florian in after he had confirmed the room was empty. They had seen the necromancer use this room earlier that day, but they had watched Hrodebert put on his nightgown and climb into bed an hour earlier, and according to their observations, the zombies didn't enter the tower.

From the trapdoor was a ladder, down into a study or laboratory that took up the whole floor of the tower. Bookshelves lined the walls, filled with leather bound tomes and rolled parchments. On one wall was a display cabinet filled with stuffed creatures mounted on wooden bases, organs in jars of floating liquid and rows of eyeballs glaring at the intruders. In the center of the room was a small desk and a large wooden table; the two separated by little less than an arm's length. The table was a ghastly scene, the partially decomposed body of a man lay there, eyes closed, right arm severed at the shoulder and draped over his chest like the arm of a lover in sleep.

Motega did not like the undead. True, he was visited by the spirits of his ancestors in his dreams, but they did not get up and walk around and try to eat his brains. *Why do the people of the Jeweled Continent insist on burying their dead when burning, like they do on the plains, would stop this from ever happening?*

Trypp led the way, knife in one hand, Motega and Florian following silently behind, as they descended the open spiral staircase to the bedchamber below. The staircase creaked as Motega, at the rear, stepped down from the landing. They froze, waiting to see if Hrodebert would awaken. A moment passed, and Trypp signaled that the necromancer had not stirred.

Urrghh.

The groan came from behind Motega as his face was level with the floor. His head turned to see the body from the table swing its legs to the floor, bloodshot eyes open, left hand grasping its right arm by the elbow.

"Shit. Trypp!" whispered Motega. "Do it now. We've got one behind us."

Motega reached the bottom step as the zombie behind him started its descent. "Stop! Who are you?" it called out in a rasping voice.

Trypp was already halfway across the room but Hrodebert, with a sprightliness unexpected for one of his obvious age, threw the bedspread in the direction of the knife-wielding assailant closing in on him.

"Help! Intruders!" called Hrodebert.

Motega braced himself, for the inevitable attack of the zombie behind him and for whatever magic the necromancer would unleash.

Much to Motega's surprise, but not necessarily his joy, the necromancer pulled a small loaded crossbow from his bedside table and pointed it at his friend as Trypp fought valiantly to untangle himself from the bed linen.

~

"Who are you?" screamed the old man in his blue and white striped nightshirt. "What are you doing in here?"

Motega, Florian, and especially Trypp—who didn't take his eyes off the crossbow bolt—did not move. The questions on Motega's mind at that moment were:

How long has that crossbow been loaded and so has the string stretched?

Does this old man know how to fire it?

Can he hit a barn door from six feet away?

Chances were good that they could kill the necromancer. The real question was: could they do it without Trypp getting a quarrel in the chest? And the potential answers to his questions left too much chance of that occurring. Motega slowly inched his hand down to his belt to pull a throwing knife.

"I don't think so," came the rasping voice of the zombie behind him, tapping Motega's hand with the outstretched severed arm. From the doorway below came sounds of movement. And then Hrodebert was surrounded by zombies, wielding mallets and hammers, chisels and awls.

"For the record," said Motega, the need for quiet obviously past now, and more than a little pissed off that things were going so suddenly pear shaped. "It was not my fault the stairs creaked. Who was supposed to check the body?"

"Don't matter now, Mot," reassured Florian. "It'll be ok."

"Leave him alone!" barked a zombie, shorter, fatter and maybe more feminine than the others, though it's state of decomposition made it difficult to tell. She pushed through the other zombies and took up a position in front of the old man. "What do you think you're doing? We're not doing anything wrong."

The old man seemed calmer surrounded by his undead bodyguards, though he still kept the crossbow pointed at Trypp. "I think it's time to talk. Explain yourselves," he said.

"We're here because Stableford knows what you're up to. You're planning to invade again. They don't want your zombies," said Motega, tensed and ready to get to work with his axes. "One of them ran through the town last night."

"Zombies? Zombies! These are not zombies, you heathen. They are wights," said Hrodebert. "Some of my finest work. Zombies are so dull to be around. And they are useless workers."

"Workers?" asked Trypp.

"Why, yes. She told you we're not doing anything wrong."

Hrodebert puffed himself up, the effect somewhat lost in his nightclothes. "This is a legitimate place of business."

"Yeah," said the dead woman. "We like it here. Been years since I was useful."

Motega and his friends exchanged confused glances. *Workers? What was going on here?*

"I'm sorry," said Trypp, putting words to the thoughts running through Motega's head. "What?"

"This is a factory. A legitimate place of business," repeated Hrodebert. "I was never into the whole conquest lifestyle. I tried it once, but it just wasn't me. All I want is a nice life. Creature comforts." He waved his hands at the undead around him with evident pride. "This here is my workforce. We make the finest furniture around. If you don't believe me, take a look for yourselves."

∼

Motega was grateful the wights had not tried to relieve them of their weapons. That would have accelerated the required decision making and for the moment, he wanted to learn more. As they descended the stairs, wights in front and behind the three friends, Florian glanced in his direction, looking questioningly at his axe, obviously thinking now might be the time to attack. Motega shook his head.

They were guided out into the large building they had assumed to be a place used for the production of implements of war. Now they could see it was a factory being used for the production of nice places to sit and have a good natter.

The female wight took up the role of guide, introducing herself as Sheila, before a flurry of other names were called out by the assembled wights, most of which Motega didn't catch.

"...we make couches, arm chairs, tables, desks. Every piece is unique. We can do whatever type of decorative work we like. All the iron work is hand forged by Sren over there. He was the smith when I was a girl..."

Motega walked around the factory floor, clucking along admiringly as Sheila continued explaining their work in her sandpapery voice.

"...it's much better work than we would do when we were alive you know. We don't need to eat or sleep, so we have a lot more time. And Master Hrodebert gets much better materials than we had. Oh, it's such a joy to be proud of your work."

"You like it here?" asked Motega to the assembled walking morgue, genuinely intrigued about their welfare, his brain having just come to terms with the whole crazy situation. A nodding of heads and general grunt of agreement came in reply. "And you don't plan to invade the town and take it over?"

"Oh no, lovey," said Sheila. "Why would we do that? We were all born and raised there. Lovely place. Our families are there." The other wights nodded again. "The only reason Adum went into Stableford last night was because we'd just dug him up and he wanted to see his wife. Got too far away from the master, he did. Made him stupid before he likely just fell right over. Am I right, lovey?"

It was Motega's turn to nod and grunt.

"Well, I guess that settles it then," said Florian, slapping his hands at a job well done. "Nothing for us to do here. Right lads?"

"I guess," said Motega, a smidgen of disappointment

creeping into his tone that there wouldn't be an exciting end to their mission.

"Do you get paid?" asked Trypp, eyes narrowing as he looked at the workers. Motega realized he'd been quiet since they left the necromancer behind, assessing the situation.

"Of course not, lovey. In case you haven't noticed, we're dead," said Sheila, her fellow wights chuckling at her joke.

"Is that fair? Hrodebert's making a lot of coin from your work. He doesn't even need to feed you." Trypp paused for a moment, letting the words sink in before putting the proverbial head on top of the pike. "You've got it worse than slaves."

The wights became silent and looked at each other with what Motega thought were quizzical expressions—but it was difficult to tell when half of their faces were exposed down to the skull.

"It's not right," said one wight, breaking the silence, slowly beginning to understand what Trypp had said.

"We work ourselves down to the bone for him," said another, without a hint of irony.

Calls of 'aye' and 'hear, hear', came from the two score workers.

"You own the means of production!" said Trypp, pumping his fist into the air. "You need to stand up for yourselves!"

"Yeah!" they cried. Trypp broke into a big smile—it was clear to Motega he was enjoying himself.

"We're not working anymore," said another, who put down his mallet on the nearest worktable. The others followed.

"What's all this commotion?" said Hrodebert entering the workroom, now dressed in long voluminous black velvet robes more in keeping for a necromancer. He looked around at the wights assembled before him, their hands on their hips and with a few things on their mind.

"Master Hrodebert," said Sheila, wagging a finger in his direction. "Me and the lads have a few things we need to talk with you about."

The necromancer sagged after scanning the faces in front of him. Motega thought he heard him mutter, "At least zombies don't bloody talk back."

~

"AND SO, YOU HAVE NOTHING TO WORRY ABOUT SHERIFF," said Trypp, finishing his explanation. Motega could tell she was finding it all difficult to process.

"Let me recap to see if I understand everything," she said, massaging her temples with her fingertips. "Hrodebert has been taking our dead ancestors, not for an army, but to make furniture?"

Trypp nodded.

"And they like being there, what with being alive again, even though they aren't paid. But now they've formed a union? *The Guild of the Working Dead* you said. So they can get a better deal. And he went along with this?"

"Oh yes. Sheila is very persuasive," nodded Trypp, a grin plastered to his face. He'd been smiling all the way back to town at the thought of his rabble rousing. "And Hrodebert seems like a pleasant old soul, actually. Sheila negotiated a quarter share of all profits back to the workers, which they can give to their families on their twice monthly visits to town."

The Sheriff paused again, contemplating the regular visitation of two score dead folk into her town. "What about the grave robbing?"

"He said he will stop. From now on there will be an opt-in process, and interviews pre-death for new positions. Hrodebert can only maintain so many live wights, so there is a limit."

"But people can interview for a job for after they die? What if they can make more money when they're dead than when they're alive?" Her mind was obviously racing now with the repercussions of the story these three strange foreigners had relayed. Her life turned upside down in ten short minutes. "And what's this going to do to the local still-breathing craftsmen who can't compete with his prices?"

"I don't know Sheriff. I'm not a scholar or a businessman. I know that most of this stuff is heading down river to Carlburg, anyway. Maybe you can just shift your problem? Anyway, a factory of the dead has to be better than the alternative. Am I right?"

The Sheriff, dumbly, nodded her head.

"Now, on to the payment," said Trypp. "I believe we have qualified for the clean-up bonus you mentioned..."

JYUTH ON MAGIC - NECROMANCY

I am by no means an expert in the matters of the walking dead but from what I've discovered, necromancy has more than a passing resemblance to the magic I practice. Now, zombies, wights, specters, all manner of undead, can sometimes occur naturally. That is, without the assistance of a necromancer. Usually, as a result of the dead body being in close proximity to a strong source of magic for an extended period of time. For example, an artifact or locus point.

But necromancy, in my mind, is the practice of magic focused on the creation and control of the undead. It is fairly apparent that the necromancer imbues the corpse with energy to make it a mockery of its former life— and that the level of power provided has some influence on the strength of the undead creature. But where this energy comes from I do not know.

It is inconceivable that the necromancer's energy comes from living things. In fact, I recall I have read that the necromancer feels the well of power inside them. Who knows if we all have this dark energy within us, just waiting to be called? Are necromancers chosen by plan or chance?

I have looked inside me and found no dark pit. I will admit I've tried to raise the dead. All in the name of research of course. And I do not have any proclivity to necromancy. Which is a relief, as I find the undead to be quite tiresome.

Just because you are dead, does not make you wise! Far from it. If you were wise then you'd realize that eternal slumber sounds like the lie-in that most of us dream of.

HOLLOW INSIDE

"**H**ey, Fin," called the red-headed girl across the long oak table from where she was going to sit. "Did you hear about Devereaux?"

That was Jilesa. One of Finabria's 'friends'. And the most potent nexus of gossip and information that Fin had ever come across. Jilesa seemed to know everything that was going on at the school, most of the jobs that were underway in the Syndicate, and even had a pretty good feel for what was going on outside the walls of the Hollow House in Kingshold.

Jilesa was completely neutral in her information sharing; everything she heard, she told, without discrimination. Some other students didn't like that about her. Fin had heard the mean-spirited rumors about how Jilesa came by her information—how she used her looks, and her skills from love-craft classes— but Fin knew that wasn't the case. Fin watched people *carefully*. She could tell what their strengths and weaknesses were. And with Jilesa, it was her smile. A smile of apparent simple joy, that made you happy when it was aimed in your direction; a smile that made the sun shine and daffodils bloom. That was all it took for Jilesa to get most people to blather all of their secrets; they just kept talking to keep the smile aimed in their direction.

And now the smile was aimed at Finabria, who hooked a leg over the bench and sat at the long communal table across from Jilesa. Where Jilesa had long, curly red hair; Finabria's was brown, straight and always tied away at her neck. Where Jilesa had grown into a shapely body with curves in the right places; Finabria was all sharp angles, muscle and sinew giving her an athlete's physique from years of extra training. And where Jilesa was known for her smile, Fin was known for her intensity.

"No, I haven't heard anything about Mr. Moran," said Finabria, referring to Devereaux by his last name, as they were supposed to for all full members of the Hollow Syndicate. Devereaux was young, and though they had known him before he had won the trial, she thought there was no excuse for not paying him the proper respect. But Fin had lost that argument with Jilesa before. "What's he doing?"

"He's dead!" said Jilesa, her eyes sweeping from side to side conspiratorially, as if she hadn't already told everyone around her (which of course she had). "He was brought back to the House in a wheelbarrow this morning. Or what was left of him anyway."

"Wow," said Fin, her brain beginning to kick into gear from the combination of the coffee and the news. "What happened?"

"Well, he was assigned to Lord Bollingsmead," said Jilesa. "But Bollingsmead's guards killed him when he was trying to execute the job."

"Why did Lady Chalice send Moran for such a high-profile target?" asked Fin, thinking out loud. Lady Chalice led the Hollow Syndicate and she fascinated Fin.

"I heard he'd been under Bollingsmead's nose for a week or more before someone paid the contract price. I don't think anyone was paying attention to Bollingsmead as a serious candidate but Chalice must have chanced her arm. Got him into position just in case."

"What are you talking about" said a short, skinny boy, whose cheeks were covered with red pimples, as he swung his leg over the bench and took a seat next to Jilesa. That was Tom. Her other 'friend'. Fin zoned out momentarily as Jilesa repeated herself for him.

"Wow," said Tom too. "So, with a spot opening up, there's going to be a trial. Can't wait." He clapped his hands together, rubbing them with undisguised glee at the show that was soon to come.

The trial. Or for that matter, the very nature of schooling within the Hollow Syndicate, was why she thought of as Jilesa and Tom as 'friends' only; not real friends. After all, only one in twenty children who started at the most famous school for assassins in the Jeweled Continent would become a member of a Hollow Syndicate, and fewer still would be admitted to the home of the Syndicate in Kingshold. This was known as the winnowing; occasions when students would be set challenges that risked life and limb, or when they would duel each other for the privilege of continuing their schooling, all the way until they graduated. At that point they would be ABT—All But Trial— and it would be the trial that would determine who would gain admittance to the Hollow Syndicate.

And so why get attached to people when you're only going to have kill or at least maim them later? It would be a waste of all of the favors that her father had to cash in to gain her admittance. It was not often that a pupil was admitted from Ioth, typically it was the reserve of Edlanders only.

But it was important to maintain the facade of being friendly. Of not standing out as a loner, and she had to admit that Jilesa was the best source of information she could hope for outside of a peephole into Lady Chalice's office. So Finabria ate her three meals a day with Jilesa and Tom. She helped them with their studies occasionally. And she listened very carefully.

"It's been nearly two years since a trial here in Kin—" began Jilesa

"One year and two months," corrected Fin.

"Oh, someone is keeping track," said Tom, laughing. He was right. She was keeping track. These opportunities didn't come up very often, and it weighed on her that she could go through the years of schooling and be sent to a Syndicate House away from Kingshold. Like Redpool or, Arloth forbid, back to Ioth.

"About a year then," said Jilesa. "And we've got three ABTs. Qeturah, Dorien, and of course Argo." Jilesa smiled as she mentioned Argo's name. He was the object of affection for many of the students; he was tall, muscular, and had the looks of a marble statue from the palace grounds. Fin thought he tried too hard. "I'm sure Argo will win," concluded Jilesa.

"It all depends," said Tom. "Argo is a great fighter, but it depends on the trial. Qeturah is really impressive, I don't think I've seen anyone faster. She can pick a lock quicker than I can knock on the door. And who knows about Dorien." Tom's eyes flicked from side to side as he finished that sentence, checking to see if Dorien was in the long, wood paneled dining room with them. "He creeps me out; I'd be scared competing against him just because I'd have to see his face." Dorien did not appreciate people making jokes about his scars. Luckily for Tom there were only a handful of other students eating breakfast, and Dorien was not one of them.

"So, Fin, who do you think will win?" asked Jilesa.

"I don't know... I'm going to have to give that some thought," said Fin.

"What I can't wait to find out is what trial is it going to be?" said Tom, ignoring Fin's reluctance to answer. "Chest, needle, vine, pit or dart? I hope its needle. I love it when they poison themselves."

The trial could be one of five different challenges and each was designed to test multiple skills of the potential Syndicate member. Needle was a test of poison making and detection. Contestants would brew poisons that were as close to undetectable as possible, coating a needle for each competitor with their concoction. And then each trialist would have to select a needle from the choices presented to jab into their skin, with only one being safe. Needle was not particularly brutal, but it could be quite deadly. It wasn't surprising that was what Tom was excited about, he loved the potions and poisons class. Fin would begrudgingly admit that he was a better natural brewer than her, too.

"I want vine," said Jilesa. Tom shook his head, about to speak. "I know what you're going to say, 'that it's difficult to watch when they're away from the House', but there have been some exciting finishes."

Vine was a race; and the rooftops of Kingshold was the course. The only rule was that the contestants could not touch the ground. From Finabria's prior research, and seeing two vine races herself, she knew it was not uncommon for the race to turn into a fight high above the streets with only one trialist reaching the finishing point back at the Hollow House.

Fin thought about what her preferred challenge would be. Pit was a race of sorts too. Most of Kingshold was not aware that the Hollow House went underground too. That was where the Pit resided—a labyrinth of tunnels, filled with traps to be avoided and places to host an ambush.

For dart the school itself was the arena, including all of the non-contestants. Each trialist received a set number of darts tipped with a paralysis poison and then had to hunt the others. Last one literally standing was the winner.

Meanwhile, chest was supposed to be a test of intelligence and weapon skill. Open the locks on a chest of your choosing to get a weapon. And then fight it out.

"So? Which one, Fin?" asked Tom, waving a hand in front of her face and dragging her away from her thoughts.

"I could do any of them," she mumbled before realizing what she said and quickly backtracking. "I mean, dart. I like dart. I have to go..." She stood up from the table—her wooden tray of bread and eggs largely untouched—and walked from the room, her mind racing.

She did not see Jilesa and Tom exchange a look of unsurprised resignation—this was not the first time they had seen Fin walk out leaving her meal untouched. Tom reached over, slid Fin's tray in front of him and tucked in.

⁓

FINABRIA WALKED.

She liked to move when she needed to think.

Walking. Running. Fighting. Any of these activities got the blood moving to her brain. Walking was good because she could roam the halls and the gardens of the Hollow House without having to pay attention to her surroundings, and more importantly, any of the other students, allowing her mind to also roam freely. She had perfected the facial expression of a person who is occupied elsewhere, and you'd best move unless you wanted to collide. It had given her a certain reputation for 'not being all there' with some of the other pupils, but she didn't care.

She didn't care what others thought of her. And if they underestimated her then that was only for her own good. In her estimation she was of a fairly typical height for a girl, pretty with the potential for beauty though she didn't have any inclination to paint her face as others did, and she was not loud and outspoken, nor quiet and shy.

She was normal. Unexceptional.

Just as she intended. Hiding in plain sight.

For she was also top of all of her classes; fencing, acrobatics, heraldry and history, potions and poisons (though Tom had more natural talent, Fin worked much harder), locks, love-craft, stealth, infiltration and espionage. She had read a third of the books of the library (though she took that as a personal failure—she had hoped to be halfway through by now). And Finabria had studied her fellow students. Her competition.

She had been playing the long game. There was still another year of classes and tests before she would be ABT. Being an assassin for the Hollow Syndicate was not without its dangers and she had discovered, that on average, a new place opened up every two years. There had been two trials in the year before Devereaux had won his trial. And now that there would be another opportunity for admittance to the Kingshold Syndicate it could be a long wait until the next opportunity arose.

"Fool," she exclaimed out loud.

A passing couple of third-years turned to look at the crazy older student talking to herself. Why couldn't Devereaux wait to get himself killed until next year?

She considered the ABTs who would be competing in the trial.

First there was Qeturah. Tom had been correct when he said she was quick. Fin was the fastest in her year but Qeturah was faster. Qeturah didn't have the strength of any of the other ABTs, or even Fin, but she could avoid the blades of all but the most experienced Syndicate blade masters.

Then there was Argo, the crush of half the school. Fin thought he was in the wrong place. He should have been down the road in the Royal Infantry Academy, using his minor title to jump the ranks and see where his pretty face might lead him. It's not that he wasn't a good trainee assassin —he was. Argo was strong, probably the best all round fighter in the school, and he seemed to possess the necessary amount of ruthlessness. But he loved the light of attention, when they must embrace the shadows.

And that took her to Dorien, someone who definitely favored the shadows. When she had arrived in Kingshold from Ioth, he had been a popular child in the year ahead of her. But then in her second year at the school, a batch of acid he had been brewing had exploded in his face. It left his appearance looking decidedly... melted. Like a candle left to burn all night. Most of the school had expected him to leave and go back to his family, but he had remained. His friends deserted him and it was obvious to Finabria that Dorien bore more than a modicum of resentment. She saw him some nights in the library, hunched over his books, stealing glances at her, but they didn't talk. She said hello, his appearance not really concerning her, but never received much more than a nod.

It was Dorien that would be the one to watch. He was a thinker. And Finabria knew there was no deadlier a weapon than the brain.

She wished again that Devereaux could have avoided getting himself killed for just another year. This could have been her chance. These three were formidable, sure. But she felt on a par with them now; she would be guaranteed of winning in a year.

"Are you waiting for something, Miss Bracaccia?" asked a voice which snapped her out of her introspection. Without thinking, she had wandered to the heraldry and history classroom, the location of her first class. "Are you going to keep waiting?" asked Mr. Chapman, the teacher holding open the door for her.

His voice echoed in her mind.

"No, sir. I'm not going to wait any longer."

~

HERALDRY AND HISTORY PASSED IN A BLUR. LARGELY because Finabria didn't pay it much attention.

She was considering her options.

She was considering whether her options were really options at all.

And so by the time that class ended and she, along with

her classmates, were told to congregate in the courtyard, she was feeling a little dislocated.

The courtyard of the Hollow House was a square, surrounded on three sides by wings of the school and on the fourth by the House proper—the home of the full members. The buildings were constructed of smooth stone blocks, thin lines of mortar almost imperceptible. There was no ornamentation, carving or filigree or otherwise—after all there was no need to encourage students, thieves or other assassins to be climbing their walls. Finabria looked up to the blue sky of a late spring morning and waited for what she knew would happen next.

A door opened on the second-floor balcony of the House and out stepped two figures. Their appearances contrasted so sharply that it brought to mind a red flamed candle and the ever-present darkness; each dangerous, though in different ways. Lady Chalice, leader of the Hollow House, and Steppen, the man with the second most coveted role in the Syndicate, that of treasurer.

"Good morning to you all," projected Lady Chalice, her voice carrying clearly across the courtyard. "Opportunity awaits. The Syndicate has need of a member, and in accordance with the articles, I announce a trial. The winner shall be admitted with full Syndicate privileges. Who here submits themselves to enter?"

As expected, Finabria saw Argo, Qeturah and Dorien raise their hands.

"Four hands!" boomed Steppen. "Step forward trialists."

Four hands? There were three ABTs...

Finabria saw Jilesa looking at her from a few rows in front of her. She had a scowl on her face and was mouthing silently. "What are you doing?"

And that's when Finabria realized she had her own hand in the air.

She moved through the crowd and stood with the other three volunteers for the trial, under the gaze of the two syndicate leaders.

"Ms. Bracaccia," said Steppen, "you are not yet finished with your studies. You do realize the trial could be fatal for one without the knowledge required."

She nodded, but didn't move. Lady Chalice regarded her without comment.

"Last chance, Ms. Bracaccia. No one will think any less of you if you step out now," said Steppen.

"Thank you, sir," said Fin, finding her voice. "I intend to compete."

"Very good," said Lady Chalice. "Steppen, shall we get on with it?"

"Yes, I think we should." Steppen turned back to look out across the courtyard and showed a small velvet bag to the crowd. "In this bag are five balls, each with a different symbol." He pulled five balls in succession from the bag and held it for all to see. "Chest. Needle. Vine. Pit. Dart. One of these will be the challenge that these four will face in the trial."

Steppen put the balls back into the bag and shook them up, the clacking of the painted wooden balls echoing in the quiet courtyard. *Which challenge would it be?* Fin was hoping for dart. It was by nature the least potentially deadly of the challenges, and she felt confident in her ability to go unnoticed in the student body and be difficult to target.

Lady Chalice reached a hand into the bag and pulled out a ball clenched tightly in her fist. Holding her other hand palm up she placed the ball, symbol outwards.

"It is chest," she declared. "The trial will be tomorrow, two hours after noon. Anyone caught fighting, poisoning or harming their fellow competitors shall be eliminated. Good luck."

~

STEW AGAIN? THOUGHT FINABRIA, RAISING HER WOODEN tray for the lunch lady to ladle the brown liquid over her boiled and buttered potatoes, as she ignored the looks of the other students around her.

It seemed like she had become the center of attention.

That was not something she had expected—she had been thinking more about the potential mortal danger of entering the trial, not the social implications—but she now realized it was not an unsurprising reaction. It was not something she appreciated.

Fin walked into the dining room and toward the end of the long table where Jilesa and Tom were waiting as usual. They hadn't been to fetch their lunch yet.

"Fin, what are you doing?" hissed Jilesa as Finabria sat.

"I'm eating my lunch. I still can't understand how you Edlanders eat stew in the summer."

"I mean, what are you doing entering the trial," said Jilesa. Tom nodded along. "That's for ABTs!"

"There's nothing in the rules that says it's for ABTs only," said Fin around mouthfuls. "A first year could enter if they want."

"But they would die..."

"Probably. But I'm not going to. I'm as good as those other three."

"You're good, Fin," said Tom. "But the ABTs have had

nearly a whole year of school more than you. What if there is something in the challenge that you don't know? What if there's a lock mechanism you don't know yet?" Tom's expression suddenly changed from concerned to earnest and he reached out a hand across the table toward Fin. "I'm sure if you go and see Chalice, tell her it was all a terrible mistake, she'll let you back out."

"What!" The noise that erupted from Finabria was rather like a squark, punctuated with a cavalcade of crumbs from the bread she had just been chewing through. The other students in the dining room stopped what they were doing (which she suspected was talking about her anyway) and turned to silently stare at her.

"Listen, Tom. I'm going to do this. And if I die trying then at least I made the attempt." She put her hands on the table and pushed herself up, her voice little more than a whisper as the color rose to her cheeks—from anger, not embarrassment, she told herself. "At least one way, or the other, I will escape the crushing boredom of classes and spending time with people like you."

Fin snatched the apple from her lunch tray, and stalked out of the dining room. She matched the stares randomly on the way, and it gave her some small pleasure to cause each child to flinch away.

"Well," said Jilesa. "I guess she's not coming to potions and poisons."

❧

FINABRIA WAS MOST DEFINITELY SKIPPING POTIONS AND poisons. She was never going to take another class again. One way or the other. Never again would she have to feign attention and interest when she had already learned what the teacher had to offer from her own independent research at the library.

The library. The source of so much knowledge about the Hollow Syndicate but frequented by so few of the students. That had been her destination when she left the dining hall; to the histories and treatises that awaited her.

She had done much research on past trials over the years, thinking about what awaited her at the end of her studies. Each contest was well documented. Who competed. Which trial was chosen at random. Who won, what occurred and what injuries were sustained. And though each contest was different, it seemed there were some constants that she could discern.

For example, the chest challenge always had a minimum of four chests—more if there were more than four competitors. The weapons that were in the chest appeared to be consistent too—long sword, pair of sai, crossbow and rapier. She felt confident in her martial prowess and the sai were her favorite weapon, she just needed to be able to find them. The problem was that the means of opening each chest was different and they changed with every contest. There could be locks of tumblers, rare rotary combination locks, puzzle boxes without visible means of entrance, pressure plates, swivel panels, and in one case she even saw reference to the chest being trapped. Some of the locks mentioned she hadn't worked with yet, in particular the more complicated puzzle boxes, and she knew there were possible traps that they had not practiced disarming as yet. The older students could potentially have an advantage there.

What stood out most though, were two fleeting references to how the chests were identified. In most of the histories the boxes' appearances weren't described, they were referred to only by the weapon that were inside them. However, in the two descriptions that had attracted her eye they referred to the chests using symbols. A diamond for the sai. A cross for the longsword. A circle for the crossbow. And a square for the rapier.

She drummed her fingers on the leather-covered desk.

Was it reliable? It was mentioned by different authors more than fifty years apart, so maybe it was. If so, it would help her identify her favored weapon; but it didn't help with whatever would be keeping it inside. The lock definitely seemed to be random. She would need to be prepared for anything.

Fin closed her histories, stacking them so she could re-shelve them in their correct places, when she noticed that she was under observation. How long had that person sat at the desk in the shadowy recess been watching her? She picked up the books and walked a course that took her close enough to see her spy.

Sitting at his own desk, books scattered around him, and clearly identifiable from his scarred face, was Dorien. His head turned, following Fin as she walked past, but his face was impassive. She flashed her most brilliant smile to him, the one they had spent weeks practicing in love-craft. He almost jumped in his seat—her smile as unexpected as a slap across his cheeks.

~

GETTING INTO THE BOX, FAST, WAS GOING TO BE CRITICAL. The first trialist to be armed was going to have a distinct advantage. Fin knew she was good at working with locks. She had the steady hand, sensitive hearing and touch to be able to open any mechanism; and she had the patience to keep on trying when the first attempt didn't work.

Of course, that was all in a classroom setting; would it be easy, knowing that being slower than the next person could lead to a bolt between her ribs?

Oh, she'd been out on school jobs in the past. Those contracts given annually to fifth year and above. The students not knowing if it was a real contract or a dummy one that would end with a teacher turning the tables on the student. She'd had three of these contracts, two real and one dummy, and there had been some element of breaking and entering required; but the locks that she'd come into contact with in the real world were not going to be a good proxy for the test conditions.

These were going to be hard. Real tests.

And the person responsible for this element of the test had to be Murcher. The Lockmaster.

Fin knew Murcher well. He liked the students who showed an aptitude for his class, and he liked the girls in particular; so Fin checked his two primary boxes. But the intensity of his stares and his lingering touches made her shudder. She wouldn't exactly call him her favorite teacher, but she was always careful not to get on the wrong side of any of the faculty. Those relationships could be useful in the future, or in this case, tomorrow.

The locks classroom was at the end of the east wing and Fin knew there wouldn't be class at the moment. The perfect time to see Murcher on his own.

Except, as she rounded the final corner before the doorway to the classroom she heard a murmuring of voices. Fin kept to the shadows without thinking, years of study and practice combining into conditioning so complete she could stalk the shadows like a vampire of legend shying away from the sun.

She could see Murcher talking to another student. Qeturah. That little humming bird had got there before her! Her and Murcher moved around some tables, objects arrayed before them, but it was impossible to hear what they were saying. Their backs kept turning toward her, muffling the conversation and making it impossible to read their lips.

And then the conversation ended. Qeturah leaned forward and placed a small kiss on the teacher's cheek, before she rushed out of the room, passing Fin without even noticing.

Finabria gave it a few seconds before revealing herself, thinking to wait for a longer period of time, but Murcher started to clear away the mechanisms that he had been showing Qeturah.

"Ahem, Mr. Murcher," said Fin, pouring sugar on every word. "I was hoping you could help me."

The Lockmaster turned at her announcement, looking flushed and he doubled the pace of his clearing.

"Miss Bracaccia. I heard you nominated yourself for the trial," he said. "Very commendable. Very... brave to think that you won't learn anything else in another year of class. But I don't think it is appropriate for us to be talking. I would not favor one student over another."

Fin was momentarily lost for words. *He wouldn't favor one student over another? Liar.* She had just seen him with the other girl! But she could hardly challenge him on that fact.

"Of course, Mr. Murcher," she said. "I was merely hoping to borrow a new set of picks. I'm afraid that mine may break during the trial."

Murcher muttered his agreement. He stopped picking up the various mechanisms and went to a cupboard at the back of the room, bringing out a roll of blue leather that Fin knew would contain tools inferior to her own; after all, her father had paid more than a pretty penny for the set he had gifted her last Wintertide. She had at least managed a few seconds to look at the locks that Murcher had been working with.

"Thank you," said Fin, taking the roll of picks and trying her best to leave the deference in her tone when inside she seethed with anger. *Murcher is helping Qeturah. It's not going to be a fair contest. The others probably have help too.*

Well, she was just going to have to help herself.

~

"DOUBLE HELPING?" ASKED TOM, LOOKING AT FIN'S TRAY, their previous exchange apparently forgotten.

"I'm hungry," said Fin between mouthfuls. "Busy afternoon. Going to be a long night too."

Now that she had made her mind up about leveling the playing field, she knew there was a lot to do. What she had planned might not leave much time for sleep, which was hardly ideal before the trial, but Fin had always been able to substitute food for sleep. And so a double helping of roasted chicken was the boost she needed.

"Where have you been?" asked Jilesa.

"Library," said Fin, tossing perfectly round new potatoes into her mouth.

Jilesa leaned in conspiratorially, and whispered, "What did you find out? Anything important?"

And so began step one of Finabria's plan. Misinformation. She knew anything she told her friends would be around the student body before lights out. It was a long shot, but worth the effort.

"Well, there was one thing. You promise not to tell anyone?" Fin waited for Jilesa and Tom to nod. "I read the accounts of the chest trials over the last hundred years, and there is a pattern. On each of the boxes is a symbol—a diamond, cross, circle or square—and it relates to the type of lock. The code changes from challenge to challenge but it repeats." Fin paused and looked around, as if to make sure no one else was listening. She waited for them to bite before continuing. "And I figured it out. Circle is the easiest lock, Cross is the most complex. Square and Diamond in between. If I can get the circle chest open fastest then I'll be the first with a weapon."

Jilesa and Tom did not make a sound though their mouths hung open in tandem, appearing much like carp regarding their own reflections.

"Remember, don't tell anyone!" said Fin as she rose from the table. Her friends nodded.

Finabria took her tray to the kitchen hatch where the staff of the Hollow House waited. She picked up an apple for later and turned to leave the dining room when she came face to face with the tall, dark, handsome form of Argo. And for the first time ever, he was noticing her.

He looked at her, cocked his head and smiled a thin smile, like the merest scraping of butter on a slice of toast. Behind him hovered a lackey, a boy a year younger than Argo by the name of Barrag; his constant shadow. Argo leaned in toward Fin.

"I heard what you told your friends," he said. "Very interesting. Very interesting indeed."

Yes! She thought. *That was quick work.*

But then Argo winked at her. Not a quick wink. Not a blink and you miss it, I-want-to-sleep-with-you, kind of wink.

No, this was one of those big obvious winks you gave a child when they thought they were being cunning.

Crap. Well, that's one of them that isn't buying it.

∿

Sleeping arrangements improved as you progressed through the school. In the first year there was one dormitory for boys and girls, bunks stacked three high and studying done at communal tables. By your third year the group was split into boys' and girls' dorms, hormones and contrasting approaches to personal cleanliness creating too much potential distraction. Fin had been in the third year's boys' dorm once, and she was quite sure that some girls in ages past had complained about the stench; stale semen and sweaty socks, the two likely related.

By the fifth year, students shared a private room with a bunk mate and it was only when a student was ABT did they receive their own room, cloistered high away in the steepled attic.

Fin didn't have a bunk mate though. She had one of the large rooms that were typically shared, but here was another thing she had to thank her father for. She wasn't sure who he had to bribe, but Fin's roommate was officially a girl called Gharesa—however, she had died two years ago and no one had seen fit to change around the sleeping arrangements.

Yes, she was very grateful to her father. For Fin, privacy enabled her to excel. She studied when others wanted to sleep. She used the extra space in her room to spar with shadows and practice intricate movements, half dance and half hand-to-hand combat. And her room gave her the privacy to prepare for her evening's activities.

From a black lacquered chest, emblazoned with the letters FB (another gift from her father), she took out neatly folded piles of clothes, none of which where her school uniform. No, these clothes weren't for studying. These were for working.

∽

THE MAID CARRIED A BROOM AND DUSTPAN, TUTTING TO herself as she hustled past the senior girls' bathroom. It was an hour to lights out and the maid noticed Qeturah, as usual at this time, wiping away the paint and powder from her face in front of a bathroom mirror.

Past some third-years, who didn't even give her a first glance, let alone a second, the maid continued to a spiral staircase. Ascending to a small landing containing three doors, one of which was wide open. The maid slipped through the open door, muttering about the dust, though she knew that none of the other rooms were in use to hear her.

The room was small, but neatly organized. A bed, a small side table, wardrobe, desk and a book-laden shelf were the only furniture. All plain but solidly built.

The maid went over to the bedside table and inspected an octagonal wooden box a little larger than her hand. Flipping the lid revealed a brush resting on a container of white powder. The maid took out a small spoon and a square of parchment. She delicately scraped away a layer of powder from the box, careful not to take too much, and emptied it on to the parchment. Five times she did this before being comfortable with her work.

Putting the spoon down, the maid pulled a small glass bottle topped with a vaporizer from a pocket in her skirts. She squirted it three times, sending tiny rain clouds on to the box's store of powder, careful not to disturb the fine particles.

The maid froze from a noise from downstairs. It sounded like Qeturah talking to another student. Quickly she put the bottle back into her pocket, lifted the parchment and its cargo of powder and swept it back into place with the brush from the box.

The box was back on the table, precisely where it had been found moments earlier, when the rooms occupant appeared in the doorway.

Qeturah observed the maid sweeping the floor for a moment. "Isn't it a little late for sweeping?"

"Yes, miss," said the maid, not looking up from the patch of floor she was cleaning. "Please don't tell, miss. I was running late today."

"Don't worry," said Qeturah. "Come back tomorrow. After the trial of course."

"Thank you, miss," said the maid, hurrying out of the room and down the stairs. Leaving the trialist to her solitude.

～

IT WAS A COOL, CALM NIGHT. AT LEAST AS FAR AS THE weather was concerned, anyway. Across the city Finabria could see and hear the evidence of rioting. Voices crying in anger that became a meaningless blare in aggregate. Bonfires illuminated the city in patches.

She sat atop the pitched slate roof of the dormitory gazing out across the city, momentarily forgetful of why she was there.

Fin had gone back to her room and changed from the maid's clothes, temporarily satisfied that stage two of her plan had been executed; though there were still a number of unknowns, so she wouldn't know its efficacy until tomorrow. The maid's costume went back into her trunk, and out came her nighttime clothes.

Some girls her age would consider their nighttime clothes to be a cotton gown, adorned with frilly lace. Others might have considered it to be something constricting, and made to present their assets to potential customers. Fin was neither of these girls. She had pulled on black hose and buttoned up her black shirt, wriggled her fingers into the soft leather gloves (also black of course). Her feet slipped into the soft leather boots, the soles thin and supple so her feet could feel for purchase. The black cotton face mask, buttoned at the side of her face, completed the look.

She smiled, though there was no one there to see it. A shadow in the night, this was where she felt at home. Alone. Above the seething ranks of humanity. With power over others. This was why she knew she would be part of the Syndicate.

Absentmindedly, she listened to the rioters in Kingshold. Who knew what their concerns were? And why would she care? They had business tonight, and so did she.

Creeping along the slate roof she peered into a protruding attic window, the glass laced with lead. She saw a young woman sleeping—Qeturah—doing what many would have suggested she should be doing too. Getting a good night's rest before the day to come.

Qeturah was not the target of her mission though. Merely a navigation point. Two more windows down.

She cupped her eyes, shielding the glare of the bonfires from the dappled glass, as she inspected the room beyond. Another sleeping figure.

Fin slid a thin length of metal silently through a gap in the window frame and flipped the latch. Security was not exactly top of mind for the Hollow House—who would be stupid enough to burgle a nest of vipers?

She climbed into the small cell and perched on the stone window ledge, regarding the sleeping figure. He faced the wall, but she could see his chest rising and falling as he breathed. She wondered whether he dreamed. Did he imagine himself victorious tomorrow? Inducted into the Syndicate and a new family that would look past his scarred face and appreciate him for his black heart alone.

Hah!

Dorien turned in his sleep at the slight sound of her laugh but did not wake. Finabria coughed. "Ahem."

Now the young man awoke. Like a triggered mousetrap he sprang into a crouch on the bed, a dagger, glinting in the moonlight, appearing from beneath a pillow. Fin did not move.

"Don't worry, Dorien," she said. "I'm not here for a fight."

"Who are you? What do you want?" he asked. His voice was deep and smooth, like a well of crisp clean water. Dorien was shirtless, wearing only breeches that bunched up around his groin as he squatted. She could only see the contours of his body, the shape of his broad shoulders and muscled legs.

The voice. The body. Fin was sure Dorien would have been quite the favorite of the girls if it wasn't for his face.

"It's Finabria. I just wanted to talk, and didn't know who else would understand. Understand what it was like to be so... lonely."

"What do you mean?"

"You know," said Fin, as she unbuttoned the mask and pulled it from her face. "We could die tomorrow. This could be my last night. It seems so... pointless. Spending it sleeping."

Fin slid off the ledge and stalked across the room to his bed. Dorien backed up against the wall like a frightened child. Fin knew that Dorien had been excused from the love-craft classes that began at the age of fourteen after the first lesson—his classmates refusing to engage in practical study with him because of his face. She wondered whether that rejection had scarred his heart more than the acid had his face.

"Why are you here?" he stammered.

"I told you, Dorien. The others, they don't understand. They don't know what it means to be dedicated to succeeding like you and me. I've seen you watching me, Dorien. And I've watched you. I see you on the training ground first and leaving last. I see you in the library, study-ing, when others are socializing. I see the freedom that having no friends gives you and I'm... jealous." She touched his arm, the hairs tickling her palm. He looked into her eyes, and she saw those of a frightened dog. Up close she could see his face—the left side devoid of eyebrow, eye lidless and watery above a cheek that was rippled with deep scars down to the jaw line. She did not flinch.

He reached out to touch her, a hunger in his eyes, before he drew back. "I don't know what to do," he said.

"Don't worry," said Finabria, as she leaned in to kiss him. "I can show you."

∼

SHE HAD REMAINED FOR A LITTLE WHILE AFTER THEIR coupling. At first it had been tentative, but then urgent and it had not taken long before they were both finished. Dorien had fallen asleep holding her, whispering Tigran love poems. Who knew he would be such a romantic?

Once she was sure he was asleep she slipped out the way she had come and back to her own bed.

It was late. By her reckoning only a couple of hours until dawn. The riot still raged. But her bed called.

Slipping naked between the sheets, she was asleep before her head hit the pillow. She dreamed of the trial. Four young men and women battling, blood spilling onto the cobblestones. But she wasn't one of them. She watched the contest from an elevated vantage. Finabria stood where Lady Chalice had been earlier that day, watching while her students gave their all to be part of her house.

∼

"THAT'S QUITE A PLATE OF FOOD YOU HAVE THERE, FIN," said Tom, apparently unaware of his repetitiveness. Another example of why she needed to be rid of these idiots and their grating small talk.

Fin looked down at the wooden tray, laden with gloriously brown sausages and beans cooked in a tomato sauce, and decided to play along. "I'm hungry."

"I don't know how you can eat," he said. "If I was you, I would be shitting bricks this morning."

"Didn't get much sleep. Need to eat."

"Have you noticed that there aren't any other trialists here?" asked Jilesa.

Fin looked around. She was surprised to find it was true. She hadn't noticed that before. In fact she hadn't really noticed anything other than how the sausages tasted so delightfully of hot fat (and not much else), occupied as she was with filling her belly and thinking about how she wasn't sure what to do about Argo. Now she noticed that she really was the only trialist there. Had they all slept in? She hadn't even considered that might have been allowed. And some additional sleep would have been welcome given her nocturnal activities.

She also noticed that everyone in the dining room was looking at her.

"Huh," she said. "They must be too soft to get out of bed. They'll still be sleepy by this afternoon." Fin grinned a toothy, pork smeared smile.

"Fin," said Jilesa, "I hope you win." Her friend looked earnest. Caring even.

It made Fin vomit a little inside her mouth.

Then the call was taken up by the other students chewing at their breakfast.

"Go on, Fin, you can do it!"

"You're one of us."

"Show 'em what you can do!"

What was this show of camaraderie? Half of these kids

had never spoken to her in the past. What did she care about what some snot-nosed first-year thought of her chances?

Her breakfast thoroughly spoiled, Fin pushed the tray away from her and fixed her friend with a cold stare. "Thanks," she said, the sarcasm dripping like the fat from the unfinished sausages.

Fin swung her leg over the bench and, eyes fixed on the doorway, she departed the room, calls of encouragement echoing around her.

～

She wasn't doing this for anyone but herself.

Why were the other students supporting her? And why should she care what they thought one way or the other?

Fin reflected on why it bothered her as she entered the courtyard, morning sparring drills starting for those already finished with breakfast. If they had laughed at her, sneering at her chances, she would have shrugged it off as them not knowing their arse from their elbow and moved on.

But their support troubled her. She wasn't a champion. She wasn't an example to others. And she sure as hell wasn't a martyr.

The day was gloomy, a mist or a fog, or even smoke from the riot of the night before—she wasn't sure which—hung in the air. Fin walked briskly across the courtyard, paying half attention to the students pairing off for sparring practice. She usually liked nothing more than starting her day with a little action, but today she had a mind to skip it and conserve her energy. She snapped to attention at the voice of one person talking with the drill instructor.

"I haven't got a partner today, sir. Argo is saving his energy for this afternoon."

It was Barrag, Argo's shadow from yesterday. The boy she recognized as his usual sparring partner.

"I'll fight him, Master Laith," she said without thinking.

"Are you sure you don't want to shadow train, Miss Finabria?" said Master Laith. "Or are you hoping to get yourself injured?" The old bastard chuckled to himself. Fin ignored it.

"I'm good thanks," she said as she walked on to the training ground in front of Barrag. "So, what's your choice of weapon?"

Barrag looked momentarily taken aback, but he glanced up to the building high behind her and then grinned. "Saber," he replied, picking up a blunted curved length of steel.

Fin nodded. "Daggers for me," she said, picking up a pair of similarly blunted training weapons. She tapped them together, a ringing sound echoing across the courtyard as she took an open fighting stance. The other training partners stopped what they were doing to watch the trialist in an unexpected show.

Barrag had a reputation as being good with a blade. Almost as good as Argo—that was why they sparred together daily. And so Fin was not surprised when Barrag leapt forward, beginning a series of rapid slashes at her legs and arms. Each blow she deflected with a dagger. And with each blow she took a step backward, ceding ground.

As she neared the wall of the courtyard the crowd parted to give the fighters room. Barrag, sensing a quick finish, lunged at her torso.

Fin rolled away, coming to her feet as Barrag turned and came at her again. This time she was on the front foot and closed with a series of slashes at his upper body. He was quick. Sliding away from a blow, or parrying it on his saber, he fended off her attack. But something stood out to her, in the way he moved, that was... strange.

After each of her strikes, his hands dropped. Like he was expecting a low attack after a high. Each time he recovered, but only just in time.

Barrag took advantage of a split second's hesitation from Fin and pushed forward again. Thrust and then parry her follow up strike. Thrust and parry. Fin danced to the side, watching her opponent's eyes.

He practically sent a herald, trumpets blaring, before he slashed high at her neck, normally off limits for sparring, as even with blunted blades it was possible to kill with head blows. Fin swung back at the hips, the saber sweeping past where she was moments before, so close she felt the displacement of the air on her wide eyes. Dodging the blow, she slipped in close.

Again he dodged. And again she noticed him move to pre-empt an expected low attack.

It came to her then. It was not just expected. It had been trained into him. Like a dog expects a treat after a trick. Too many times only training with the same opponent...

She struck low and he parried the blade across her body, tying up her arms and allowing him to flick the sabre forward and jab into her chest. It hurt. She could tell there would be a peach of a bruise. Maybe even blood. Fin fell on her backside in the gravel.

There was an audible "ohhhh" from around her as the crowd collectively exhaled, disappointment that she had been bested so early in the day, and not even by a trialist. Barrag meanwhile looked like he had caught the greased pig.

Fin got to her feet. This had been useful. It had taken a few moments but her brain caught up to why her mouth had gotten her into this trouble. She reached out and shook Barrag's hand stiffly.

"Well fought."

Fin threw down the daggers in mock outrage and marched out of the courtyard, all eyes on her for the second time that day.

~

IT WAS TIMES LIKE THESE THAT SHE MISSED HER HOME. HER father's house on the grand canal of Ioth was one of the grandest palaces not owned by the ruling merchants. It had four enclosed gardens; a spectrum of aromatic flowers arranged in geometric shapes, walkways, benches and other quiet secluded spots which had been havens for thinking and planning, even at a young age.

The Hollow House garden by contrast was small, singular and green. Herbs used by the kitchen flourished in pots. Ivy crept up the walls. And a square of grass lawn, maintained at a house-mandated three inches in length by men with scissors (she knew because she had seen them with said implement and a measuring stick).

It was on this lawn that she lay. Arms and legs akimbo, a human starfish in a sea of green. Fin looked at the sky, or least where the sky would normally be if it wasn't for the unending grey. The disappearance of summer was hardly an encouraging portent for her fate.

But Fin did not move.

The ground felt good beneath her body. The grasses cradled her. She imagined thousands of tiny green hands holding her a sliver above the ground. It was lunchtime but Fin had no desire to see her fellow students. She did not need their unwanted support. Just the comforting feel of the lawn and the memories of her father, as she contemplated her completed work.

People loved routine. Their actions recurring in a circle of inevitable regularity, whether they realized it or not. Her father had taught her this lesson. He was a powerful and successful merchant, but he was also a feared player of card games, and he ascribed his success not to mathematical prowess, but his ability to study people. Business and cards were two different forms of the same game to him, and his opponents fell into categories of people that he had been refining his whole life.

Finabria remembered afternoons sitting in the piazza with her father, watching the great and good go about their business, and he would point and whisper in her ear his prediction for what they would do next— "he's buying flowers for his mistress, not his wife", "he's walking quickly because he needs a glass of wine to stop the tremors", "look at him there, he looks well-to-do but he is going to steal that woman's coin purse". Her father's ability to predict the future had been like magic to her younger self.

Before she came to Kingshold, her father had sat her down and shared his secrets with her, though he warned her not to blindly trust his learnings, but instead to develop her own approach. Just remember three things he had said, "the sun will rise, the days will turn, and people can't help betraying themselves."

Her future success was reliant on this fact. Her life potentially relied on this. She breathed deeply and trusted that this lesson was true.

~

THE SQUARE COURTYARD WAS EMPTY SAVE FOR FINABRIA, her three fellow trialists, and four chests positioned at the points of a smaller square—scratched into the center of what would pass for the arena. Every window lining the courtyard was flung open, her fellow students hanging out and jostling for a good view. On the balcony where yesterday had stood just Lady Chalice and Master Steppen, were the other full Syndicate members currently in residence at the Hollow House.

Fin stood in one corner. In the corner to her right was Dorien, who stared intently at her. She flashed him a brief smile and let her gaze roam. In the opposite corner was Argo, standing tall and looking maddeningly confident. In the corner to her left was Qeturah, and as usual her pale face showed that she had recently applied powder. Fin breathed a sigh of relief. Wearing make-up for a fight was inconceivable to Fin, but Qeturah was nothing if not predictable.

Which was good, as Fin had rested her hopes on the predictability of her competition.

Fin focused her attention on Qeturah, who swayed slightly instead of standing at the ready. Fin could see how her eyes seemed slightly unfocused.

Another thing that was predictable were the effects of desiccated greeber slug when applied to the skin. Drowsiness. Lethargy. Delayed reflexes. Fin almost laughed at the ease of the small victory.

She noticed that Dorien had been looking at Qeturah too. Would he see what she had done? If you didn't know what to look for then it would not be obvious that the other girl had been drugged...

A loud clap bounced off the courtyard walls, and the murmuring from the windows stopped. Finabria turned to face Steppen, who clapped once more.

"Trialists," began Lady Chalice, "there is one place in the Syndicate and there are four of you. In each chest is a weapon, and on each chest is a lock. Last one standing wins. Try not to kill each other." Without further ceremony Chalice rang a small glass bell and the trial began.

Fin wanted the diamond chest, where she expected the sai to wait within. The bell rang and she set off at a sprint to the chest in front of Dorien. He was moving toward the same destination, but instead of stopping at the diamond chest he leapt over it and continued his run.

Dorien was heading for Qeturah. He must have noticed her looking slightly dazed too.

She reached the chest and examined it. It was the same size as the other boxes, inlaid with stained and polished wood in a herringbone pattern, the pattern interrupted in the center of each panel to contain a diamond shaped piece of lacquered black wood. But it was without any obvious locking mechanism.

A puzzle box. Not what she had been hoping for, but she could do this. She knew she could.

Fin dropped her lock picking tools to the earth—they wouldn't be useful now—and slowly swept her hands over every surface of the chest, with the gentleness of a lover's caress.

As her hands felt for seams, tell-tale changes in the solidity of the panels, she assessed the battlefield. Argo, now to her right, was on his knees working at the chest in front of him, peering into a lock as he probed it with his tools.

Across the courtyard, Dorien had engaged Qeturah in

hand to hand combat over a chest decorated with squares in a checkerboard. Qeturah dodged his leap and downward punch as Dorien jumped over the chest and skidded to a halt in the sand. Qeturah turned, swinging a roundhouse kick at Dorien's head, but it was too slow and he blocked it easily, catching her ankle in one hand. He stepped inside her leg and brought his elbow down on the kneecap—it popped audibly and Qeturah squealed. He released his grip on her foot, letting it drop. Qeturah, unthinking, bent over to touch her wounded leg. Dorien thrust a straight arm punch into her exposed temple and she crumpled to the floor. One down.

She felt the diamond on the right-hand side of the box give slightly at her touch. A firmer touch and it depressed a quarter inch, but nothing happened.

Only seconds had passed since the bell, but Argo would crack his box soon and Dorien was at work now too. Fin redoubled her search.

Another section of herringbone pattern on the front gave way, a third on the left-hand side of the box. She kept her ears sensed for the tell-tale clicking sound of a mechanism, blotting out the cries of the crowd, calling on their favorite. But she couldn't hear anything. *Why wouldn't it open!*

Fin rechecked the right side of the box, sliding her hand over the wood and the chevrons of the pattern shifted, moving into the empty space of the diamond. Quickly she slid the panels of the wood at random—each panel connected to the other with small perfectly crafted grooves like a child's puzzle—unsure what would be revealed or what the answer would be. Finally, one panel slid to reveal a key hole.

She grabbed her roll of tools, pulling a slender pick,

inserting it into the lock and feeling it pop with a simple flick. So the lock wasn't the challenge, not judging by its simplicity; the trouble was finding the keyhole. But the chest did not open. There must be more. Shifting her attention she set to sliding the panels on the front of the chest.

Argo cried "yes!" as he flipped the lid of his chest in triumph and pulled a short sword from within. He drew it from its scabbard, throwing the latter to the floor.

Another keyhole! Fin inserted her pick as Argo assessed his options, looking in turn at her and Dorien.

Argo advanced toward her, sword raised in a fighting stance. She tried to put him out of her mind and concentrate on the box; it felt like time slowed as she focused fully on the challenge at hand. The lock clicked, but the lid would not budge. There must be still another lock. She began to slide the wooden panels around on the left side as Argo neared to within ten paces. Thoughts raced through her mind. Should she try to fight him hand to hand or focus on the box until the last minute?

Five paces.

Slick. Slick. Slick, went the panels as she flipped them around, trying to avoid becoming frantic.

Three paces. Still no key hole.

Argo was bearing down her. Suddenly, the blade of a rapier was being fended away from his stomach at the last moment. Dorien had freed his weapon and now flicked his longer-reaching rapier at Argo's cheek, drawing a scratch. The scarred man smiled.

Predictable. Dorien should have joined with Argo to finish her off, but he had allowed himself to be influenced by his emotions.

Slick. Another keyhole appeared and Fin gratefully thrust

her pick inside, catching the tumbler almost immediately. The lid to the chest popped up. Fin flung it open to reveal a pair of sai inside. She grabbed the weapons, exhaling in relief at the weight of the steel in her hands.

Now it was time to finish this.

Dorien and Argo fought frenetically, parry and thrust, dodge and riposte. They were an even match. But the odds had changed now.

Fin advanced toward Argo, one sai held high above and behind her head, the other held at the ready in front of her chest. Argo parried a thrust from Dorien, the heavier weight of the short sword deflecting the blow, leaving his side exposed to Fin. She struck, leading with her high blade toward his chest. He swayed away, the sharp tip narrowly missing, but his feet were twisted and he wasn't able to easily avoid her follow up which pierced the triceps of his sword arm. Argo fell backward, rolled away and leapt back to his feet once more. Blood dripped to the sandy floor, but he wasn't about to quit with just a scratch.

Dorien ran to re-engage, Fin a half step behind him. Argo backed up, attempting to keep his space as he defended against the attacks of the rapier. Fin rounded the wounded man, drawing his attention in two directions. She swung a couple of times lazily at his head, and she had to be impressed by how Argo could parry her attacks and keep Dorien at bay. At least for now.

She thrust high and low, extending her arms and her sai through his guard from a half-crouched position. Argo knocked the high attack aside, but the low scored his thigh and she saw the blood well. Dorien sensed his opportunity, and from the look in his eyes, she thought he may well kill Argo, even though that wasn't required. Dorien was almost by her side, and she could sense him tensing to thrust once more, his blade held up in front of his face.

Fin twisted, and thrust the sai through the side of the man's gut, above where the kidneys should be and away from the essential stuff in the middle. It would hurt like hell but shouldn't be deadly.

Dorien fell to the floor, clutching at the wound with his free hands, his rapier lying on the sand next to him. Blood flowed freely. He looked at Fin aghast, his face awash with pain. Fin wondered what hurt more, the attack or the betrayal? *Predictable.*

Fin skipped back a couple of steps. Argo was wounded but not out of the game, and she wanted some space to play with. He came forward and Fin could see that he was trying his best to ignore his wounds. It was nothing more than many of her friends had received on the training field, but she doubted that Argo was used to fighting wounded—he had always been *too good* to be hit.

Argo's weapon had the advantage of length; the short sword six inches longer than her sai, and its edged blade gave it more area to wound than her sharp-tipped piercing weapons. But she had the pair, her favored weapons, and it gave her confidence. He didn't stand a chance.

The sword danced forward, Argo maintaining a duelists stance, the blade a blur from the speed of his attacks. *Ting. Ting.* The courtyard was silent except for the clash of metal on metal as the audience held their breath. The strikes came high, at her chest, her arms and her face. An overhand came at her head, and she dodged to the right, not wanting to block the attack from the stronger man and get tangled up at this stage.

And there it was. What she had been waiting for since

fighting Barrag earlier that day. The low thrust following the high attack. The move that Barrag had been programmed to anticipate.

She could have stepped clear. She could have jumped over the slash, for Marlth's sake. It would have looked good, but it wasn't going to finish this fight. She blocked the short sword with one sai, meeting the blade in the air. He was strong though, and there was a lot in that swing. Though she took much of the momentum out of the attack, Argo's short sword bit into her thigh. But no matter, because her other sai was already moving. It pierced his chest near the shoulder of his sword arm and she pushed with the weight of her body until the blade met resistance against his shoulder blade.

"Aaargh!" he roared.

The short sword hit the sandy floor with a thud, Argo's backside doing likewise shortly afterwards.

It was only a couple of seconds, but the moment of silence seemed like an eternity. Fin breathed deeply, her heart pounding in her ears. She raised her bloody sai in the air, feeling as high as the Finger of Heaven on the Sanctum of Arloth in her home city. And then the audience erupted. Her fellow students cheered and pounded on the window frames. The Syndicate members standing on the balcony clapped enthusiastically.

"Bravo!" called Lady Chalice.

～

THE AFTERNOON WAS A WHIRLWIND. THE INFIRMARY TO stitch her leg and bind her wounds. A trip to the baths to ease her aching muscles. Congratulations from her fellow students that she found hard not to find pleasure in. She packed her belongings into her chest; now she could leave the dormitory and move into the House proper.

"Finabria, you may stop packing," said Steppen from the doorway. "Lady Chalice wants to see you. Now."

Wordlessly, she followed Steppen through the hallways of the school wing like a troublesome schoolgirl. Which could be exactly what she was. *Had Chalice discovered her actions before the trial?* They descended a long stairway to the entrance to the courtyard. Fellow students came out from their rooms and stopped what they were doing to watch her walk of shame. Fin's face drained of blood, worry eating at her stomach. She had everything she wanted within reach, but now it could all be taken away from her.

Steppen led the way across the courtyard and into the Hollow House. He led her through a sitting room—cushioned seats arrayed in clusters, portraits of past House leaders adorning the walls—to an oak doorway. Without knocking, Steppen opened the door and ushered her in. "Miss Bracaccia, Lady Chalice."

"Thank you, Steppen," she said. "Come in and have a seat, Finabria."

Lady Chalice leaned against a desk and directed her to a chair in front of her. She looked as she had earlier that day; dressed in green trousers and white shirt, her long curly red hair tied behind her head. She looked nothing like the most feared assassin in the Jeweled Continent; Fin admired her disguise.

"I wanted to talk to you, Fin. You did well today. There hasn't been an admittance to the Syndicate from someone who has not finished their studies for a long time. Since me, actually. Tell me, when did the trial begin?"

Fin blinked. Had she heard her right? "At the second hour of the afternoon?"

Chalice laughed. "Are you pretending to be the fool, Fin? When did your trial begin?"

She sat silently for a moment. From the open window Fin heard the sound of bells tolling in the city. Lady Chalice must have heard it too but she did not let Fin out of her gaze.

"It started when I raised my hand. Yesterday. In the courtyard," she said, more afraid now than anytime this afternoon.

"Good," said Lady Chalice. "That's right. It was obvious, to me at least, that you had prepared." She raised a hand to cut off Fin as she opened her mouth to defend herself. "I don't need to know how. I don't care—it was nothing obvious enough for others to detect. Right now you are probably feeling pretty good about yourself, am I right?"

"Yes, Lady Chalice," she conceded.

"Well, you need to remember that you still have a lot to learn. And now you are answerable to me, and let me warn you, Miss Bracaccia," Lady Chalice leaned forward, moving her face closer to Fin's, her eyes narrowing. "You don't want to disappoint me."

Fin nodded as the door to the office opened again. Without acknowledging Fin, Steppen gestured to Lady Chalice for a word. She could not hear what they said. Their whispers did not carry and she was still trying to process what had happened. Chalice knew what she'd done! But she was still going to be in the Syndicate!

"Finabria," said Lady Chalice. "Get prepared. It appears Kingshold is under attack. By pirates of all things. I don't know what this place is coming to. But I'll be damned if they're going to take my city unharried."

FROM THE DESK OF LORD MARCHIAL EDEN

Dear Amphrey,
    I write this to you before I depart Kingshold for Aria, and I apologize for my tremulous script. I find myself unable to fully come to terms with what happened today.

You and I have been friends for many years, more decades than I wish to count; and I know the events of today were probably as great a shock to you as they were to me. I am still frankly aghast at how the younger Bollingsmead has been able to corrupt the sanctity of this election process. I smell the taint of that wizard.

My lands and titles have been passed down in my family for more than four centuries. I refuse to kowtow before Jyuth. I find it impossible to recognize his authority to strip me of mine in the absence of King or Queen. I ride for home to muster my good men and welcome others to bring their banners in support. I know I will be able to count on you to support me in this time of trouble and, once this meddling usurper is taught a lesson, I look forward to being able to work with you at my side to make Edland a shining beacon for the rest of the Jeweled Continent once again.

Yours faithfully,

MARCHIAL

~

1st Seventhmoon, 1085

DEAR HALTON,

I sit here in the keep at Aria, your note in my hand confirming the election of that pretender Bollingsmead and the disappearance of the wizard. What a foul corpulent thief to disappear with the funds held in trust during this election. This truly proves to show that the whole process was little more than a confidence trick and a sham.

I assure you, I have no plans to flee Edland, a country that my family and subjects have sacrificed their life for in years past. Nathan, my beloved son, currently rides our lands raising the men to be ready for any assault that may come.

Can I count on your support in the coming months? You are one of my oldest friends, and my neighbor in the north. Have you discussed my need with others in the past weeks? I am sure their support in terms of letters and men are on their way.

My best wishes to you and Meredith. Keep the faith in these troubled times.

Yours,

MARCHIAL

~

20th *Seventhmoon, 1085*

DEAR NATHAN,

Your reports of criers spreading the false news of my downfall to our villages and towns are of grave concern. It is of the upmost importance that you root out these peddlers of lies and base falsehoods where you find them.

Hang them from the trees and let them cry the truth about that disgusting bard as their tongues stick out from their mouths!

Already there has been one attempt on my life. Dirty bounty hunters from Ambrukkhar infiltrated Aria and fired on me with crossbows. The only reason I am still here to write this letter to you is the good actions of our selfless steward Rambotham (Arloth rest his soul) taking the quarrel in my place. Now the gates to our fair town are closed and all strangers have been expelled.

I have heard word that Uthridge has raised a force that is already marching north to our lands and we must be ready for their arrival. If you are able to harry them along the way then that will truly prepare them for what they are in for when they arrive in the north. I take no pleasure in fighting fellow Edlanders and I pray to Arloth that they will see sense as they face our defenses.

Remember, that you are an Eden through and through. You share the blood of strong military commanders like myself. Have faith my son. This will be the making of you.

Your father,

LORD EDEN

~

20th Seventhmoon, 1085

TO MY DEAR LADY CHALICE,

I do not know who gave you the contract on Bollingsmead during the election, but now I gladly commission the contract. I insist on only the best to execute the task. As we arranged for Hoxteth, only you are suitable for this job.

Additionally, I want those three thugs who accompany Bollingsmead to die slow deaths. And Lady Grey, obviously the brains behind both Hoxteth and the disgusting bard. I should have eliminated her previously.

It is no exaggeration to say that I will pay any price for this to happen. I will empty my coffers for the chance to dance on their graves.

I am prepared to forgive you for your public display of praise for the brawler that supported Bollingsmead in the duel. For what is more important in these times than friendship and loyalty?

Please confirm the acceptance of the contract at once, and provide me with details on logistics.

Your ever-grateful patron,

LORD MARCHIAL EDEN

∽

20th Seventhmoon, 1085

TO GUILDMASTER WREN,

Sir, I grieve for your loss during the recent election. The theft of thousands of golden crowns by that wizard Jyuth must be a significant loss to your house and those of your guild. Though I am sure you received adequate collateral in exchange for your demon-loans, the impact to the economy must be nothing short of a catastrophe! This kingdom only runs because of the deployment of capital by people such as I and the venerable institutions of your guild.

I have many thousands of crowns on deposit in your vaults, and my family have been valued and loyal customers for many generations. I trust that my funds remain readily available to me, though it would be appreciated, and of course adequately compensated, that my financial dealings remain discreet. Additionally, if you are able to assist in the sourcing and hiring of talented martial professionals then I know I will be doubly grateful.

Yours sincerely,

LORD MARCHIAL EDEN

~

5th Eighthmoon, 1085

LADY CHALICE,

It was with great sadness that I received the news that my friendship and patronage is no longer good enough for you. I thought we had developed a strong understanding in recent weeks.

Has there ever been a customer more forthcoming in such a short space of time than I?

By your actions, it is clear that you have joined with the usurper. The collection of noble cast offs and petty murderers that make up the Hollow Syndicate have suddenly discovered 'morals'?

Hah, I say to your hypocrisy.

Now that your country needs your services, and even when it

would make your house wildly rich, you refuse to help, pleading patriotism with this ideologue bard.

Your lack of loyalty disgusts me.

LORD MARCHIAL EDEN

~

5th *Eighthmoon, 1085*

To THE DUKE OF NORTHFIELD,

I apologize for the delay in sending my condolences for the death of your nephew, our rightful King, and his graceful Queen at the fell hand of the sorcerer. I truly understand the trauma you must have suffered and I feel your outrage that the proper rules of hereditary law have not been followed. I assure you, that had I been made Lord Protector, I would have seen it as only a short-term appointment enabling the transition of rule back to the royal family and yourself. Alas, my good intentions have been foiled by more foul scheming from Jyuth.

But I will not go down without a fight! Though it seems my friends have forgotten me, I refuse to let this sham continue and I shall never give up my lands or this realm to the hands of usurpers and charlatans. I am a rich man, and the banks of Kingshold are venerable institutions who are solid in their dependability. Mercenaries and sell swords are on their way from the continent as I write.

My wife and daughter bring you this message and I ask your aid in helping them find a good home to purchase, and in the hiring of dependable and trustworthy servants. They are the light of my life and I want to ensure their safe keeping while my son and I protect our home.

For the good of Edland, and your throne.

Your servant,

LORD MARCHIAL EDEN

～

12*th* Eighthmoon, 1085

TO MY DARLING ELIZA,

It is with great sadness that I write to you today. The ignominies visited on our family know no end.

What does Arloth hold against us that we must suffer so?

For now our son has been taken away from us, cut down on the road by the men of the Second. The army that I commanded for many years, used as the weapon to take away the light of my life.

Nathan was a good boy and left this world in a way that brings me pride to mix with my tears. He personally led a night-time raid on the encamped army some fifty miles from Aria. The raid was initially a great success, sowing discord and crippling our enemies in the dark. It was only an opportunistic arrow fired from a sentry as he and his men melted away into the night that coldly took him in the back.

I know your grief will nearly match mine and I wish we could be together during this troubling time.

But now the defense of our home rests on my shoulders. We have *supplies, our walls are secure and I know I can rely on the love of our people to fight for the defense of our home.*

We will be together soon my love, once this is over with.

MARCHIAL

~

22nd Eighthmoon, 1085

GUILDMASTER WREN,

These are sorry days indeed. I miss our games of Queens over a glass of fine brandy but, alas, I fear that it will be some time until we can repeat these more pleasurable activities.

The usurper's army attacked Aria, and I am proud to say that my people defended it well, giving their lives to keep their countrymen from the door. I led from the front, of course; prowling the walls and commanding the defenses that we relied upon, hardly sleeping for days until I sensed that Arloth called out for me.

I retired to my chapel, letting my captain know that I sought counsel from our lord and to defend the town at all costs until I returned. Truly, I was ready to lay down my own life, and all of those who swore service to me, in the name of this most noble cause. But while I fasted and prayed in the chapel I was visited by Arloth himself.

I don't believe it is fitting to attempt to describe on such a poor medium as ink and paper the vision that I received, and I find myself unable to do glory to his words; but he showed me a terrible vision for the future of Edland if I was to perish and not be in place to stop the chain of events from happening. And so I left my home, by secret tunnel during the dead of night, to the coast where a boat that I thought I would never use lay waiting for me. While my friends and subjects continued to fight for my survival.

I am now bound for Pienza, so that I may fulfill this calling that Arloth has laid out for me. I have lost so much this summer, but let me assure you that I remain resolute in what must be achieved. I will contact you through other channels in the future, to organize further our plans of liberation and salvation. Arloth himself chose the symbol I will use. The Red Hart, most noble of the beasts of Edland, synonym for the courage that we must all show to make this world better.

Yours sincerely,

LORD MARCHIAL EDEN

CIRCLES

The walk from Kingshold to Wombourne on the coastal road, and then on to the Dark Forest by the pathway known as The Spine, had taken the better part of a fortnight. Though the roads were paved, well maintained and free of bandits, Motega's insistence that they travel on foot had turned a few days ride into something of an expedition. Not that Neenahwi was against the quality time with her brother; she had only just been reunited with him after many years apart, and now she finally had him to herself.

Neenahwi walked hand in hand with Motega—like they used to as children—and found the physical presence to be reassuring in a way that she had not realized she missed. In Edland it was considered strange for people to hold hands, but in her homeland her people were not afraid of being close to each other. Though it had been many years since the death of their parents and the tribe, she could still remember seeing her father walk hand-in-hand with his champion.

Traveling in this manner also brought back bitter sweet

memories of their flight from the Pyrfew raiders who came with fire and steel to their happy little village. Back in those days, Motega was little more than a boy, and though he rarely got scared, she remembered their escape, traveling hand-in-hand during the day and holding him until he would fall asleep at night. Thinking about that time, after so long pushing it down deep inside her, brought a tear to her eye.

Neenahwi looked at the man walking by her side, so different than he had been back then. Now he was a few inches taller than her, and he walked with a confidence that made her think of her father. His hood was down, exposing his short hair, close beard and the markings on his face; his two-tone skin pale white except for bird wing shapes around his eyes. On his face was the same content smile that she remembered from her mother as she would play with them; Neenahwi found herself mirroring that smile.

"What is it?" asked Motega, noticing his sister's attention. "Do I have breakfast on my chin? You know I'm too big for you to clean my face with a spit cloth."

"Hah! Like you'd ever let me do that anyway," she said. "I was just thinking about how familiar this feels. I missed it."

"Me too, sis. And it will be so good to see Kanaveen again after all this time."

She was feeling a little apprehensive about seeing Kanaveen again, even though she was no longer a child relying on her father's champion to help them escape their pursuers, or to act as a conspirator in her teenage yearnings for revenge. Now she was a sorcerer; battle tested and independent. She'd just fought a draco-turtle during the recent troubles in Kingshold, for Marlth's sake. But the thought of seeing the man who had been like a father to her for many years made her stomach squirm.

Motega had seen Kanaveen most recently, when he had
undergone the Quana, the traditional vision quest where he
had been gifted with the falcon spirit animal that circled
above her head. And though she was older than her brother,
and many years past officially coming of age, she was about
to tread the same ceremonial path to adulthood that all of
the members of her tribe had followed.

"I only wish we didn't have to walk the whole way," said
Neenahwi.

"Yep, it's a long way on foot. But Kanaveen said in his
message that you needed to reconnect with the earth before
you can start the ceremony."

"I could transform into a wolf and be there in half the
time you know," she said, though she had no intention of
doing so. Being out in nature, the air clean and fresh, was a
marvelous change.

"Hah, you read the message. No magic," said Motega.
"And you'd leave me behind then, so what would be the fun
in that? After the past few weeks, it's a relief to settle into a
peaceful rhythm. Even for me."

She had to agree with that. The election of a new ruler of
Edland had been an intense affair. Riots, assassinations and a
pirate raid—hardly the most auspicious way for Mareth to
come to the role of Lord Protector, but she still believed he
was the best option on the table. Not that she didn't have
concerns about his ability. After all, a tavern bard is not
typical training for running a country. And now that Jyuth,
her adopted father and wizard of Edland, had disappeared,
she was left feeling responsible for Mareth and the nation.
Motega nearly had to physically drag her away from court to
come on this particular trip, reminding her of the promise
she had made on their reunion. But now she was on the road,

she had to agree that the tiredness in her legs and feet, and the feel of her brother's hand in hers, was an excellent way to forget about other troubles.

∾

THEY LEFT THE SPINE LATER THAT DAY AND MADE OUT across the foothills toward the eastern edge of the Dark Forest. The Edland countryside was beautiful; rolling hills covered in green grass, fluffy white balls of sheep idly going about their business, and only an occasional stray summer shower blotting out the sun. Their pace slowed as they strode up hill and cantered down dale. At night they camped on soft beds of turf, the wayside inns only lining the well-traveled roads.

On the fourth day from The Spine, Neenahwi and Motega crested a hill to see the land fall away slowly to a line of tall dark trees. Nestled close to it, visible by the thin trail of smoke rising from a chimney, was a small wooden cottage.

The sun was nearing its zenith as sister and brother neared the house—close enough to see a figure chopping wood, a string of animal pelts hanging from a line nearby.

"Ho!" called Motega. "Kanaveen!"

The old warrior turned at the call. He still looked just as she remembered him. Tall, with weathered brown skin and long hair tied behind his neck. She knew he must be approaching eighty, but still looked as fit as any of the soldiers in Kingshold. Her people, the Alfjarun, were like the humans of the Jeweled Continent in many ways, but being constrained by such a short life was not one of them. Kanaveen wedged the axe in the log he was chopping, waved, and walked over to greet them.

"Motega!" said Kanaveen, his voice deep, emanating from his broad chest. He enclosed the younger man in a tight embrace. "It is good to see you. What happened to your hair?"

Motega rubbed at his shorn hair self-consciously. Neenahwi knew that it had hit him hard when he had lost his braid in a work-related accident (that is, getting stuck escaping from the scene of a crime), but he did seem to be getting over it.

"Oh yeah," said Motega, "it was either my hair or my neck. My neck won."

Kanaveen nodded, as if in understanding at such a choice. Then he turned to face Neenahwi. "So, Neeni. Finally, you have come to see me. Or have you just come to inspect your property?"

Neenahwi paused in reaching out to hug her old protector, taken aback by his words. "Oh Kanaveen, it is so good to see you. I am sorry I have been absent, but what do you mean?"

"This house is yours. It belonged to Jyuth and he has let me live here for as long as I like. He sent me word of his retirement, and told me that his property is yours now."

More surprises from Jyuth. He hadn't see fit to mention this in his going away letter. "I don't want it, Kanaveen. I am just here to see you."

"Well I am very happy to have you here, Neeni," he said, as he finally took her in his arms, lifting her in the air as he squeezed her in one of the bear-hugs she used to love so much. "And I am glad that you will finally come of age before the World Tree. You are chief of what remains of the Wolfclaw clan. Us three here. But you can both add to that number one day, eh? Come, you both must be weary. Let me prepare you lunch and we can talk about what comes ahead."

~

LUNCH OF ROASTED RABBIT WITH STEWED FIDDLEHEADS was simple but enjoyable, and Neenahwi found herself reveling in being able to rest her feet. They sat in Kanaveen's house, a simple construct of sawn logs and daub, with a stone chimney reaching out from a pitched thatched roof. The interior was just as functional; a single room with a bed, small table and a chair, and a few cushions on the floor by the fireplace. Neenahwi sat cross-legged, a wooden cup of chamomile tea in her hand as she watched Kanaveen clear up after their meal, her protestations at not being allowed to help being waved away.

Eventually Kanaveen joined her and Motega on the floor. Kanaveen sat opposite them both, a serious look on his face.

"Tomorrow, you will start your Quana," said Kanaveen, his back straight as a rod and head held high. "As all other Wolfclaw clan members have done for centuries. The shaman should lead this ceremony but you will have to make do with me. He would tell you tales of how it started and the connection to our ancestors and gods. These stories alone could take days and I do not know them anymore, but what is important is that we do this for two reasons. Do you know why?"

Neenahwi considered this, unaccustomed to the note of formality in his tone. It had been a long time since she had heard Greytooth welcome the tribe to celebrate the beginning of a Quana, and she had been but a child then, with a child's habit for finding other things to consider during long monologues. "We believe that you can't rejoin your ancestors when you die, unless you have been formally admitted to the tribe," said Neenahwi, playing along with Kanaveen's role of teacher. He nodded his agreement. "But I don't know the other," she admitted.

"The other reason is the most important. It is for you to find your purpose in life. How will you help the tribe?" Kanaveen paused, letting the words sink in. Neenahwi considered how that had not been in her thoughts for a long time and it did not sit well. "We all have the potential for great things; and your Quana, your vision quest, helps you to see what that is. Some people discover it through their own introspection. Others have spirits who help them. But it is always your choice, Neeni, to decide whether you accept it."

"Did you find your purpose in your vision quest?" she asked, wondering if he had known where his path would take him.

"Yes. I knew I was to protect the tribe from great challenges," said Kanaveen. "And so I dedicated my life to being a great warrior. I thought I would be protecting our people against other tribes, or the horrors that can roam the plains. When our tribe was attacked by the demon and the men in steel, I thought that was my moment of testing—that I would protect our tribe or die trying." He paused for a moment, tears visible in his eyes. "But I was wrong, my purpose was to protect you two. To take you to safety so the tribe would survive. Sometimes I think it would have been easier to fight and die with our friends."

Neenahwi leaned forward to give her old protector a hug and brush the tears from his cheek. "I understand. I think the same sometimes. Thank you for taking the hard path, Kanaveen."

Kanaveen forced a weak smile, and took a deep breath to steady his voice. "Who knows what your vision will tell you? And from my story you can see that you may think it is one thing and it could turn out to be something else. Don't let your certainty of what your vision tells you turn you into a rock. Stay flexible like the reed, bending in the wind of life; continually question your destination." He paused, and Neenahwi nodded in understanding. "Now, there are certain rules you must follow. Are you ready to hear them?"

More rules. She'd spent more than a decade with Jyuth learning not to accept rules. She was sure 'no magic' would be part of it. Nevertheless, she said, "I am."

"Good. You will remain in the wilderness for four days and nights and you will not eat anything. This was your last meal until you are reborn. You will use no magic to make the time less arduous." There it was, as she had expected. "You will walk into the wilderness with the clothes on your back and a small knife. Nothing else. The land here is different than where I did my Quana, but the forest seems to have been a reasonable place for your brother's ceremony."

Motega nodded. "That forest is a wild place; you'll need to stay alert," he said.

"On the first day you will choose your home in the wilderness. Build your shelter.

"On the second day you will spend your time as you wish. Walk, sit, sleep, wait. It matters not. Time will slow and it will test your patience.

"On the third day you will build a stone circle. Be thoughtful on the stones you choose. Place them like so." Kanaveen drew a circle on the dirt floor with a stick, indicating stone placements at each of the eight primary points of direction, two stones placed in the center.

"And then on the fourth day you will enter your stone circle and wait."

"Wait for what?" she asked, still unsure of what was going to happen.

"For your enlightenment. When you leave your circle, you are reborn and like your physical birth, you cannot return. So leave only when you know it is time."

"I understand, Kanaveen," said Neenahwi.

"At dawn tomorrow, I will walk you into the Forest and then leave you to your journey."

"Be careful he doesn't hit you on the back of the head as you walk, sis," said Motega, chuckling.

"Do not worry, Neenahwi. I will not do that." He shot Motega a scowl.

"Then why did you do that to me?" asked Motega, his brow furrowed.

"You were always a difficult child," said Kanaveen, waving his hand in irritation. "You don't listen to what you are told. I had to make sure you weren't taking tools that would spoil the ceremony. As I remember, you had four knives, string, flint and a biscuit in your pockets. It was for your own good." Motega looked sheepish at the litany of contraband, avoiding Neenahwi's appraising, but amused, gaze.

Kanaveen got to his feet, his knees clicking as he rose. "And now, we should finish our preparations. You will need water, Neeni. Let us fetch it. And, Motega, I look forward to sparring with you these next few days. I have been restricted to shadow fighting for too long."

⁓

DAMN DEER TRACKS.

This was the second path that Neenahwi had followed that had disappeared a few hundred yards along, right before a thicket of thorns. Of course, if she was allowed to use magic, then she could become a deer and leap over this collection of evil vegetation. Or she could be a wolf and her fur would provide protection. But Kanaveen had warned that magic was not allowed. He'd even reminded her this morning as he escorted her to the edge of the forest—the sun just starting to peak up over the horizon. He had handed her two waterskins and reminded her of the rules, before he had embraced her, and told her how proud of her he was. Hearing those words from Kanaveen had brought back a rush of emotion. Again! *What was it about this journey that was turning her into a blubbering wreck?*

Now she was on her own—not that she was unused to that. She'd explored far and wide by herself in the past. In particular she'd hunted the trail of various demon stones until she'd finally found one. But then she'd always had her arcane talents at her disposal; to defend herself, or to flee if necessary. She supposed that there probably weren't many monsters or great beasts still lurking in the forest that she would have to worry about.

Probably.

The sun would have been fairly high in the sky then, but she couldn't see it under the tree canopy. Neenahwi was sure that she was feeling the benefits of it though; dappled sunlight came through breaks in the trees and the air was full of the sounds of birds and other creatures going about their woodland business. Her job now was to find a place to make camp and build a shelter. So the only thing on her mind was where should it be? How far should she keep walking?

It was her stomach that informed her to stop some hours

later, likely around lunchtime, when it gurgled to let her know that it was still there and was usually fed by then. Neenahwi gave a silent apology to her body and took stock of where she was. It was a small clearing, the sun peaked through a gap in the trees, and from the ground sprouted great green leaves shaped like the feathers of a giant phoenix. She had passed a small stream a half hour before, and she was fairly confident she could find it again to collect rocks for her stone circle, and also to refill her waterskins if she needed.

This will be a good place, she thought, and set to work cutting down the ferns with her small knife.

~

IT TOOK THE REST OF THE DAY TO CLEAR THE GROUND cover and weave the large green leaves into panels. These she fastened to frames of wood, built of live limbs she cut from trees around her new home. She didn't notice the time passing with her hands busy and work to occupy her. At times, Neenahwi had found herself frustrated at her first attempts at creating her own building materials, fashioning twine from vine or fibrous plant material proving to be particularly bothersome. But she persevered, and tried again. After all, what else was there for her to do? At least it had the added benefit of keeping her mind off her empty belly.

As the light in the forest started to dim, she stood, hands on hips surveying the product of her craft. An A-frame structure butting up against a great chestnut tree, the vivid green of the screens blending in with the undergrowth behind it. It was large enough for her to lie down inside, and to sit up cross legged, but not to stand upright. The floor was lined with other green leaves, and a pile of the same leaves was reserved in the corner in case she needed covering at night.

"Home," she said to herself. "If only I had my cat."

~

THE FOREST GOT DARK QUICKLY THAT NIGHT, LONG BEFORE when Neenahwi suspected the sun had actually set. And her environment changed markedly. The shadows between the trees were impenetrable pools of black. The quiet peace replaced by a cacophony of insects chirruping and owls hooting, interrupted by the rustling sounds of some ground creature walking close by but completely unseen. She cursed herself for spending so much time on a shelter and not thinking of preparing a fire—at least to have some light. That would need to be a focus for tomorrow.

Without light, and work for her hands, time once again slowed to a crawl. She sat cross legged in her shelter and took up her typical meditating position.

She usually spent many hours each day in such a pose, working through the mental exercises that were essential to wield the magic of the world. Splitting her consciousness to do more than one thing at once, drawing energy from her environment in threads that sparkled to her arcane eye, weaving it into the forms and effects that she could call on at a moment's notice. These exercises were like a swordsman's drills—essential if she was to continually improve or even maintain her current level of skill. But she supposed the ban on magic during her vision quest extended to this routine too.

So she closed her eyes with the intention to contemplate the events of the past few months; the new leadership of

Edland, stepping into her adopted father's ancient shoes, and most of all, what was Llewdon, self-proclaimed god-emperor of Pyrfew, up to? But, for the first time since she was a teenager, the combination of her aching muscles and the monotony of the forest noise, pulled her toward sleep instead of into thought.

∼

NEENAHWI WOKE WITH A START. A TICKLE AT HER FEET, accompanied by a snuffling, and she snapped upright, briefly unsure of her surroundings.

Whatever beast had been in her clearing disappeared before she could see it, but she heard the sound of it running away through the vegetation.

She wasn't the only one to be startled this morning.

Sunlight was starting to filter through the trees as Neenahwi unfolded herself from the shelter. Stretching, she briefly gave thought to making breakfast, before remembering that wasn't on the agenda. In fact there wasn't really anything on the agenda. And that emptiness of purpose was concerning to her. Not having a thousand things to do was completely unfamiliar. The irony of finding her purpose in life while feeling completely purposeless was not lost on her.

Fire.

Remembering the lack of light last night, she was suddenly thankful for her prior oversight.

Something to do.

∼

THREE STACKS AND A CIRCLE SHOWED THE EVIDENCE OF

her work. A small ring of rocks to act as a hearth. A small pile of tinder tucked away in her shelter out of any wind or rain that might come. A larger stack of twigs and small branches for kindling, and a final pile of larger branches for fuel that she had tried, with varying degrees of success, to snap to manageable sizes. Completing her preparations were two sticks that she had prepared with her knife to act as a fire starter.

Neenahwi realized that she hadn't made a fire by rubbing two sticks together since she had fled Missapik with her brother and Kanaveen, more than fifteen years ago. Making a spark had been one of the first applications of magic she had discovered. She still remembered that night; they had been caught in storm that had lasted two days, they were soaked to the skin and though they had found a cave in which to shelter, there was no dry kindling to start a fire. Neenahwi had been despondent, and her brother thoroughly miserable, both of them staring intently at the pile of twigs they had tried to use. Her anger and frustration at their predicament had welled up inside her, releasing suddenly like a whistle from a kettle. And the fire had burst to life, consuming the sticks. She'd fainted from the exertion and awoke to find Kanaveen tending a roaring fire, a rabbit roasting on a spit to finally feed their bellies.

As she thought about it, she realized she hadn't been as hungry since then too.

It had been nearly two days since the lunch that Kanaveen had prepared and she wondered now if she would ever eat again. If she'd have known it was going to be her last meal then maybe she would have asked for seconds.

Her thoughts turned back again to that night and their flight. The Wolfclaw clan was native to the broad plains of

Missapik which they shared with other tribes—mostly in peace but war was always just a disagreement away. When her tribe had been destroyed by the Pyrfew invaders, Kanaveen had led them east to warn the other tribes.

They had traveled to places that were only stories to members of her clan. Over mountain passes into a great forest that she didn't know the name of, like this one in many ways, but so unalike in others. The people of Edland would describe it as 'wild', though she thought untamed was a more fitting depiction of its raw beauty.

More times than she could count on her hands she had thought they would perish in that unending forest. Monsters. Quick sand. Swamp. And that sorcerer they had stumbled across, living alone in a cave, who had cursed her brother and damaged his sight.

And the hunger.

Moving fast, they had gathered what food they came across as they traveled—rarely stopping to hunt—and there were many evenings when she went to sleep hungry. Kanaveen would often give his share of food to her and Motega, and when he wasn't looking she would share further with her younger brother. Strangely, though she was sure it was due to the benefit of time passing, she looked back on those days with a fondness now. She had been so close to her brother, something which slipped away as events had taken them to the Jeweled Continent. Neenahwi felt some of that connection to Motega coming back in recent weeks but she didn't know how reliable it was. Would she abandon him again for the pursuit of knowledge? Would he disappear in the night once more to seek adventure?

Finally, they had broken out of the forest to see their first sight of the ocean, and to meet other Alfjarun peoples, those who lived in harmony with the sea. Their villages were bigger, their ocean-going canoes larger than what her people used on the rivers and they were fitted with sails, though nothing like the vessels she grew accustomed to in Kingshold. At first, they had been welcomed by people she thought of as distant cousins. She had been so happy to be around normal families again. And to eat the abundance of fish and sea food that was those peoples' bounty.

Then the Pyrfew ships had come. But not in conquest this time.

Neenahwi had watched in growing horror as the same men in steel that had killed her parents and torn her world asunder were now welcomed by the people she had considered friends.

Trading partners. And it was not long before she, Motega and Kanaveen were goods to be traded in exchange for gaudy trinkets, and bundled onto a ship bound for Pyrfew and its Emperor.

Tears streaked down her cheeks as the memories flooded over her. So long these experiences had been hidden away, replaced by a burning desire for revenge and the need to learn the power to execute it. She cried until her soul felt as empty as her belly. And the emptiness felt light. It felt good.

~

DRUM. DRUM.

The rain beat a tattoo on the roof of Neenahwi's shelter.

It thrummed through the canopy of trees above.

Puddles of muddy water formed on the cleared ground before her.

The wind swept through the trees, circling through the

ancient trunks, creating eddies in the air and bending the younger saplings that reached earnestly toward the sky.

Neenahwi watched the unexpected summer storm with a sense of detachment.

Branches ripped from bows above came tumbling to earth—sticking into the muddy ground at an angle—but it gave her no concern.

Leaves woven into the side of her shelter became separated by natures breath, allowing the rain to soak through her purple robe, causing it to stick to her skin.

But she paid no mind.

An earthworm had burrowed to the surface, escaping a death by drowning. She watched it squirm and wriggle as it sought the dry. Neenahwi reached out to pick it up and cradled it in her hand as the storm blew around her.

The humble earthworm. An alchemist of the ground, able to turn death and decay into the fertile soil needed for everyone's survival. She was reminded of the early days of her study with Jyuth, when he refused to train her in the use of magic until she had absorbed many dusty volumes on the myriad of beasts and plants that inhabit the Jeweled Continent. One fascinating entry was on the purple worm; the gigantic cousin of what she held in her hand. The purple worm lived hundreds of feet below the surface of the world, and was itself many millions of times greater in size than the wriggling brown creature of the forest. But they were essentially the same. And she had got to see those beautiful creatures just last year in Unedar Halt. Great and small sharing many characteristics; a body of interconnected rings, able to move objects many times it's bodyweight; eating, digesting and excreting all it came across as it burrowed through the land. Both were beautiful in their simplicity and purpose, but she had come to admire the purple worm's capacity for friendship and bravery. Was this tiny creature the same?

"Ah, dear worm," said Neenahwi. "You and I are much alike. I am no more important in the scheme of things than you are. But you know your purpose, and I, as yet, do not. Am I here to make the world better for things to grow and live as you are?"

The worm tilted its head in a shoulder-less shrug and she felt compelled to agree with it. After all, what business did she have demanding such answers of him? She tenderly placed the worm on the earth at the back of her shelter where she hoped it could stay out of the rain before resuming its work.

Water dripping from her face, the rain continued. And Neenahwi continued her watch.

~

THE STORM BLEW OUT SOME TIME LATER, THE SUN following behind, and steam rose from the forest floor. Neenahwi sat a while some more, watching the wildflowers opening their blooms once again to entice the butterflies and bees, before she remembered that today was the day she had to build her stone circle.

At the stream, she refilled her water skins and then set to wading barefoot through the water. Deliberately, she picked stones half the size of her head, smooth from the flow of the river, inspecting them without any specific intention, though afterward it was striking how they were all distinct in appearance. Ten stones in total she carried one-by-one back to her camp, eight for the compass points, one for the sky and one for the earth.

The bare ground in front of her tattered shelter was already dry; the rain gone, evaporated into the air or sucked into the thirsty earth like a beer set in front of a farm worker after a long day in the field. Standing in the center of the space, she turned on the spot, marking a circle with the point of a stick. Neenahwi placed the stones around the edge, not giving much thought to which would go where, letting her subconscious guide their selection. She was left with two stones; one sparkling white, smooth and round; the other black with lines of grey swirling through it like smoke, vaguely cuboid with sharp edges. These were placed inside the circle to represent above and below.

Her job done, she took her seat inside the shelter once more. Her belly, empty of ballast, left her feeling untethered, like a projection of herself, floating above the solidity of the ground.

∾

THE LIGHT DISAPPEARED AND THE FOREST WENT ABOUT IT'S now customary transition from day to night, two worlds occupying the one space. One set of creatures replacing another—a changeover of the watch—roles of sleeping and eating switched. The moon was high in the night sky, silvery light filtered through the trees bathing her stone circle in unexpected illumination.

Approval? she thought.

Neenahwi stood in the stone circle, craning her neck to look up through the gap in the canopy, then closing her eyes she let the moonlight bathe her clean. She didn't know how long she stood in such a way. But she sensed there was someone else there with her.

Opening her eyes she saw a figure silhouetted before her. She was not afraid. She did not call on her magic. Neenahwi knew that she was safe inside her circle. The figure stepped closer to the circle of light until she could make out his appearance. He was tall, powerfully built—naked except for a hide loin cloth—but his face was anything but human. Upward from his chest, tight curly hair carpeted what there was of a neck and all of the face and head. Large intelligent eyes peaked out from the fur above a short stubby nose with flared nostrils and a broad mouth with pointed cuspids jutting out over thin lips. Neenahwi was taken with how much he looked like a buffalo, though there was none of the bovine indifference.

"Welcome," said Neenahwi, giving a small bow.

"It is I that welcomes you, child. I have been waiting for you," he said, every word enunciated clearly, at odds with his beastly appearance.

"Who are you?"

"I am no-one. I am not your guide in this awakening. Merely an observer."

"You will watch over me?" asked Neenahwi.

"Yes. No man, nor creature, will enter this clearing while you stay within this circle. I will ensure it."

"Thank you," she said, unsure what else to ask this strange man in front of her.

"Good bye, Neenahwi. I will leave you to your solitude, and your other visitors to come. I will see you on the 'morrow."

She nodded silently and watched as the buffalo-man turned and melted into the darkness.

∽

"WAKE UP, LITTLE WOLF."

Neenahwi opened her eyes. She must have drifted off. Or given that she was lying in the middle of her stone circle, her arm as a pillow, she must have completely flaked out. Did she hear someone speak? Was the buffalo-man back? But she thought she had heard them say 'little wolf'. Only one person had called her that...

"Mother?" Neenahwi scrambled to a sitting position. Before her was a woman that she had not seen for so long, except in dreams. Her memory had become fuzzy, given the passage of time. Now she saw a woman standing proud in a simple brown dress and Neenahwi's memories came flooding back. Neenahwi inspected the face of her mother, gorging on the sight of her. They looked so alike! The image of what she would see when she looked in a mirror.

"Yes, my Neeni," said her mother, smiling broadly, a tear trickling down her cheek. "It is so good to see you. How you have grown!"

"Oh, mother!" she cried, scrambling to her feet to take her in an embrace, longing to feel her, have her stroke her hair like she used to—

"Stop!" said the older woman. "You must not leave the circle. Regain control, Neenahwi."

Neenahwi stopped, one foot raised above the west facing stone. She so wanted to hold her mother again. It struck her that she could see the silhouette of the tree through her Mother's form. She wanted to scream at the unfairness of this, but she did not want to appear immature before her mother. She wanted her mother to be proud of her.

"You are a vision? Are you here to tell me what I should do?"

"Little wolf, no one is going to tell you what to do," said

her mother, a kind smile on her face. "I am to share your vision. To guide you. Though I had thought your father would be here too. I don't know what we will see here today, but do so with confidence that I am with you. That I will always be with you."

Neenahwi felt unsteady on her feet—hunger and warring emotions taking their toll—so she slid to the ground and rested on her knees, her eyes never leaving the apparition before her. She wanted to have time to talk to her mother; discuss her life, tell her how people always left her. But she knew that was not why her mother was here. "I am ready, mother. How do we begin?"

"Your readiness is enough." Her mother called out in an ululating cry, a wavering, high pitched song, the call used in her tribe to mark momentous occasions; a birth, a death, a marriage. And now her mother called it out to welcome her awakening. Neenahwi found her voice rising in communion.

And the visions came.

∾

BLUE STREAKED WITH WHITE, ABOVE AND BELOW.

A pelican flying across the ocean, arriving at shores of unspoilt beauty, descending to land on a strip of clean white beach.

Sand under feet, though there was no familiar crunch of her feet in the shifting sand. The pelican stretched and bulged in impossible ways, the rest of the world faded away as she found herself transfixed on a horrendous transformation. Legs extended to many times their initial length, sprouting fur and ending in cloven hooves. The wings grew too, but each spurt of growth added a new joint like a twisting vine, until they ended in pointed shards of bone. The pelican's head was pushed off its neck, falling to the beach, as an insectile head took its place, antennae cleaning away ichor that covered its multi-faceted eyes. The feathers across its body fell away too, replaced by a shiny hard black surface.

She had seen this creature before, and only too recently. The demon that had gone unnoticed in human form as Gawl Tegyr.

The demon Gawl stood at full height, twice as tall as a grown man, and looked toward a range of mountains that appeared in the distance. It launched into a lurching run, and the world sped by.

Was this how fast this creature really traveled, or did time move differently?

She did not know. Grassland gave way to thick forest and the demon did not stop or slow. The forest ended and the demon clambered up sheer mountain cliffs to reach snowy peaks, then descended by a series of leaps from rocky crags that would make a mountain goat ashamed. The mountain range behind it and vast grasslands ahead, the demon picked up the pace—running on all fours, its scythe-like arms reaching to the earth to pull it forward.

Neenahwi knew this path. She had walked it in the opposite direction with Motega and Kanaveen, though it had taken her many months. This was her homeland.

The demon stopped. Trails of smoke rose into the air near the horizon. A settlement. Was this when the Gawl demon had led the attack on her home? But he was alone, not accompanied by soldiers wearing steel. The demon crawled through the grasses, moving much more slowly, until Neenahwi could see the outline of buildings ahead. And then the demon was gone. Her presence had been right by its shoulder, like she was dragged along by a short leash. Where could it have gone?

And then the world melted away...

...TO BE REPLACED BY GIGANTIC BLADES OF GRASS THAT swayed in the breeze all around her. She shrieked in surprise, as she turned to face a giant flea. It leapt forward and she felt herself tugged along with it.

The flea was the demon. It's fore limbs still wickedly sharp and extended.

It hitched a ride on a field mouse, then a hawk which snapped up the mouse from the grass. They flew in the air, circling over the plain before sweeping over the settlement toward the bird's roost.

And then they were falling, the flea bounding off the bird's back into the open sky. For a creature so small, the fall seemed like forever. But as Greytooth, their tribe's shaman, had taught her: the earth waits for all, and the tiny insect landed with a bounce. It lay still for a moment, until its massive rear legs kicked and brought it upright. A camp dog wandered by and the flea jumped into the matted fur...

...THEY WERE IN A DARK CIRCULAR HUT, A FIRE BURNING in the center, the smoke rising out from a hole in the center of the roof. The flea demon's epipharynx was stuck in the dog's flesh, and Neenahwi watched in revulsion as instead of sucking blood from the dog, it pumped a green liquid into the animal.

"Get out, you mangy animal," cried a voice beside the fire.

The dog whined and approached, its head down and tail between its legs. A figure came into view. A man, head shorn completely of hair, with swirling tattoos covering his skull.

Neenahwi recognized him. This was her old teacher. Her father's advisor. This was Greytooth, the Wolfclaw clan's shaman.

"OK, you can have some dinner," said Greytooth, reaching out a hand to scratch the dog behind the ear while he fed it something from his hand.

The flea withdrew its needle-sharp proboscis from the dog and leapt onto the shaman's foot, bounding up his body, unfelt and unseen in the poor light. It reached his shoulder and the nape of his neck. The saw-like mandibles of the flea cut open a tiny incision in Greytooth's flesh and the epipharynx plunged in, green liquid flowing into the wound...

...GREYTOOTH SAT WITH HIS HANDS HELD CLOSE TO THE fire as if warming them, but the flames leaned forward to lick around his fingers. The shaman's face was contorted, as if in pain, interrupted occasionally by violent spasms that would start around his eyes and reverberate through his body. To Neenahwi he looked like he was at war with himself, and it was some moments before peace came. When it did, the flames rose further around Greytooth's arms, rising around his bare muscular shoulders and then down to cover his entire person. Neenahwi screamed for her old teacher, in fear he would be consumed by flame, though he raised no alarm himself and did not hear her cries.

The flames fell away and Neenahwi sighed in relief.

But it wasn't Greytooth sitting there now. It was her father. Sharef, chief of the tribe.

Her father stood and walked out of the hut, Neenahwi tugged along into the darkness behind him. He walked purposefully through the village of the Wolfclaw clan, quiet in the night, until he reached the wooden building that was the meeting hall of her tribe.

And Neenahwi's childhood home.

Sharef walked through the open area where the tribe came together to a doorway hung with an animal hide. He pulled it aside, traveling through two more rooms until he reached an area she recognized well. Her parents' sleeping room.

Lying on a pile of animal furs on the hard floor was a sleeping woman, bare skin exposed where a blanket had fallen away. Her father walked forward and undressed, pooling his clothes on the floor. The woman stirred.

"Sharef, is that you?" asked Neenahwi's mother. "I didn't think you would be back from the hunt until tomorrow?"

"I missed you, Manari, so I ran home," he said as he slipped under the covers.

"Hmmm," Manari purred as the man who was not her father touched her. "I am the luckiest one." Her mother turned and pulled her father's mouth to hers...

...SHE WAS BACK IN GREYTOOTH'S HUT NOW. SHE FELT untethered. Gawl was gone. She did not know where, but she felt she was no longer attached to his presence. Neenahwi moved around the hut in the pitch black, sure she was alone until she heard a shudder and a wet sniffle.

There, in the corner, was someone curled into a ball,

rocking gently backward and forwards. Neenahwi approached, crouching down in front of him, unable to see his face as it was buried in his arms and facing the floor. He was muttering something to himself.

"I'm sorry, my love. I'm sorry, Manari," he repeated, his shaven tattooed head shaking back and forth...

~

"No!"

A scream of utter pain ripped through the night and pulled Neenahwi gratefully from Greytooth's hut and back to her stone circle. The ghost of Neenahwi's mother, Manari, was on her knees and looked like the world had just been pulled out from under her.

"No!" she screamed again. "You bastard, Greytooth. You bastard."

Neenahwi struggled to process all she had just seen as the buffalo-man materialized from the shadows to stand beside her mother.

"Come with me," he said to Manari. "You have seen enough."

"Why?" she asked. "Why did you bring me here to see this? Why?"

"Because you deserved to know the truth as much as Neenahwi. Truth is hard but ignorance is a dream. You can go now to your rest."

Her mother faded away, her keening wail lingering after her as Neenahwi reached out for her, distraught.

The world swirled around Neenahwi, nausea rising in her throat. "Tell me," she said. "What did I see?"

"You don't need me to tell you what your own eyes saw,"

said the buffalo-man. "What you did not see, is that you were born nine moons after that night."

"My father is Greytooth?"

"Who can say for certain? Sharef returned the next day."

"Did the demon compel Greytooth to do it?"

"Greytooth had loved your mother since they were children. Though shaman cannot marry, he still loved her with all of his heart. But he was not simply compelled to follow these urges; it was more than that. The demon possessed him. The green venom you saw was the method of the demon's invasion, and though Greytooth tried to fight it, he was weak." The note of distaste in the buffalo-man's voice at the shaman's inability to resist was unmistakable. "He saw all that happened—detached, separate from his own body—and he was unable to do anything. At least the memories of his evil actions tormented him until the day he died."

Neenahwi's chest heaved in shuddering gasps. Who was she? *What* was she? She leaned forward until her forehead touched the cold bare earth and closed her eyes.

~

SLOWLY, HER PULSE RETURNED TO NORMAL AND THE pounding vein in her temple reduced to an occasional flutter, the deep breaths brought calm to her body while the cold of the earth cooled her brain. Neenahwi lifted her head and saw the buffalo-man standing motionless.

"You're still here?" she asked wearily. "Are we done? Can I go?"

"You can always leave," he said flatly, "but you are not done. It is necessary for you to understand your past, and eventually accept it, if you are to decide on your future course. Do you wish to continue?"

Neenahwi considered the question carefully. Right then she wanted nothing more than to run to Motega and Kanaveen and hold them in her arms. Her one link to her past life that hadn't been torn away. But should she tell them about who might be her true father? That was something to think on later. Now, she had to know more. If there was knowledge available then she knew she could never pass it up, even at the risk of physical danger, or here, with her sanity on the line.

"Yes," she said, sitting upright, trying to project determination, even though she suspected she failed.

"Good!" boomed the buffalo-man. His hands came together with a wicked clap and the clearing disappeared.

～

NEENAHWI STOOD NEAR THE CENTER OF A DIFFERENT stone circle. This was many times larger, and the floor was made of slabs of marble. She turned slowly on the spot, taking in her surroundings to see ancient trees fringing the circle, six equally spaced thorough-fares in the forest showed the way to and from the circle. And at the center of the circle was a round stone table, with six chairs and six occupants.

They looked vaguely human, but stretched. Though they were seated she could tell they were over six feet tall, and they were slender, with long thin faces and high brows. Their ears were pointed and their eyes were cat like, almond shaped pupils in iridescent irises. This was where the similarity in their appearance ended; the attendees varied in skin color—pale, dark, even grey—and they dressed in differing styles. Neenahwi peered at them closely from her vantage point behind the nearest elf, for that is clearly what they were.

They did not move, as if time had stopped for everyone but her, allowing her a moment to think.

Elves. Gone from the Jeweled Continent for more than a thousand years. The first settlers of the great wooded lands to the south; she had read how they had been isolationists but largely peaceful toward the other races. Jyuth had told her of his attempts to visit with them in his youth, but never being able to penetrate the forest. All that remained of the elves were their lands and just one of their kind.

Llewdon. The smiling, foul-minded beast that had destroyed her life.

"Why have you called us here, Llewdon?" asked a dark-skinned elf across the table.

Neenahwi jumped, doubly surprised as this counsel of elves came to life, and in hearing the name of the person she had been quietly cursing. The elf whose back was to her, the one closest, answered. "How like you, Thalander. Getting to the point as quickly as possible."

"How like you to be long winded. Get on with it," said Thalander. "We have shared enough chit chat about our families, the state of our people, and I for one do not want to hear any more about Gabrial's travels." An elven woman to his right furrowed her brow, though Neenahwi thought she looked more amused than angry.

"Fine," said Llewdon. "We have lost delight in each other's company. I see. I shall *get to the point*. The wizard Myank has disappeared in, how shall I put it, strange circumstances."

Myank? Neenahwi had heard that name recently. She racked her brain, forcing down the swirl of emotions so she could concentrate. *The letter!* Jyuth's letter had named him as his teacher.

"What strange circumstances?" asked another elvish woman, her long brown hair tied atop her head in a bun, accentuating her long neck.

"A better question would be, what do we care?" said Thalander.

"We care because he is powerful, he is human, and he has been teaching students," replied Llewdon in evident frustration. *Students.* So Jyuth was not the only one. Neenahwi's mind raced; are there others out there somewhere like him? "We have discussed this before. Our magic keeps our lands safe from invaders, but the humans continue to spread like a plague. Myank could threaten our border if he was so inclined. We do not know his like and he warrants our attention."

"Hmph, don't lecture me Llewdon," said Thalander. "Continue if you must."

"Tell me," said Llewdon, looking around the table, "did any of you notice something strange two days after the last full moon? For want of a better description, a flare, at the edge of your perceptions?"

The other elves looked at each other before Gabrial nodded, the others following suit, even Thalander.

"I thought so. It came from the region of the Sapphire Sea. I believe that Myank has left this world."

"He's dead?" asked Gabrial.

"Sounds like that solves our problem," said the elvish woman with the bun.

"Fionara, I think it only makes our situation more troublesome. I don't believe he is dead. His six apprentices have scattered. But Myank, I believe, has ascended." Llewdon let those words hang in the air, looking each of his compatriots in turn. "I believe he has become a god."

"Oakblight!" exclaimed Thalander. "Through all of our studies, none of us have discovered evidence of gods. Our fair share of demons. But gods? Stories for lesser beings who need to understand why their crops fail."

Neenahwi moved around the table so as to be better able to see Llewdon, who now regarded his tormentor in chief with a steely gaze, but she could tell he tried his best to keep his voice in check. "Whether you want to call them gods or not, I do not care, Thalander. These are beings of more energy than we can muster, and a *human* has achieved this. What foul treachery will he bring on us now?"

"How do you know Myank bears us ill will? He has never born us ill before," said Fionara.

"It sounds to me like you are jealous," said an elf who had not spoken yet, his voice deeper than all of the others', pale skinned with hair cut close to his head.

"What are you talking about, Rananon? Why would I be jealous?"

"You tell me," Rananon growled. "I just heard the way you talked about him. We know you are the strongest of us in the ways of magic, and that is a fact that most of us don't really give a fig about. But I've long suspected that your obsession with Myank developed from a fear he was better than you. And now you have your proof."

Llewdon slapped his open palms down on to the table. "You dare accuse me of selfish motives. I bring this to your attention because I care about our people."

Rananon and Llewdon stared across the table at each

other, neither speaking. It was Thalander who broke the silence.

"What Llewdon tells us is of concern, *if* this human wizard now has more power at his fingertips. They are a fickle lot who shift with the tides," Llewdon shifted his attention, visibly surprised at the unexpected source of help. "It at least warrants more study. We may need plans to improve our defenses. My people are closest to the humans and we will be at the front line of any war."

"I think, Thalander," said Llewdon smiling, "that what you propose is the perfect course of action."

THE WORLD MELTED AWAY ONCE MORE, THE OPEN AIR replaced by a round white chamber, crafted of marble with no visible seam. Tall windows, open to the warm air, spaced the walls, and through them Neenahwi could see white towers reaching high above a dense forest. The room was empty except for two figures. Llewdon, standing tall and dressed in robes of white and silver, and before him a woman suspended a foot from the floor, chained hand and foot. She was naked, and her arms stretched at her shoulder sockets from her own hanging weight. Neenahwi screamed at the elf to free the woman, the memories of how Kanaveen had been imprisoned flooding back to her. She thought momentarily to attack the elf; with her fists, her teeth, with whatever she could lay her hands on. But Llewdon did not turn at her cry.

"You tried to enter our forest," said Llewdon, interrogating his prisoner. "Why?"

"I-I-I was only looking to explore," said the woman. "Myank told us to gather knowledge in the world."

"What is your name? And stop trying to struggle. These

chains stop you from weaving. I can ask my Incisitor to return if you wish."

"I am Tarra. I meant no harm," she stuttered. Neenahwi surveyed the prisoner's body with pity, seeing it crossed with cuts that had been roughly healed. *Was this the work of this Incisitor?*

"So, Tarra, you are an apprentice of Myank?" The woman nodded. "I don't recall seeing you before, but you all seem so alike to me how does anyone tell the difference? What are the names of the others? How many of you are there?"

"S-s-six. Serenus, Ridwan, Kirjath, Wilpert and Jyuth." Neenahwi's ears pricked at the mention of her adopted father. She had only just discovered that his teacher had been this Myank person. A name she had never heard of before a few weeks ago. But there had been other students like her father?

"Were they with you?" asked Llewdon. The woman shook her head in answer. "Good. And it is fortunate for you that you are telling the truth. I can tell if you try to deceive me." His lips parted in a manic smile, his voice softer. Suddenly, he snapped, "Where is Myank?"

Tarra closed her eyes and turned her head, refusing to answer.

"Tell me!" cried Llewdon. "Where has he gone?" Tarra shook her head, unable to look Llewdon in the eye now. Neenahwi's magic eye, the part of her sensitive to the use of sorcery, saw a tendril of green leap from Llewdon like a sharp needle into Tarra's breast, creating a connection into her life force. Llewdon channeled that energy into himself, taking it and weaving the threads of magical energy into a thousand tiny sharp nails that materialized and pierced Tarra's flesh.

Neenahwi saw the skin depress under the force of one nail until it ruptured, blood flowing around it.

Neenahwi's hands went to her face in horror. *The pain must be enormous.*

With a small movement of Llewdon's hands, the nails began to push downward, dragging long jagged rips in Tarra's body. "You are nothing to me girl. I can steal your mana to torment you. Take your own life and use it to give you the most excruciating death you ever imagined. Tell me where Myank has gone, and how he did it."

Tarra screamed, eyes bulging wide. Her head nodded in agreement.

THE MARBLE STONE CIRCLE APPEARED AGAIN AND Neenahwi's head swirled at the changing scenery and what she had just witnessed. Llewdon was there, along with the other elves from the last vision, though the circle was bare of furniture now. She turned, surveying the edges of the forest, thinking that something looked different... and she noticed with a start that between the trees stood many more elves, keeping their distance from the conversations of their elders.

"Friends," said Llewdon. "This is a momentous day. The day when we ensure our safety and our future."

"Are you sure this will work, Llewdon?" asked Gabrial. "We have brought all of our people, even our children, for this undertaking. It can't all be for naught."

"I have spent the past year practicing, perfecting what must be done. I know it will work. Together, we will create a golden wall that will keep out all other races, and our home will be safeguarded. Will we step away from this opportunity to finally be protected from the wider world and the chaos it brings?" A chorus of 'nays' came in answer. "Good, then let us begin. Stand with your people. I will take only what is needed."

The elven leaders bowed to each other before walking over to the forest circling the stone slab, taking their place in front of their people. Neenahwi slowly stepped back to the edge of the marble, sensing that something was coming.

Five threads floated out from Llewdon, like yarn on the breeze, attaching to the elders. The threads split thousands of times, arching into the air and snaring the other elves standing nearby until all of the elves were connected to Llewdon. And then he began to draw on the vast well of life force that Neenahwi imagined lived within all of these beings. *What power! How could he use so much?*

Llewdon shone with a bright white light. One elf fell to his knees. It was one of Thalander's people, and he called out, "Enough, Llewdon. You take too much. Build the wall!"

"Do not worry, my friend. I take only what I need. When I become a god I shall bring you all back. When I am a god, I will be the ultimate protection for the elves."

"Treachery!" called Rananon.

"You are mad, Llewdon," called Gabrial. "Stop this!"

"You mistake my greatness, Gabrial. But I forgive you."

More elves fell to the floor, some unmoving, some shaking with the tremors, and still the energy flowed into Llewdon.

"I curse you, Llewdon," cried Fionara. She screamed, and her nose and ears began to bleed. "You, who of all of us is so enamored with destruction. I curse you. Though you have my life you shall destroy no more!"

Calls of 'I curse you' swept around the wooded circle, elder and follower crying out.

"Enough!" cried Llewdon and he pulled the remnants of their life from all who surrounded him, the power moving with such force and speed that Neenahwi felt her ears popping. She watched, distressed, as many thousands of elves tumbled to the ground, unmoving. Llewdon raised his arms in the air, his brilliance intensifying by the second. A beam of light shot into the blue sky, and then, he was gone.

Neenahwi found herself alone. It was eerily quiet. No animals or birds had remained to witness this slaughter. No mothers or fathers remained to keen their lost children. All were dead. She had never seen such a display of magic before. Or the depth of Llewdon's trickery. She buried her eyes in her hands, hiding from the devastation, wondering why the vision had not ended.

Crack.

Displaced air buffeted Neenahwi. The noise echoed in the empty world. She took her hands away from her eyes, and lying in the center of the marble circle was Llewdon. Broken. Bloodied. And not looking very god like.

~

THE FOREST CLOSED IN ON HER. THE MARBLE BECAME BARE earth. The circle was now the river stones she had spent so much time selecting. It had been night here a moment before. Now the sun was shining down from directly over-head. And the buffalo-man towered over her.

"History repeats itself," he said. "Lessons are not learned. Now, Neenahwi, what will be your role? Do something. Do nothing. This is your choice." The buffalo-man turned and walked into the undergrowth.

"Wait!" called Neenahwi. But the buffalo-man had gone.

~

SHE HAD LAIN CURLED UP IN HER STONE CIRCLE FOR SOME
time after the buffalo-man had deserted her. At first her
thoughts went back to the revelations around her birth and
the possibility of Greytooth being her father. *It seemed her
father issues began earlier than she recognized?* She knew that
Sharef was still her father. He was the man who had brought
her up. Greytooth had always been there for her too, like a
favorite uncle. When they had both gone, Kanaveen took on
the responsibility of looking after her and her brother, but it
was different. He saw her as his chief, as well as a child he
had to protect for the memory of his best friend.

Finally she had Jyuth, the ancient wizard who had done
more than anyone else to help her discover her talents and to
master them. Most importantly, he had been the one to
rescue her from Llewdon when they had been captured,
risking his life to save an unknown girl. And now he had
gone too, slinking off to who knows where and leaving her
with this mess of a world.

Neenahwi was struck by the memory of her mother's
face as she had shared the revelation. It was a look of horror.
Was it the discovery of her rape by a close friend? Or was her
mother now ashamed of her? Not the child of her loving
husband as she had thought she was? These thoughts
brought back the tears. She cried at the sheer unfairness of
everything. Hadn't she been through enough? Things had
been getting better. She had been controlling her temper.
Enjoying her studies. And in the space of a few months, her
life had been turned upside down once more.

Anger burned away her tears at the thought of the
demon possessing Greytooth. Why hadn't he fought harder?

Pieces started to tumble into place. Only now did Gawl's words make sense, from when they fought in Kingshold. *You look so much like her.* Damn, she should have left some part of him alive to find out why. Why did Llewdon have him travel so far to her tribe? What was special about them? About her? She should have spared him when he pleaded with her, but killing the destroyer of her people had felt so... right.

Llewdon. Thinking of the crazed elf sparked a burning fire in her empty belly, driving her to her feet. Her fists clenched by her side as she thought on how this had all started.

Jealousy.

Of another man's achievements. And he was willing to sacrifice his entire people to attain them himself. Tens of thousands of elves died on that day, whole families brought together in the common goal of self-protection, candles snuffed out to make the bonfire bright. And for all that he had failed. His broken body testimony to that. Neenahwi considered the power he had absorbed, unable to process what would be able to withstand such an onslaught.

Neenahwi cursed whoever didn't finish the job and kill him then. How her life would have been different.

The curse! A thousand curses from a thousand dying souls. *You shall destroy no more.* Neenahwi didn't know what that meant, how that had impacted Llewdon; but maybe it had been enough to throw him off his stride at a crucial moment. Llewdon still lived, and he still destroyed. Maybe not through magic, but his armies and agents sowed salt around the world. She was evidence of this.

Two visions, of two different times. And only one thing connected the two. Llewdon.

History is repeating itself. The buffalo-man had said that.

Jyuth had written that in his good-bye letter too. And she had a choice; stand by and watch whatever is repeating happen again, or do something about it. She had wanted a purpose. A meaning in her life. Jyuth had pointed her in this direction too, but it had felt like another instance of cleaning up his mess. Now she understood that this was something even greater than her father. She wanted a purpose. And now she had it, though she knew not how to proceed.

"On the spirits of my ancestors, on all of the gods of *my* home," she said out loud, "I swear I will kill you, Llewdon."

Neenahwi threw her head back and let out a great primal scream, a circle of force expanded out from her, breaking her circle, stones sent flying across the clearing.

The ceremony was over. Neenahwi was reborn.

~

THE WOLF SAT ON ITS HAUNCHES, WATCHING MOTEGA AND Kanaveen spar. Both were stripped to their waist, the sweat shining on their bodies evidence they had been at it for some time. Both wielded steel shod wooden staves and the sound of parried blows had carried into the forest. The wolf had run with abandon, happy to feel the rush of the air in its fur, all the way to the edge of the trees and this little wooden house.

It trotted over to the two men. Kanaveen had seen the wolf, pausing to look more closely and allowing Motega to strike him in the gut. He doubled over.

"Ufff," grunted Kanaveen. "Foul, little hawk. Look who returns."

Motega looked in the direction that Kanaveen pointed and went into the wooden house, returning with a blanket.

The wolf's image shifted and warped, the air turning hazy and distorted, and out of the miasma stood Neenahwi. Motega wrapped his naked sister in the blanket.

"Hello, sis," he said. "How are you? Hungry?"

"I ate on the way back," she said, the taste of bloody hare fresh in her mouth even after reverting back. But the sight of her brother and Kanaveen were a meal for her soul. "Been keeping busy?"

"You could say that. Kanaveen is still beating me five out of ten spars, even at his age."

Kanaveen poked Motega with one of his sticks, breathing a little heavier than he used to after training. "Watch it. Next time I'll actually try."

Neenahwi felt the older man's gaze on her but said nothing. Kanaveen nodded and then sat on the grassy earth cross legged, beckoning her to follow suit.

"Tell me. What did you see?"

Neenahwi had resolved not to share all she had learned during her time in the stone circle. In particular the revelations of who her father might be. Not yet. She had to... come to terms with it first. But she had questions that she hoped she could get some answers to. "Kanaveen, who is the buffalo-man?"

Kanaveen looked quizzical and shrugged his shoulders. "He was part of your vision?"

"No. He watched over me outside the stone circle. And he knew what the visions were. He was tall, half covered in tight curly fur, and his face resembled a buffalo."

"I don't know, Neeni," said Kanaveen. "I have not heard of such a person before, though I have heard many strange stories of the Quana in the past. It sounds like he meant you no ill will though. Maybe it is a question that will be answered in time."

"What about you, Motega, did he appear for you?"

"No. Just father. And he's been bothering my dreams ever since. Did you see him too?"

"No. I saw mother," she said, ending that line of conversation. "I also saw Llewdon."

Motega tensed. It was not only her that had suffered at the elf's hands. All three of them had been captured and taken to the emperor in his city of Fymrius. All knew who was behind the death of their family and friends. Kanaveen nodded, betraying no other reaction.

"That does not surprise me, Neenahwi," said Kanaveen. "What did you learn?"

"I have to stop him. He killed all his own people trying to become a god. The buffalo-man said history is repeating itself. I have to stop him."

"What is he going to do?" asked Motega.

"I don't know," she said, shaking her head. "I don't know. We have to work that out." Neenahwi looked directly into her brother's eyes and reached out to hold his hand. "Motega, get ready; it's time that we had our revenge."

GLOSSARY

Groups

HIGHER GUILDS:

Engineers
Law
Merchants
Money Changers
Shipwrights
Weavers
Hollow Syndicate (Unofficial Status)

LOWER GUILDS:

Artists
Bakers
Brewers

Butchers
Craftsmen
Doctors and Druggists
Ironworkers
Saddle Makers and Tanners
Stonemason
Twilight Exiles (Unofficial Status)

KINGSHOLD DISTRICTS AND SUPERVISORS

Fishtown - Eldrida
Warehouse - Gonal
Central Market - Aldo
Docks - Colbert
Garden - Hertha
Cherry Tree - Jules
Fourwells - Win
Golden - Geary
Lance - Row
Redguard - Ifig
Whiteguard - Garet
Inner Narrows - Dyer
Outer Narrow - Lud
Four Points - Lowell
Garmond - Yetta
Bottom Run - Denley
Woodton - Odam
Randall's Addition - Nara
Arloth's Acre - Paine
Beggar's Point - Medwyn

CAST OF CHARACTERS

AIOLA: Sister of Florian
ALANA: Palace maid, sister to Petra
LORD AMPHREY : Former friend of Eden
ARGO: Student at the Hollow House
ARTUR DANWEAZEL: Merchant, dealer of under-the-table wares and giver of extraction jobs to Motega, Trypp and Florian
AYMER: Dyer's friend
BARRAG: Student at the Hollow House
BEKAH: Fence and dealer of fine objects. Resident of Carlburg
CARLISS: Pirate in charge of the galley slaves aboard *The Scythe*
LADY CHALICE : Managing partner of the Hollow Syndicate, rescuer of Neenahwi and Motega
CREED: Wannabe pirate, friend of Karr
DIBBLER: Purveyor of pies
DORIEN: Student at the Hollow House
DUBH: Pirate of *The Icicle*
DUKE OF NORTHFIELD: Brother of King Roland, Pienzan duke
DUG: Squad member of the Ravens
DYER: District supervisor for The Inner Narrows
LORD EDEN : Savior of Redsmoke, war hero, richest man in Edland
ELIZA: Wife of Lord Eden
FINABRIA: Originally of Ioth; student at the Hollow House
FIONARA: An elf
FLATHEAD: Squad member of the Ravens

FLORIAN: Friend to Motega and Trypp, originally introduced by Jyuth. Veteran of foreign wars, including the liberation of Redpool, mercenary for hire
FOLA: Leader of a cleaner squad
FORGER: Elected leader of the dwarves of Unedar Halt
GABRIAL: An elf
GARRELONT: Sheriff of Stableford
GAWL TEGYR: Bearer of Light, Bringer of Peace, Ambassador of Pyrfew
GILSTRAP: Captain of the pirate ship *The Icicle*
GREYTOOTH: Shaman of the Wolfclaw clan
LORD HALTON : Former friend of Eden
HRODEBERT: Necromancer and entrepreneur
JILESA: Student at the Hollow House
JOE: Squad member of the Ravens
JULES: Owner and landlady of the Royal Oak
JYUTH: Wizard, founder of Edland, adopted father of Neenahwi
KANAVEEN: Wolfclaw champion and protector of Neenahwi and Motega after the flight. Lives in the wilderness of Edland.
KARR: Pirate
KOLSEN: Pirate King
KYLE: Chiseler of Unedar Halt
LLEWDON: Emperor of Pyrfew, wizard, ancient, elf
LAY: Pirate of *The Icicle*
LUD: District supervisor for The Outer Narrows
MADGE: Wife of Lud
MANARI: Mother of Neenahwi and Motega
MARETH: Son of Lord Bollingsmead, bard, former adventurer, former pirate.
MIDNIGHT: Squad member of the Ravens

MOLEY: Squad member of the Ravens

MORRIS: Sergeant of the Ravens

MOTEGA: Warrior and archer of renown from the wild continent, Brother to Neenahwi, mercenary for hire.

MYANK: Wizard, teacher of Jyuth

NAIL: Pirate of *The Icicle*

NANNY EARMA: Dyer's great-aunt

NATHAN: Son of Lord Eden

NEENAHWI: Of the Wolfclaw clan, wizard, adopted daughter of Jyuth and older sister to Motega

NINI: Lud's grandmother

ORMAN: Lud's best friend

PAVAK: A purple worm

PETRA: Bar maid at the Royal Oak, sister to Alana

QETURAH: Student at the Hollow House

RANANON: An elf

SHAREF: Former chief of the Wolfclaw tribe, Motega and Neenahwi's father

SHEILA: Undead

STEPPEN: Treasurer of the Hollow Syndicate

TALBOT: First mate of *The Icicle*

THALANDAR: An elf

TOM: Student at the Hollow House

TORKEL: Priest of Varcon and juggernaut pilot

TRYPP: Friend to Motega and Florian. Former thief with the Twilight Exiles

TUFT: Neenahwi's cat

VIDIN: A purple worm

WENDA: Wife of Dyer

WREN: Guildmaster of the Money Changers guild

XATANIEL: Selkie sorceress

CALL TO ACTION

Thanks for reading the further adventures of Mareth, Alana, Neenahwi, Motega and a few new characters. I hope you enjoyed it. I would appreciate you leaving a few remarks or comments on Amazon or Goodreads, and of course, telling your friends the good old fashioned way. It's this reader led communication that helps to spread the word and get others interested in trying this book.

You can sign up for my newsletter to be notified of future releases, opportunities to become a beta reader, and behind-the-scenes discussion of what went into the making of my books. Also, if you want to drop me a line, please do. My email address is dave@dpwoolliscroft.com.

ABOUT THE AUTHOR

Born in Derby in England, on the day before midsummer's day, David Peter Woolliscroft was very nearly magical. If only his dear old mum could have held on for another day. But magic called out to him over the intervening years, with many a book being devoured for its arcane properties. David studied Accounting at Cardiff University where numbers weaved their own kind of magic, and he has since been a successful business leader in the intervening twenty years.

Adventures have been had. More books have been devoured; and then one day, David had read enough where the ideas he had kept bottled up needed a release valve. And thus, rising out of the self-doubt like a phoenix at a clicky keyboard, a writer was born. You can keep up to date on all new releases, and get exclusive stories and excerpts of works in progress, at www.dpwoolliscroft.com.

He is married to his wife Haneen and has a daughter Liberty, who all live with their mini goldendoodle Rosie in Princeton NJ. David is one of the few crabs to escape the crab-pot.

f 𝕏

ACKNOWLEDGMENTS

It has been six months since I published Kingshold and it's been an exciting time. I truly wasn't sure how it would be received, as I know that it is a little different than the typical fantasy novel. But I am pleased to say that it has been well received and it has given me the much-needed boost to keep writing (if you haven't noticed, authors are an insecure lot).

I'd like to take a moment to call out some of the bloggers who have supported Kingshold and encouraged me to carry on; Nick Borelli, Olivia Hofer, Patrick Kansa, Jordan Rose, Timy Takács, Esme Weatherwax, and any others that I may have apologetically neglected to call out.

One of the most wonderful things I've encountered is the support from fellow authors; thanks to Dave De Burgh, Phil Parker, William Ray, Travis Riddle and a special thanks to Mark Lawrence for organizing the Self-Published Fantasy Blog Off.

As ever, the book in your hands would not have been possible without the help and support of a number of people.

Firstly, my wife Haneen and daughter Liberty, putting up with me getting up at five in the morning every day to write.

Bethan May is my new editor and she has been a joy to work with, challenging me where it is needed and making this a much better work than it would be otherwise.

I'd also like to thank Jaya Balasubramaniam, Erin Duncan-O'Neil, Ryan Ehrlich, James Polledri, Joe Smith, Mark Watkins and Bernie Zimmermann for their immense help as beta readers once again. I feel for them because they always get to read the unedited version.

And last, but not least, Jeff Brown my illustrator and cover designer who has once again produced the amazing cover to this book.

Thanks again to everyone.

D.P. Woolliscroft
October, 2018

COMING SOON

Ioth, City of Lights

Uncorrected Preview

CHAPTER 1
THE DRAKE

Thrum. Thrum. Thrum.

Bolts a yard long, topped with steel barbs, launched across the hundred feet of sea from *The Drake* to crash across the prow of the lone Pyrfew ship. Neenahwi watched with a mixture of regret and grim satisfaction as sailors were ripped apart by the flurry of missiles from the score of repeating ballistae. She clenched her teeth as the bolts passed through the soft obstacles until they smashed into the wood of the mast or the aft castle.

Admiral Crews had told her that this Pyrfew ship was bigger than what was typical; this beast of creaking wood and sail, five decks, three masts and towers fore and aft, must be a product of the Ioth shipyards. Easily the size of a first-class vessel of the Edland navy.

Neenahwi turned to watch a sheep-sized boulder splash into the water between *The Drake* and *The Orca* following neatly in line behind. The catapult positioned on the aft castle of their prey—it's second shot spent without effect—begin to crank back the arm for a second salvo. But *The Orca* came into range and bolts from its rail-lined ballista tore the catapult to pieces under sustained fire. *Dwarven armaments. Well worth the expense.*

Men ran to the railing on the Pyrfew ship, as if to wave to a passing pleasure cruiser. A dark cloud, moving unnaturally, launched into the sky, a blemish on the brilliant blue sky.

"Take cover!" went the call from the barrelman of *The Drake*. Edland marines and sailors alike ducked under whatever cover was close at hand; shields, lids of barrels or crouching behind timber walls. But Neenahwi did not duck, or cover, or even move.

Arrows thudded all around her. She saw one arrow take a woman armored in hardened leather just below the ear, slicing through her neck and coming out the other side. The marine fell, gurgling, reaching uselessly to her throat as her lifeblood bubbled up from her mouth. Neenahwi instinctively reached out a hand to move to help but she knew she could do nothing. She knew this woman would be but the first of good men and women to die in this conflict; Neenahwi clenched her fists and knew it would be worse if they couldn't prevail.

Above her purple robe, high on her chest, rested a red stone pendant. Blood trickled between her breasts, staining her clothes from the small wound it caused. And arrows that should have rightfully left her looking like a hedgehog stopped a few inches from her person, ricocheting uselessly to the floor. Hardened air surrounded her, one aspect of Neenahwi's mind concentrating on the shield as she watched the attack of the Pyrfew vessel. She knew if she called on the full power of the demon stone that she could have stopped this barrage of arrows—by Marlth, she could have blown this ship out of the water—but she was still mindful of the advice of her father not to draw too deeply on its power. She could feel the rage nagging at the edge of her mind with even this modest use.

"Clear!" went the call from above as *The Drake* passed out of bow range. But the Pyrfew vessel was not so safe. *The Drake* was just the first ship of the line, the flagship of Admiral Crews. Behind came two more first class vessels and another pair of smaller second-class ships. All armed with dwarven made repeating ballistae - the most feared weapon on the three seas. The crew of *The Drake* rushed to the railing or the stern to watch the carnage unfold behind them and Neenahwi found herself calmly drawn to follow.

She climbed the stairs up to the aft castle, noting Crews standing with an eyeglass to his face, calmly dictating orders to both the wheelman and a girl whirling a pair of flags in semaphore. From her vantage point, Neenahwi saw the second ship come under fire from a volley of arrows, but less so than the steel-tipped hail storm they'd just endured—no doubt the archers had been wounded by another broadside of missiles.

The third Edland ship neared within a hundred feet, with its smaller shadow of the next second-class ship close behind, and more destruction was unleashed. Neenahwi couldn't see the bolts flying through the air—their speed was too great and the distance too far. But she could see explosions of wood and flesh as they ripped across the deck. Screams carried in the air over the noise of the sea. The second mast of the Pyrfew ship came under repeated fire and with an audible crack, the tall length holding three sails split like a tree struck from the heavens. The mast buckled, sliding into its tall neighbor before it slid slowly down, ripping down the sails, rigging and the seamen who had been climbing them. The sailors hit the deck of the ship, or the water around them, before the mast finished its journey to crash down.

"Well," said Neenahwi more to herself than anyone in particular, "that should do it."

"Not yet, my lady," said Crews without turning from his lookout. "Let us be certain before we board her. Ensign, signal *The Otter* to engage."

∾

THREE MONTHS HAD PASSED SINCE THE ELECTION. SINCE her father had disappeared in the night—though to be fair, he had warned her he was going to do that.

It had been two months since her Quana, the vision quest where she had to finally accept who she was and why she was still alive. She had to stop Llewdon, god emperor of Pyrfew and destroyer of his own race, before he unleashed who knew what cataclysm on the people of the Jeweled Continent. Or on the remnants of her own people, so very far away.

The visions had brought on a rage within her, seeing Llewdon up so close, even though the events she had witnessed had occurred more than a millennium ago. Seeing the man, or in this case the elf, responsible for the destruction of her family and friends, for her abduction and captivity—even though that seemed trifling given his other horrors—and gaining an understanding that this was all due to some petty jealousy, incensed her.

She wanted his head.

And if she had to go through the people of Pyrfew, the fools who followed and revered this monster, then so be it.

Now, as she walked across a gangplank to the stricken Pyrfew ship, following a few steps behind Admiral Crews, she saw Pyrfew blood bathing the wooden deck. The first blow. Something she had been impatient for. And though the scene disgusted her, she had to remind herself that acts like these would be *necessary*.

Once she had completed her visit with Kanaveen, she had gone back to Mareth, now Lord Protector of Edland, and assumed her father's old role of adviser. She had strategized with him and his counsel; Lady Grey the new chancellor; Crews, the new admiral after that unfortunate incident with Ridgton and the burning brothel; and Lord Marshall Uthridge, another man she thought of as family. They had expected that the new Pyrfew fleet that had set sail from the shipyards of Ioth would mean an attack on Redpool would be forthcoming, but instead it had been quiet seas. Merchants who called Kingshold home had spied Pyrfew ships on the Sapphire Sea, but they had been surprisingly unmolested. And the Edland navy had been frustratingly unsuccessful in their hunt; the Pyrfew fleet proving elusive.

Her father had preached patience. But she needed to do something. Her visions had been for a purpose and she was not achieving anything sitting in Kingshold. So she had lobbied that they take the fight to Pyrfew. Shore up Redpool. Take to the Sapphire Sea in greater numbers and hunt down the fleet. That she could personally cover hundreds of miles a day with a fair wind to find these bastards had swayed the counsel to her side.

The fight that followed the boarding was not much more than a few minutes in length. Two hundred marines from *The Orca* and *The Falcon* had grappled the Pyrfew ship after coming alongside. Pyrfew resistance had been limited after being greatly softened up from the barrage of missiles. But any who had put up a fight had been put down with crossbow or axe. The scene before her was a madman's abattoir; limbs ripped from their owners by the force of the siege engines lay scattered around. Heads caved in by axes or falling timbers presented a grisly welcome. Neenahwi couldn't help but think of her own massacred tribe. Who had stepped through the carnage there once morning had come? She pushed aside a momentary reflection that she was no better than the man she was determined to bring to justice. *No. This had to be done. And it will not be the last.*

She had found this ship. It was Neenahwi who had soared the skies. Not as a goose, but as an albatross, a solitary bird known to be bad luck to sailors. And she had most definitely been the bearer of bad fortune for this vessel.

The Pyrfew crew looked much like that which escorted her; humans of light and dark skin, some old enough to be fathers and others young enough to be their children. Were they evil? Who knew what they may have done in the dark? What they might have done in the future? But she doubted it. This was chattel to Llewdon and she would add it to the list of his crimes.

A man wearing a coat of bright green decorated with brass buttons was pushed through a crowd of captives by a pair of burly marines.

"So, Edland attacks solitary ships at sea, now? Showing your true colors as the pirates you are?" The captain of the captured ship spat at their feet.

Crews ignored his phlegm and his barbs. "What is your name and what are you doing in these waters?"

"I am Captain Bhaga," the man said proudly. "We were patrolling against pirates. We were no threat to you!"

"I find that difficult to believe," snorted Crews. "Since when has Pyrfew had an interest in trade on these seas?"

"What will you do with my crew?" asked Captain Bhaga, ignoring the question. Neenahwi twirled the braid of her hair with her fingers. She didn't believe his story either. But why was there a lone ship when there should be a fleet many times its size?

Crews' voice increased in volume; he wanted the captives on deck to hear this. "Any who have surrendered will be taken to Redpool. From there you will be free. Free to choose to stay in Edland if you wish. Free from your tyrant!"

From the looks on the faces of the prisoners, it didn't seem that most were too excited by this prospect. Real love for their ruler? Or a reluctance to leave their families behind and be branded a traitor?

"Now," said Crews, his voice returning to a conversational tone, "Captain Bhaga. You will be well treated. My personal guest. Tell me, why are you alone? Why leave the safety of your other ships?"

"And spoil any surprise?" A dark smirk spread slowly across Bhaga's face. "I don't think so. I will speak no more."

"Get him out of here," snapped Crews impatiently. "Put him in a guest room on *The Drake*. Two guards at all times." The marines nodded in acknowledgment and marched the captain away. Crews looked at Neenahwi and then guided her toward a quiet area of the deck with a light touch. They stepped over discarded butcher's scraps; Neenahwi lifted her purple robes up around her ankles so as not to spoil the hem. The laundry facilities at sea were not the best.

"Do you know what he hints of? Did you see other ships?"

Neenahwi slowly shook her head. "There was nothing in

sight when I came across this one. But you said it yourself, it's pretty stupid for one ship to be alone."

"Hmmm, sometimes I hate to be right—"

"Sails! Four o'clock!" came a cry from the lookout deck high up the mainmast of *The Drake*.

"Blast." Crews brought his enameled looking-glass to his eye and peered at the horizon. He rested one foot on the ships railing, his profile statuesque with the blue skies as his backdrop; Neenahwi had to admit he did cut quite the dashing figure. What was it about sailors? "I can't see a thing. How many?" he called in return to the lookout, while he scanned the seas.

"Maybe... ten sails!"

"Double blast!" Crews turned back to Neenahwi. "We must be back to the ship, my lady. There is more work to do."

"What if we're outnumbered?" she asked, wrapping her arms across her chest.

"You saw how easily we were victorious today. These crews do not know how to sail their ships yet. My fleet is skilled. Each worth at least three of their vessels. And I do not intend for them to capture our spoils."

"Why not just set it on fire and let's be gone?" said Neenahwi. Something nagged at her. This did not feel right. Why would Llewdon send these ships out to sea that he knew could be picked off by Edland? It might be better to draw these other vessels behind them and set a trap where they could be sure of superior numbers.

Crews, however, looked aghast at the suggestion. "My lady! We do not do that in the Edland navy. They have surrendered and they are under my protection."

Neenahwi sighed. The same code of honor as her Uncle. She wondered how long it would last if war truly erupted.

"Can you conduct a reconnaissance and see what we are dealing with? So we might be prepared?" he asked.

She nodded. Now faced with another battle and the thought of more casualties—even her enemies—she found her blood lust receding. "I'll find you when I am done."

Neenahwi left Crews and crossed the gang plank once more. The swaying of the ship was still something she was uncomfortable with, and now with congealed blood coating her boots and filling her nostrils, she steeled herself not to fall or stumble. She went at once to her quarters at the rear of the ship; a simple private room with a hanging hammock and a cushion on the floor. A double rectangular window let in the light from the stern of the ship—one of her few demands for assisting with this plan. She sure as shit wasn't going to parade around naked before the crew.

She disrobed and flung open the windows. Perching on the window sill, Neenahwi took a deep breath and fragmented her mind, forming an image of the albatross. The hooked beak, the downy white feathers on wings that stretched out wide, the webbed feet; all down to the smallest detail. For those details were important; screw one of those up and the natural elegance of this master of flying would be disrupted.

Neenahwi the albatross leapt into the air, wings beating, unconcerned with the crowds gathered at the railings of the ships nearby watching their wizard at work.

~

SHE HURRIED UP TO THE DECK, STILL FASTENING THE BELT

around her robes after dressing, to find Crews waiting for her.

"There are fifteen ships. We have to get out of here."

The admiral puffed his cheeks and blew, spinning on his heel as he thought. "What do they look like?" he asked.

Neenahwi sighed, frustration and anxiety building within her. "Three as big as this one," she said pointing to the captured ship, bobbing listlessly without sails off their starboard bow. "Twelve smaller ones, with just the one mast."

"Like a scout ship? A trader?"

"I don't bloody know, Crews. I'm a wizard not a fucking fisherman." Not being able to answer his questions more helpfully was painful to her; it wasn't normal for her knowledge to be so limited. But she also thought that it didn't bloody matter given the number of them. "It's more than we have, so why not run? Let's pull them back to Redpool where we have more ships."

Crews fixed a fake smile above his strong jawline. She knew she was pushing him, especially in public like this, but she didn't imagine her father would have been quiet either.

"They won't follow, my lady. They will take back our prize and then we will lose them. We have searched for their new fleet, even a fraction of it, and now with your help we have found them."

"Don't pat me on the head, Crews. I'm not going to just roll over and let you rub my belly. Sink the ship and they'll have nothing."

"I will not!" he barked, almost forgetting his patient facade. But it was just a moment, his varnished exterior returning. "We will meet them, and we will show them who rules the waves. Maybe you would like to retire to your quarters?" He turned on his heel and walked to the aft castle without waiting for a response.

"Not bloody likely," she muttered under her breath, suddenly unsure what to do. She paced a circle as Crews dispatched his orders to the captains that had hastily assembled on *The Drake*. The men and women nodded their acceptance without a word of complaint or challenge and returned to their boats and teams of oarsmen for the short crossing back to their ships.

Neenahwi stood in the center of the main deck, sailors scurried like ants around her; industrious but to what purpose she was not sure. Marines left behind to guard their prize waved to their friends as *The Drake* pushed away. She was in the way. Neenahwi walked to the prow and rested a hand on the great figurehead of the winged drake as she watched the fleet set sail to meet the Pyrfew ships now visible on the horizon.

The breeze was stiff but the surf was little more than a lover's kiss on the hull. The fresh sea air flooded her lungs and she steadied herself. Neenahwi's hand went to her pendant and she could have sworn she felt it pulse in her grip. Releasing her hold she noticed the blood that still wept from the wound; the needle on the pendant's rear had continued to scratch at her flesh, the constant sting of the irritation forgotten. She'd gotten angry with Crews, and in truth, she hadn't really meant to. It was the demon stone. *It seems that with great power, comes the ability to get really pissed off.*

Calls for full sails chained through the sailors on duty and *The Drake* overtook the other ships of Crews' small fleet to take the lead. He was new to the admiral job, and though she was beginning to admire his bravery, she would have to talk with Mareth about getting him to hold the rear in the future

—they didn't need to lose another admiral who felt he had something to prove.

The distance closed quickly, little more than half an hour before the Pyrfew fleet became visible as independent ships. The Pyrfew ships sailed in groups of four, in what appeared to be a fairly tight formation. A larger ship such as the one they fought earlier that day with the smaller ships flanking and one at point. All except for one group of three smaller ships that was missing its big sister—surely the broken ship they had left behind.

"Prepare arms!" came the call from Woodell, Crews' first lieutenant. Marines scurried on deck from their resting places; weapons sharpened, naps taken, or prayers given; she did not know. But this was a well drilled lot. She watched with interest as teams assembled around each of the ballistae, turning the repeating crank to test the mechanism and confirm they had a full complement of armaments.

The Pyrfew ships were less than a mile away now and it felt like the whole crew was holding its breath. All except Woodell, who shouted words of encouragement or admonishment. The silence would be gone soon. The Edland ships came alongside each other, matching speed, heading face-on toward the arrow formations of the Pyrfew fleet.

Half a mile. She could see the ships clearly now. The smaller vessels looked odd—even to her now that she thought about it—quite unlike the scouting ships of Edland. But before she could give it further thought, Woodell called out again.

"Forty-five degrees to port! Line them up!"

The Drake listed as the wheel turned and the sails were set. Neenahwi looked behind to see the other four Edland vessels match course and speed, falling into procession behind them. Ships of the line against their wedge formation.

The turn sent them toward the most northerly of the group of ships. Whether this tactic took their opponents by surprise or not she couldn't say because they did not change their course. They were close now. She could see the smaller ship at the head of the formation clearer now. Its deck was completely clear and glinted in the sunlight; metal sheets? Oars appeared from their holes in the side of the smaller ships and dipped into the white flecked sea in unison, propelling them forward. All of the smaller ships had matching figureheads; something reptilian.

Were these small ships going to ram them? They were so small they wouldn't be able to do anything. So what was going on? It was not like Pyrfew troops to blindly rush to death.

Neenahwi descended from the fore-castle, taking the steps two at a time as she hurried to make her way to Crews, when Woodell called the distance to fire.

"Fire on the lead. Ready, aim, fire!"

Thwum. Thwum.

The silence ended and the chaos began. The steady sound of the ballistae repeating their action. The cranking of the iron cogs and gears. Men and women calling out to each other to adjust the aim. All of this filled the air and Neenahwi couldn't help but find herself drawn to the railing as a moth to a bonfire, eager to see their work.

It was mixed. Some of the initial volley stood out from the wood of the lead ship like whiskers on a teenager's chin, but more skittered off the armored deck to fly uselessly into the sea. *Shit! These ships have a shell.*

"Mast!" went the call from Woodell. The withering fire concentrated on the single mast of the lead ship. It was a tough shot with two moving vessels and the constant shifting of the ballista under its repeating action so most missed the mark. But one hit the target, splitting it a third of the way up. And then another struck, bringing the square-sailed rigging down onto the deck. But the ship did not stop. The oars beat a steady rhythm. It did not change course.

A great rattle of wood and metal, ropes and pulleys were audible across the sea. Neenahwi watched in trepidation as huge stones fired into the air from the larger ship of each group. Neenahwi had not rebuilt her defenses, so mesmerized was she with the action all around her. She closed her eyes and fractured her mind, once and then again. One aspect of her consciousness pulled on a thin thread of raw power from the demon stone and weaved it once more into a shield in front of her, the hardened air pushing aside marines standing by her side. The other aspect of Neenahwi remained waiting, alert—she needed to be ready.

The rock sailed through the air serenely, growing larger and larger. It was falling too close to *The Drake*, it might even hit it and she didn't want to risk that. The other aspect of Neenahwi pulled another thread from the demon stone— and she could feel it calling out to her, wanting to take more —and formed it into a thrust of counter force enough to disrupt the boulder's course; it splashed into the sea. But one of the other ships of the line was not so lucky. She heard the screams as the rock plowed through people and wood.

Neenahwi hurried up to the aft castle, pushing aside the crew and marines alike with her shield to clear a path. She had to find Crews.

The Drake, as first ship of the line, was now past the first armored Pyrfew ship, and the ballistae could not swivel far enough to fire at the ship in its wake. *The Orca* opened fire on the lead armored ship to little effect, and now its two similarly built companions were closing as well.

"Crews!" she called.

He didn't turn to face her and his profile betrayed little apparent concern. Crews surveyed the emerald green battleground through his looking glass. "They mean to harry us with the small ships. Skirmishers. And then pick us off with their catapults. These are old tactics..."

The lead Pyrfew ship quickly closed on *The Orca*, its oars tearing up the waves in time to a muffled drum beat. The ship's low design made it impossible for the ballistae to fire down at it as it came so close. Its oars picked up speed and there was a shuddering smash as it hit the larger Edland ship on the starboard side. Without missing a beat, the marines on board dropped ropes and scurried down to the metal coated deck, crossbows slung across their backs. A score of marines charged around the metal deck slippery with sea spray, looking for signs of people or their egress. Neenahwi grabbed the spy glass from Crews fist without so much as a murmur of apology. She looked through it and saw the looks of confusion on the faces of the marines. There was neither door nor defender. Crews calmly took another spy glass from his pocket and matched Neenahwi's focus.

The second group of Pyrfew ships was nearing the third ship of the line. The other two armored ships of the first group had now closed with *The Orca* as well, turning to avoid collision. Their line was being swarmed by the smaller armored ships; it looked to Neenahwi like a family of turtles nipping at the heels of the bigger ships.

Turtles? No. Surely not...

"Turn us around, Crews! We have to help them."

The flag girl looked to her Admiral to see if he would give

her new instructions. But Crews had another mind. "No. Belay that order. We stick to the line!" Neenahwi muttered a curse at the man's pig headedness. Crews' belief in Edland's naval superiority was clouding his judgement.

The Orca tried a different tactic against the turtles dragging along at its sides. Small objects arced through the air, thrown by hand, to hit the surface of the armored ships. Arrows followed quickly after; fire arrows by the streak of flame they left imprinted in Neenahwi's eye as they sliced through the air. The surface of the deck burst into flame. Pitch bombs, bringer of fire and chaos to any normal ships. But metal armor did not burn.

And the Edland ship was not the only one with fire.

Neenahwi watched in horror, her stomach sinking, as the reptilian figureheads of the two pursuing ships opened. Great spouts of fire erupted, shooting across the twenty feet of sea separating them from *The Orca*. The flames hit the side of the Edland ship like a torrent, churning and tumbling upwards and across the hull. The fire spilled over the deck of the ship and sailors ignited like human candles. Neenahwi's knuckles were white as she held the spy glass, scanning to see what was happening. Some of the sailors leapt into the burning sea, others ran around wildly. The flames did not stop coming, the tempo of the Pyrfew ships' oars increased to bring the draco-turtle ships either side of *The Orca*. The fire spewing spouts turned to bathe the ship completely, streams of flame flicking from side to side like a drunk trying to piss straight.

"What is this?" said Crews, removing the looking glass from his eye, staring slack-jawed at the devastation behind him. More flame erupted in the bright, crisp afternoon. The third ship of the line, *The Falcon*, under similar attack.

Neenahwi stared at him, momentarily at a loss as much as he was. Admiral Crews was the first to snap out of it. "Come about!" he hollered. "Signal the rear to disengage!"

"Get me close!" called Neenahwi, her mind racing, the anger building inside her. The demon stone throbbed against her chest. *So Pyrfew has some secret weapons, eh? Well Llewdon, we've got something you weren't expecting either.*

The Drake lurched as it turned. The crew scrambled to adjust sails and not stall. Marines stood still at their post. *Good training or fear?* She'd give them the benefit of the doubt today. Watching your friends on *The Orca* be consumed by fire was not something they would see every day. She was sure they would shed a tear for their fallen comrades while at the same time saying a quiet prayer to Atarah that it wasn't them. The turtle ships scoured the tall wooden sides of the ship. Flames licking up and onto the deck. Ropes lit up in a blaze; small, dancing fires raced up to catch hold of the sails.

The Orca was fucked. *Another mark against you, Llewdon.*

The Drake completed its turn, coming about with the stricken Edland ships between it and the larger Pyrfew ships that had resumed their onslaught of catapulted rocks. Neenahwi rushed down the main deck screaming obscenities to clear her some space at the railing. She gripped the demon stone pendant in her left hand and squeezed hard. The needle sunk into her flesh. It felt like the sharp metal squirmed, gouging a hole in the palm of her hand; blood dripped down her wrist.

She focused on her right hand. All of the anger, all of the power from the stone, she brought into herself and weaved into a tight ball of heat and hate. She would never have been able to do this without the stone. Here at sea there was no mana for her to draw on. Her own life force would have been spent like sparked tinder. But with the pendant and the hard-won little red rock set in it by her father, she felt powerful.

Neenahwi flung the fiery ball at the turtle's side, another aspect of her mind carrying the ball of energy straight and true where her arm would never have been enough. Though no smaller than her fist, the ball exploded satisfyingly on contact with the hull, the rear quarter of the starboard side blown to pieces in a shower of splinters. Oarsmen, little more than chum after the explosion of wood and metal, fell from the rent into the water.

"Aim for that hole!" called a voice. Woodell. Thankfully he had been paying attention and the ballista crews resumed their firing with glee to have such a vulnerable target. Bolts ripped through the breach in the hull, screams audible from the oarsmen inside. Other bolts smashed into the hull which broke off in long planks now that the turtle's shell had been cracked open.

"Set course between *The Orca* and *The Falcon!*" came a call from the rear. Neenahwi looked up to see Crews staring down at her, a steely look in his eyes. He nodded his respect at the display of her talents. She shrugged off the unwelcome attention and squared her shoulders, raising her chin to look down at her destruction. She was not just a fucking scout. She was the daughter of Jyuth. She was a Wolfclaw!

The Drake split the distance between the two listing, blazing bonfires of the Edland first-class ships. At least this would give her more chance to even the tally.

Neenahwi focused on drawing another ball of energy as she calmly made her way across deck, people scattering to get out of her way or pushed aside forcefully by the shield that still surrounded her. A turtle ship was pouring fire on

The Falcon and she could see straight down its reptilian figurehead.

The fiery ball flew out of her hand. Her attention guiding the missile—Neenahwi almost one with the ball—until it smashed into the carved reptilian neck.

There was silence for a fraction of a second, the air and all sound sucked into the impact. And then Neenahwi and her crew mates were reeling from the deep boom of the explosion. She blinked. The turtle ship was gone. Burning debris rained down on the waves from a greasy black cloud.

Printed in Great Britain
by Amazon

47189545R00192